Pirate Princess

the lost princess series, book 3

jp roth

PROLOGUE

*S*ilence drenched the night. Henry stared at her, and the world stopped spinning. In Velvet's twisting heart, her guilt battled shame and crimson rage. Henry's eyes traced the lifts and curves in her wings, roved over the long feathers that ran atop each other like waterfalls of crystal snow. When he spoke, his voice was low. A rasping whisper stained with shock and his own fury. "When did you know it wasn't a dream?"

Velvet had no words. She pressed her lips in a thin line and shook her head. She owed him nothing. Nothing! So why, oh why, did she want to fall to her knees and beg him to understand and forgive?

"How long, Marie?"

"I did not know for sure until I flew just now."

"Liar," he darkly accused. He straightened then, and black mists poured from his shoulders, filled the indigo pool under his feet with writhing darkness. "No matter, by your own choice, you are mine."

"Nay!" she cried. "You did not take me. I am still a virgin."

"Give me a moment for this water to roll off my back and I will quickly remedy that."

"I wholeheartedly beg you not to," said Zoe, sounding deeply distressed. Mid eye roll, he turned his back on them both, muttering about women and the spells and incantations they cast on all unwary men.

Velvet rounded on Henry. "You do not own me. Why would you believe such a thing? Because you shared a dimensional fantasy of mine? Or is it because you received a useless piece of paper from a mad king that says I belong to you?" Velvet kicked away the remnants of the broken irons under foot. "Or perhaps you believe such foolishness because you made a silent promise with a kiss, then put me in chains?"

"Yes, to all of the above," Henry said with disdain, then took a single step toward her, his beautiful lips twisted into a terrifying snarl. "After what passed between us that night, you owed me more than silence."

Velvet made a strange, strangled sound in her throat. She searched for an angry response and found none. He was right. She had owed them both far more. "I will not be owned by you, or any man," she finally said, speaking the only truth she knew.

His look seemed to sear through blood and bone, and she felt his eyes ravaging her very soul. He was clearly furious, and red rage painted the chiseled lines of his flawless face, but there was more. Desperate craving, raw desire, and an emotion that felt like pain. He moved again and reached her in two long strides.

Velvet wanted to skitter away from his touch. It was the craving that held her feet locked in place. She felt it too. A wretched heat coursing over her in sizzling waves. She wanted him, wanted him in all the ways it was possible to want another person. If he put his hands on her as he clearly meant to do, Velvet feared she would either submit, or burst into visible flames.

The reels of black steam continued to pour from his skin; it swirled up and around them, creating a barrier to all of the outside, cocooning them in their own hidden world. The clashing sounds of the battle above faded as the darkness encompassing them thickened. The golden light spilling off her wings tangled with shadows.

He reached out to touch her cheek, and for the briefest moment, his features softened. "Say what you will," he whispered, "there is no running from this, from us. I am irreparably trapped in your orbit. You are my fate, as I am yours. Destiny often finds you on the path you take to avoid it." He brushed a lock of damp hair from her eyes, his exhale washed her cheek, then he locked his teeth.

Velvet saw a muscle ticking in his jaw and his face was all harsh lines and dark shadows again. "You look like an angel, Marie. A truly spellbinding shell, it is a crying shame that what is inside is bolstered by deceit and lies."

Velvet flinched. It felt as though he slapped her.

Henry stepped back a pace and took her hand. "If you still don't want me, even knowing that night was real, perhaps there truly is no hope."

Velvet heard a bleak misery in his tone and knew she had hurt him in ways she did not fully understand. Again came that odd, wrenching impulse to throw her arms around his neck, fall to her knees and beg him to look at her once more as he had before he knew her truth. But the rage on his face froze her limbs and tied her tongue. He dropped her hand, his eyes flicked once more over her wings, then he looked past her—through her—as if she had simply ceased to exist.

"Come," he said, and there was a terrible chill in his voice, "let me show you the bones of your predecessors in the cave beneath the glass. The burning letters carved in the cliffside are a code, one which was fairly easy to decipher for a spy, assassin, and villain, as so oft you have called me."

"I thought you said there was no way to reach the bottom of a bottomless pool."

"Apparently I was wrong," Henry said, and dug his hand in the pocket of his wet trousers to withdraw a stone of unknown color. It seemed an ancient thing, so old it rivalled the very fabric of time.

Velvet could not contain her gasp. "I have never seen that gem before in my life. Where did you find it?" she asked, reaching for it before she fully comprehended her actions.

Henry closed his hand around the enchanted stone. More reels of black smoke seeped through his fingers and fell around them. "I found it in the cave amidst a pile of bones, and I heard words when I touched it."

"What did they say?" she breathed.

Henry's eyes found her again—black saturated the indigo in his gaze. He opened his hand and carefully placed the gem in hers. Chills instantly rushed down her spine, prickled the tiny hairs on her arm, then she heard the words for herself. They bore no resemblance to human sound, more like rushing waves crashing against jagged cliffs, or booming thunder clouds spitting white lightning, yet she understood each word just the same.

The price of life is eternal death.

The images of what she had seen when the wraiths had attacked them only moments ago bombarded her, pictures of the heartbreaking life briefly lived, and the explosion of one witches' power which had brought so much pain and death. She thought of Minerva and her hollow crimson eyes, forever cursed to wander in some dimension of this haunted island.

Velvet feared if she took Henry's hand and the final plunge with him beneath the violet water, she would never find a return to any sense of normalcy. She would be forever changed. The thought terrified her.

"And the spell to save my brother?" she whispered, trying not to visibly tremble as the power of the stone surged up her arm and through her bones. She saw that it added a touch of spilt ink to her golden glow.

Henry sighed and ran a hand through his glistening hair. "The spell is right where we expected it to be. It is written in blood on the walls."

~

They went beneath the glassy surface of the violet pool. Velvet held her breath but there was no need as the stone was in her hand, and they swam engulfed in its light. Intrinsically—as it always was when she used the magic of these stones—Velvet knew she could draw air from all the molecules of water that surrounded her. Henry's face was grim as they took the plunge, stern and stoic despite the adorable little bubbles escaping his locked lips. Behind Henry, past the procession of shadows marching along the dark cliff side, each symbol stood out like a dazzling star, glittering undaunted in their underwater world.

Henry's cold glare notwithstanding, Velvet was entranced. Rapt. She swayed closer to Henry, gazing at the burnished reflection of each symbol in his eyes. Velvet was forced to bite her lip, so she wouldn't break into a brilliant smile and make all of this so much worse. If the unyielding set of his lips was any tell, it seemed he may never smile again.

Velvet squirmed in his arms, pressed the palms of her hands against his chest, and gently pushed at him. Stern faced, he let her go. Together, they swam toward the wall. Two hard kicks, and the rocks were close enough to touch. She reached out, her fingertips skimmed the rocks, her touch reverent. Liquid lighting shot up her arm, sizzled through her bones.

Henry seemed to forget his rage. He touched the fire branded rocks and wonder quickly replaced the dangerous chill in his glare. More bubbles escaped his lips as he swung his head to search her face. Velvet saw that telltale muscle still ticking in his jaw as he came to some internal conclusion with apparent difficulty. She could nearly feel the hot energy of his warring thoughts, and assumed he was deciding—yet again—if he should help her, trust her. Velvet's hands went to her hips, and she couldn't stomp her feet, so she settled for kicking them. She made a weak sound of distress. *Don't you dare change your mind*; her heart screamed.

After a tense moment, Henry's shoulders sagged, and she knew the internal argument was won. He turned with purpose, a small wrinkle worrying the spot between his brow, then pressed his fingers against thirteen separate symbols in quick succession.

Breath held; Velvet watched his hands move. The water around her felt soft, warm, and thick, like honey that's not sticky, or one of those little puddings Nora so loved. Velvet moved her own hands, water threaded between her fingers, heavy and enchanting, like she was lost again in that alternate dimension the stones had created or caught up in a fever dream.

Henry repeated the same pattern, thirteen symbols, three times, then his hands dropped to his sides when the pattern was complete. For a second there was nothing at all, just silence and water, then the rocks began to tremble. It was like he had tugged an old book on a library shelf, only to find it was not a book at all, instead the lever which opened a hidden door. Henry kicked his way back to her; his hand was hot as he caught her own.

Velvet took a hesitant breath, staring at the stone's golden glow for fortitude. The water when it rushed through her lungs was light and airy. Shock of breathing underwater was incidental compared to the wonder of the quaking cave wall. Her eyes were locked to the way the black rocks shuddered and groaned. Cracking apart with booming sounds that sent ripples rushing. Velvet felt tears burn her eyes. She was close. So close. Since the night Queenie poured her noxious spell over Velvet's head, held the stone of Tamora in her hands and recited those terrible, ominous words, Velvet was finally here. The cave beneath the glass, the cave that held the words she had lied, fought, and killed to read. The words that would save her baby brother and exonerate her from a promise made to her dead mother so many years ago.

Before she thought to do so, Velvet tore her hand from Henry's grasp, as she swam toward the narrow opening in the cave. She swam down past more jagged cliffs all cast in watery, luminous shadows, swam over strange, tentacled creatures.

Translucent mushroom heads bobbing up and down like ghosts in the darkness. She kicked her feet and shot forward through the jagged break in the cliff face, kicked her feet once more, her body surged, and her head broke the water's surface with a frothy splash. Velvet gulped in a giant breath, wiping water from her eyes, shoving sticky strands of hair from her face. Then she saw where she was, and the world seemed to stand still. She had found it. The cave beneath the glass. She was here.

CHAPTER 1

ENCHANTING SHADOWS, DRUGGING LIGHT

December 5th, 1800

The interior of the cave was enchanting, beyond imagination, a world of fantasy absent any threat of reality. Cliffs of glistening aquamarine, rocks climbed high on all sides bathed in waterfalls that tumbled like so many falling diamonds into crystalline pools colored bronze, magenta, and violet. Smooth, rock shelves clustered together—tiered atop and beside each other—made a room of sorts to the east of the cave. Vines the color of captured lighting climbed up the shelves and ran over the walls.

The runoff of three waterfalls fell over the stones, but the large, raised shelf standing in the center of them all was dry, and strewn with the remnants of blankets, made threadbare by time. The rest, a golden set of combs, crystal perfume bottles of twined glass, the carved drawings on the wall, and a purple cloak made of gossamer threads that shimmered when the light shifted—the latter lying on the wet stones near Velvet's feet—were all perfectly preserved. Like it had been days rather than thousands of years since these items were touched. Who was the last person to breathe this enchanting air? Velvet wondered. Was it really Minerva, the goddess with the bloody eyes who had cursed and killed her sisters to save her lover, or had there been others, doomed souls such as herself?

Velvet moved toward the small room still strewn by the golden assortments of a dead girl's things, water rolling from her skin in sparkling drops, making the silk of her white dress cling to her legs. When she reached the ratty blankets, she fell to her knees. There, high on the turquoise cave walls, bracing the once make-shift bed were the words. The words she needed more than breath. The words that would save her brother, absolve her, and put an end to it all. The writing was messy and brown, the color of dried blood. Velvet looked at them for a long moment, then dropped her eyes and tried not to feel the chills that rushed down her spine. They brought with them a sense of horrible dread, as if the worst thing in the world was only seconds from happening.

"Like spiders crawling across your grave," said Henry, startling her. Velvet spun; her breath caught in her throat at first sight of him. He stood at the stone lip of the largest pool. Water traced golden rivulets down his chest, collecting in the waistband of his trousers. He held the bag of stones in his left hand, black mists raced down his legs, and around his feet. Dripping hair swung about his set jaw as he strode toward her, his eyes alternating between her face and the bloody writing on the wall. He shook the water from his hair and met her eyes. "I feel this place in my gut like a gulp of poison," he said.

Velvet rubbed her hands over the chills rushing up and down her arms. "It is rather strange and horrible," she said, hearing her voice shake. "Makes me remember what I saw, what I lived through when the wraiths attacked. They loved each other, Minerva, and the man she killed for."

Velvet spun on her heels, taking in the way the fractured aqua shine of the rocks cut through the surrounding waterfalls.

"I still feel her in the air. She haunts this place. I saw her, you know. The night you...the night we...the night..." her voice fell away. Velvet waved her hand through the glistening air. What a ninny she was! Velvet locked her teeth and spoke through them. "The night we were together."

Henry took a step toward her, his stance dominant, his aura the color of rage. "Were we really, Marie? Was all real? The wings, my mouth on you, the way you said my name?" His low voice rasped over her nerves. Velvet felt her whole-body flush scarlet. Henry drew in an audible breath and closed the remaining distance between them. Black smoke rolled off his shoulders, drenching her in a cloak of night. The air between them seemed to sizzle and come alive. "I want to hear you say it," he whispered against her cheek and wrapped his fingers around her upper arms, drew her closer. Velvet locked her lips and gave him only silence. She would not be dictated to. The sparking light deep in his eyes, the domineering chill in his voice were some of the many reasons she could not submit to him.

"Marie." His tone sharpened until it stabbed. "Say it!"

Scorching heat coursed through Velvet; she felt the burn as more blood rushed to her cheeks mere seconds before she exploded. "Yes! It was real!" she all but screamed, struggling to break his hold. "Real as any of this has been for me since the night the guillotine cut off my mother's head. In all my cognitive memories, I'm running from the king, the church, from you in a haze of confusion, panic, and terror. My brother is an enchanted stag, and not a month ago, a cursed goddess pulled me through dimensions and showed me I still had wings. *What is real?*" Velvet dragged her fingers through her wild, unbound hair. Her chest rapidly rose and fell, each breath quick and labored. Henry's hands dropped to his side, his own breaths shredded and raw. As always, absent his touch, an instant chill slid over her. The tips of her fingers felt freezing, but his eyes were hot as the sun on her face.

"Ever have I stalked you, wanted you, yet because of a single error in a moment of madness—"

"A single error?" Velvet cried. "Henry, you cannot be serious. You put me at war with the church of England and sent me to die."

He waved her words away with a sharp slash of his hand. "That night, on this island, with you, by that pool, under that tree, beneath that sky of frozen stars—it was the most spectacular of my life. I may be the worst of fools, but I am not blind. I know at least a modicum of what you felt. You are no actress, my love, and never much good as a liar." His voice dropped lower, grew tense. "I would give the heart from my body to touch you again. My hands in your hair, my mouth on your skin—there was magic between us that night. When it was done, when that tree and those silent stars faded back to whatever dimension spawned them...when it was over, you knew the choice. I demanded the truth from you and didn't choose *me!*" His tenor rose on each word, till he was all but yelling in her face. *"You didn't choose me!"*

"Because choosing you is choosing us!" she screamed. "You will take away all of me that remains. You will steal what's left of my freedom."

Henry reached out and grabbed her before Velvet could flinch away. He pulled her hard against him, crushing the aching tips of her breasts to his iron chest. She could feel the drops that clung to him seeping through the thin bodice of her sheer white dress.

His head fell until his lips hovered less than an inch above hers. "Never think it," he breathed. "Freedom is yours. I don't wish to take that from you. All I want is your soul, your body hot against mine, your hands on my skin, in my hair, your breath in my lungs. Take your freedom?" Henry shook his head, touched her chin, lifted her face closer, closer. "How absurd you are, when from first touch, I've been your ardent slave. Look at me, my love," he said, but Velvet vehemently declined to acquiesce, yet his strength thwarted her efforts to turn away. It didn't matter, they were halfhearted efforts at best; she wanted him. Molten flames seared her, pulsing from all the spots where he touched her. She wanted to submit to him, to this desire. She wanted to stop fighting. It did not seem to be doing much good, anyway. Ever she tried to run, ever did destiny pull them closer.

Velvet opened her stubborn eyes, and glared at him, saw the wild thing that sparked in his own. Henry was going to kiss her... if he did...Velvet knew her protests would melt away under the fire of how badly she wanted him.

If she thought about it at all, Velvet suspected she would be forced to admit that her elusive lady Freedom had been well and truly assassinated the night he came to kill her, put his hands on her in hate, then strangely changed his mind.

It all seemed a lifetime ago now, a story belonging to a different, frightened girl. A girl who had not battled red coats, kings, the church, Romani warriors, the sea, and this man. The girl back then had never caused a friend to die, never knelt before the executioner's blade, closed her eyes, and waited to die, her last words burning on her lips. Velvet stopped her feeble resistance. Her body fell still.

"There is nowhere left for you to hide, now that I know the truth," Henry said, making no effort to disguise the desperation in his voice.

Velvet had time to take a single, screeching breath before his mouth descended on hers. Her lips parted on her gasp as his tongue swept inside, blistering hot. Her fingers curled in his chest, she went up on her toes, and her nails scored welts down his neck, twisted in his dark hair. Henry groaned against her mouth, then the kiss turned vicious, frantic, necessary. He moved and invoked magic with his hands, clutched her tighter, dragged her up his hard body and ravaged her mouth. Velvet made a wanton, hungry sound and twisted closer.

It was always enthralling madness with him, she thought, before she could not think at all. Henry's hands slid over her hips, cupped her breasts, then gently pinched their aching tips, and bit a small spot just beneath her ear. Velvet felt a scream building in the back of her throat.

Panting like he had run ten miles, Henry drew back his head. With aching slowness, he slid the white straps of her dress down her bare arms, revealing what was hidden one inch at a time. Velvet held her breath, silently counting off each racing beat of her heart, and watched his eyes devour her. In them she saw his intent—he did nothing to hide it. Tonight, he would make her his. Velvet suspected it would come to a fight if she dared refuse him. Oh, her mind screamed for her to do so, draw back her hand and deliver a swift slap to his cheek before sending him packing—he was a traitor, liar, murderer, and trickster—but his lips and hands were spinning her world off its axis, clouding what remained of her rational mind. The moon would rise on the morrow, the sun would set, and she would want this man—in this moment, those were the only truths she knew.

Henry let the gown fall to her waist, his gaze touched hot as his hands. He reached out to drag his finger down the shallow valley between her breasts. Her nipples hardened in a visible rush. They ached, and she trembled. "God, Marie. So soft, you are so damn beautiful," Henry growled. "I should have known it wasn't a dream. For days I had the taste of you in my mouth, like roses, rainwater, and starlight." Velvet saw his crooked smile as he watched her flush to the roots of her hair. He brushed away a lock of hair clinging to the moisture on her cheek, tucked it gently behind her ear. "In all my travels, I've never seen a thing so magical as you."

Not breaking contact with her dazed stare, Henry released the tie at her waist with a deft flick of his fingers. The moment it was loosened, the dress seemed to drop like a stone. Velvet scrambled to catch it and preserve the last shreds of her modesty, but it was to no avail. Henry caught her hands and pressed her knuckles to his lips. "Don't fight me, my love, or I will be forced to put the chains back on."

Velvet's head snapped back; she felt her whole body tighten. "I hate you," she breathed, but the harsh words sounded like a caress.

"That may be true," Henry said as he took her face between his palms and spoke against her lips, "but tonight you will love me. Here in this place, on this cursed, hallowed ground, I will love you."

Velvet opened her mouth to protest, yet all that came out was a breathy, whispered assent. "Yes." It was inevitable, the like pull of the moon, or birdsong at dawn.

Henry's shoulders sagged in what seemed like crushing relief and he held her closer, kissed her lips, softly, tenderly. Nipped at her lower one, traced the top with his tongue, said her name like a prayer. Velvet should have felt anger at her weak, desperate body, instead, she felt beautiful, and strong enough to make his knees go weak, to make him shake as he pressed his forehead against hers.

On all sides, hot springs bubbling in rocky pools released their steam, moistening their skin, and seeping into her bones, until she ached and surrendered. Yet, in this moment, it did not feel like surrender, wrapped in black, moving mists, and surrounded by luminous wonder. It felt like the best decision of her life. Because she loved him, of course she did, and she had been an idiot to deny it. She loved him so insanely much. Loved his laughter and his dark side. Loved his honor and loyalty. Adored the way his men trusted him, craved the way she felt at home in his arms, and she wanted him. Come what may, she wanted him now, wanted to stay with him forever.

Wordlessly Henry carried her to where the dead lovers had once lain, now a place of ash and shadow. Words in old Latin, and symbols were scrawled in haphazard order all over the face of the largest stone shelf, covering the spot where the shredded blankets lay. In her mind's current state of flushed disarray, she could only make out a few of the words. *To have, to hold, sickness, health.* Wedding vows, she realized, inscribed in stone, exchanged between Minerva, her lover, and their gods watching in the sky.

Henry set her atop the words, and Velvet felt them branded to her skin, entwining, binding her to this man of smoke and fire. She leaned back, bracing herself on her elbows and watched him kick off his boots; his hands went to the laces on his trousers; Velvet flicked her tongue over her dry lips. He was a sculpture of golden skin stretched taut over a chiseled frame, still shrouded by the moving mists spilling from the onyx stone in his pocket.

"I suppose you have done this hundreds of times," Velvet whispered, then wished she had not.

Laughter lit the dark corners of his eyes. He knelt in front of her, cocking his head to the right and regarding her. "Are you jealous, Marie? Don't worry, I've not been able to think of another woman since the second I crashed into you. They have all been talking shadows."

Velvet lifted the tip of her nose, trying for imperious nonchalance. "I am not jealous at all, villain! How could I be? I was a bird flying the sky while you were out gallivanting with half of Europe."

"We are not about to gallivant, and if another man touched you, past or future, I would want to rip off his head."

"That's barbaric," Velvet said, censure in her tone, though she battled a smile. "And you claim to be a gentleman. I always knew it was but a veneer."

"The mirage of a gentleman is always a veneer, beware of the beast beneath," he said, then took her hands and pulled her to her knees. His fingers fell to her lower back, and he gripped her tight, tugged her close. She felt the burning length of him pressed against her stomach. He let her feel him, moved his hips, nearly grinding himself against her. Velvet's whole soul focused on the place their bodies touched until she felt weak with want of him. "I would follow you to the ends of the earth," he rasped, "chase you wherever you went, and long as I live, there will be no other man for you but me. I mean to keep you too dazzled, too breathless to ever look away. I am your fate, darling, accept it," he breathed, then he kissed her. Time and all surrounding faded from existence. There was only him.

~

Henry cradled her head in his hand when he lay her down, and he brushed the blankets away. The stone was cold and wet. Velvet gasped at the chill of the rock against her bare skin. She arched back, the sudden action thrust the tips of her breasts against his chest as he settled his body between her legs. She made a sound like crystal shattering, a sound that acted on Henry like a whip. The possibility, or truth, that Velvet shared the dream with him, that it had not been a dream at all, made his blood run so hotly, he feared to speak another word.

She stared up at him, watching him with that hawk-like gaze. Her skin was alabaster and roses, the hair that tumbled in wild abandon hallowed them in a waterfall of the purest gold. She was a treasure for a king. For a second, he felt unworthy, his bloody hands had no business touching her perfection. Then, her dark lashes flicked up, and she stared at him through eyes of crystal blue, unflinching, not bothering to hide the shiver that ran through her at his touch.

"Do what you will, Henry," she whispered, "and consider it a bargain well paid."

The rage in Henry almost broke free; keeping it leashed was an extraordinary task. "It is a bargain that comes with stronger chains than even you might be able to break."

Velvet shook her head. "A true devil's bargain. No matter, it means nothing. I am giving you one night, giving us...then it will be over."

"Destiny has no regard for those who fight it, darling. It means for us to be together," Henry heard himself say. He actually sympathized with her, for this princess, submission was no easy feat. Now that they were about it, now that she was feeling what was to come, he knew it was more than she had thought to give. He feared it was this place which had forced her to concede. The spell he suspected roved through in the air. He had tasted similar enchantment before and knew the flavor.

"No matter," Velvet sighed, "I cannot fight it tonight."

"Because you want me," he said, needing to hear it.

Two spots of color bloomed on her cheeks, but her lashes did not fall to hide her wide eyes. "I want you," she admitted, "yet, my body and my mind have been at war since the day we met. I want you here, in this moment. I do not want you for life. I do not want anyone. Perhaps I flew free in the sky for too long." She shrugged. "Or, it may be the Gypsy part of me I just can't shake."

Her words made Henry burn; red hazed his vision. "Would it be so terrible to be mine?" he asked, and her instant nod of assent hurt him more than all the rest. None of it mattered. He would have her now.

Her heart beat rapidly, fluttering like the wing of a humming-bird against his chest. How beautiful, a diamond star, unearthly witch that she was. He needed her like he needed to breathe. He was painfully hard, straining against the restraint of his britches, and she was warm as a sunspot against him. He refused to give any more credence to this fight. There was always tomorrow to wage war. She opened her mouth to answer his husky question, when he leaned in and stopped her angry lips with his own.

Velvet flinched at his first touch. He filled his hands with her rose-tipped breasts, then drank the moan he summoned. The slim column of her neck held his focus, as he lightly sucked a spot just beneath her ear. She tasted divine, like clear water and magic. He trailed kisses across her breasts, and her body went rigid when he took her flushed nipple between his teeth. Velvet cried out, the sound was angelic ambrosia, enticing him to madness.

Henry touched her everywhere, slid his hands up her thighs, stroked what he wanted to kiss. What he had kissed in that dream that was not a dream. Velvet met his eyes in silent understanding. Long legs shifted—fell apart. He stared down at the centrifugal focus of his desire, what he wanted more than anything on earth. He was a creature of instinct now, as he bit the curve of her waist, and licked his way up her silky thighs. When he dipped his head to taste her, she gasped his name.

Henry closed his eyes at the pleasure of the sound. Her hips undulated against his lips, and Velvet unraveled like moonlight under his tongue. For a time, the only sound was her breathless sighs and muted screams as he kissed and licked and sucked. When the rippling pleasure came and shook her, Henry thought he would lose control right then, all over the twisted sheets. Her moans faded to sighs as he kissed the taut curve of her waist. A fine dew misted her skin, and he tasted it, kissing her beautiful skin until she was limp and gasping. Only then did Henry move more fully atop her; his jaw clenched against the hunger tearing at his inside. His shaking hands shocked him, for he felt like an untried boy. Slowly, he settled between her thighs and looked at her. Her neck was still arched, her flushed lips parted, her eyes wide and full of shocked wonder. He would remember her like this until he died. If ever another woman ever tried to incite him away, all he would need to do is picture his princess, just like this, and Henry knew he would be hard as a rutting stallion in seconds, for her, only her, always her.

"If you take yourself from me," he heard himself pant against her throat, "I will forever remember the taste of you. Forever need you. I don't want to take you by force. I don't want this night to sour in your mind. If you want me to stop, tell me now, for later it will be too late."

Velvet tugged at his shoulders. "Don't stop."

"Are you sure?"

"Please," she begged, lifting her hips. "I want more. I want the rest. I want you. Inside me Henry...I—"

It was enough for him. Henry kissed her then, hard and ruthless. He made an adjustment between their bodies, then slowly, with aching care, he pressed inside of her. The broken gasp she uttered, her nails scoring down his back, the scorching, tight heat of her nearly drove him over the edge. He closed his eyes and moved deeper, then met a thin veil of resistance and fell still.

Velvet stiffened. "Henry, wait. You're too big. I can't...I...don't move another inch...you will split me in two. It's too much," she breathed, wriggling. Her slight struggles only drew their bodies closer.

"Hold still," he managed to grit through locked teeth, and sweat broke out across his brow. "God, Marie." Bracing his hands on either side of her, Henry leaned back to gaze at her face. He flexed his hips. "The pain is only once."

"Only once," she repeated. He kissed her hot cheeks, traced the beautiful lines of her brows with his mouth, nipped at her lips, and rocked against her, licked her nipples, lightly blew on them until her eyes went heavy lidded and a spark kindled in her deep blue eyes. Her body softened beneath him, and her nails retracted across his skin.

"Only once, then it is ecstasy, I swear. I promise to make it beautiful for you. Trust me, just trust me," he rasped and hoped he spoke the truth. He had not been with a virgin since he was one, and he wanted her first time to be perfect. He would go slow even if it killed him.

"I've always known it would be beautiful with you," she said, then, "don't look at me like that Henry, I only say these things because your kiss has muddled my mind."

"Then, I will kiss you again," he said, and made good on his word. Keeping his mouth locked to hers, he stroked his fingers over that single spot between her legs. Only when she was gasping, writhing, pleading—did Henry let himself really move. He took what remained of her innocence with a single thrust. Velvet screamed. Henry remained motionless as the sound of that breathless scream echoed, then faded. "It's done," he said.

∼

It was done, and Velvet knew she was forever changed. Forever his. His hand moved again between their bodies, and he stroked the place that was the whole focus of her world, burning and glittering like the sun. The pain was brief and overshadowed by the indescribable feeling of having Henry inside of her. He held still for a long time, just looking at her. "You're mine now," he finally said. She was. Forever.

"I want the rest," she said. His breath came faster, shaking them both.

"Are you sure?"

"Yes, I—" Her voice broke as his hips rocked.

"Oh, god!" she gasped, barely recognizing her own voice. It sounded hoarse, desperate, lusty. His thrusts were slow at first, achingly so. "More," she demanded. Henry obeyed, his hips ground into hers, fierce, rotating, caressing, until Velvet was sure her skin was aflame.

Velvet forgot all but the pleasure he wrung from her. Visions clouded her mind, beating like dark wings. Pictures of desire, Henry kissing her lips with the sun at his back, the way the golden ball had glowed against her closed eyes as she tilted her head to taste his lips. Henry, proud and beautiful, holding her close, the rocking deck of a ship beneath his feet, her love spell burning his mind. The taste of his lips under a crystalline moon beside a rippling pool...so many moments of frustrated passion all leading to this moment—this act. An act that became a little more with each of his powerful thrusts.

She clutched at him frantically, dug her nails into his biceps, scored them down his back. Henry moved like thunder, again and again until she was screaming, twisting, begging. He gave what she demanded. It was primal, necessary and the pleasure rose so intensely, Velvet wondered wildly if she could bear it. His heart beat clamored madly against her breast; his labored breaths were hot in her mouth. He whispered her name; told her she was flawless and rare. Her hands skated down his body, it was tense and hard as iron. She kissed his neck, and he went up on his knees, then lifted her hips off the ground cupping them in his big hands, squeezing, stroking, never breaking the rhythm of his maddening thrusts. The new position drove him deeper. Pain and pleasure combined. Her head thrashed back and forth; her body strained toward his.

"God's blood, Marie, I can't hold it—I—"

His choked words were cut off by Velvet's scream. Ecstasy broke over her all at once like a dark wave. Indescribable, blooming, splintering rapture. Velvet's entire body tensed, taut as a drawn bowstring. She closed her eyes and let swell after tantalizing swell rush over her. She screamed again; she couldn't help it. Her toes curled; her nails scored crimson groves down his back. Somewhere in the distance Velvet heard Henry's harsh cry, felt him shudder. Ripples ran over her body in a slow wash of what he had promised. Ecstasy. When it was over, Velvet listened to the blood pounding in her ears. It felt like she hovered just above herself, her sated body floating on a fluffy bed of euphoria. Henry's lips stayed locked to hers, as softly he whispered her name.

Bright lights flashed behind Velvet's lids, then faded to swaths of merciful darkness—she gave herself to it with a satisfied sigh. It felt like a net of shimmering gold ensconced them. Unbreakable. Forever. Thus entwined, with Henry's hands wrapped up in her hair, and they slept—slept the true sleep of the enthralled and deeply enchanted.

CHAPTER 2

THE CAVE OF LOVERS

*N*o time came to part them, no day or night with all their varied demands, only misty darkness threatened by muted reals of glowing aqua light. If beyond the boundaries of water, the moon or sun rose, they did not know it. Soft breaths, panted, burning whispers, blistering pleasure, and the heat in Henry's eyes were all the elements that constructed Velvet's world. She did not disentangle herself from his arms, so he had her, again and again. Took everything she had to offer, and more. With his kiss, he stole so many pieces of her soul, gave her his in return.

Later, when their skin was damp, their lips swollen from kissing, Henry rolled onto his back and pulled her head to his chest. His fingers threaded through her hair, spreading the golden strands over his heart. "You read about this," he whispered, pressing his lips to her damp temple, where only thoughts of him dwelt. "Lord Byron can't shut up about the wonder of this act. I always thought it was a bit much. I've never had a mistress, women aplenty, never one I cared for...never one I—" Henry broke off sighing. "With you, in this place?" He shook his head, then softly pressed his lips to hers. "I fear I am forever changed. I also fear we are the victims of another damn enchantment, and when we leave here, this violent reality will feel like a dream."

From her perch in the crook of his shoulder, Velvet smiled up at him, biting her lip to hold back a giggle. "Really? Is that why you did it so many times?" She laughed at his expression, unable to help it. "I didn't know a man could...I thought more time was needed to..." Velvet broke off and breathed through her nose until she found her nerve. "I thought you," her eyes flicked below his navel, "I thought *that* needed time to recover."

Henry smiled wryly. "So did I." He growled into the curve of her neck and rolled her beneath him. "Maybe it's just that I wanted to have you under me since the day you kissed my cheek in the garden of a storied French castle, all those years ago."

"I had been watching you for days," Velvet shyly admitted, not able to meet his searching stare. "Earlier that day, I nearly toppled from my bedroom window trying to catch a glance of you sparing with my father's men at arms."

Henry leaned back to stare in shock at her flushed face. "You remember?"

Velvet drew in a sharp breath and thought the air tasted like starlight and him. "I remember everything, this island, it seems, has given back what Queenie's spell stole. I remember your squire's garb, and the way the sun touched the deepest black strands in your hair and turned them midnight blue. I remember the filth of the dungeon where they held me. I remember my mother's screams when they took her, and I remember the black blade Queenie used to draw her own blood the night she first changed me." Velvet blinked when hot tears stung her eyes. "I remember the fear in my brother's eyes when her blood dripped over his golden head. That was the last time I saw my brother's true face. I don't even know what he looks like now. Sometimes I believe if I saw him again my heart would know him, but...I wonder."

She swallowed hard and shook the shadows away, focusing on the sharp, beloved lines of Henry's face. "You dazzled me,

Henry. In a court filled with the most beautiful, desirable men in France, it was your emerald eyes and swarthy skin I saw in my dreams. All my ladies stayed in a perpetual swoon at the thought of you, but I was never jealous. I was the first princess of France and, if I wanted you, I foolishly believed you could be mine," Velvet snapped her fingers, "just like that."

Henry stared down at her, she could see the shock her unexpected honesty had brought. "I never knew," he whispered, "I am, you know."

"You are, what?" she asked.

"Yours," he said, and the words fell like a stone on her chest. Terrified, Velvet met his gaze. Henry shrugged. "I always have been, and you needed no magic stones to bewitch me. Could be why I was so angry with you that night on the Bacchus." He threaded his fingers through her hair, captured her face between his palms. The dark light in his eyes seemed to pierce her soul. "Little princess of France, gypsy girl, fugitive witch, or winged angel. I love every version of you, Marie-Thérèse Charlotte of France, with every piece of my scared, unworthy heart," he said, his voice impassioned. Velvet thought her own heart may burst from her chest.

Around them, waterfalls continued to pour, keeping their own counsel with whispered, splashing sounds. Steam rose endlessly from the surrounding pools and the air they breathed was bathed in heavy, churning mist. Impossible, surely, but Velvet thought she saw stars nestled in the rocks overhead. Feeling tears burn in their corners, she screwed her eyes shut and shook her head. Unable to say the words screaming in the back of her throat, clamoring for release. "I do not want to love you," she finally whispered, her voice breaking over unshed tears. Between them passed a look of understanding and inevitability. Words were useless.

Velvet pulled his head down to hers so she could speak her truth in a kiss. A kiss that was tender, fierce, and devout. When they came apart, they stared into each other's eyes. Gently she touched her lips to his again, unable to bear the slightest distance, once, twice. "You are my sun, Henry. Before you, there was only confusion and darkness."

"Despite everything?" he asked.

"Perhaps because of it," she admitted. "I've always wondered how to fight my enemy if I became a part of him, but I know the answer now."

"Do you?"

"Yes, when you become a part of your enemy there is no more cause for battle. We are a part of each other. Two pieces of the same whole."

"Marie." His hand brushed her cheek. "My love, my brave, strong princess." He touched the tears gathering in tiny droplets at the corners of her eyes. The moment of silent, shared understanding suffused her with feelings of warmth and fear. It made her want to trust him, belong to him in some unbreakable, fundamental way, now...always. Velvet hesitated, still locked in his eyes. He had somehow replaced all else and become her world. He could have stood in a crowd of giants, or winged, horned dragons, and he would have towered over all of them in her sight. It was the way he looked at her when they were thus entwined, heightened awareness flowed between them like invisible chain lightning. Binding, eternal.

Velvet opened her lips, but no words came. Henry saw or sensed her struggle. He fitted his mouth to hers, the touch of his hands hot and urgent. Velvet was flying without wings, her body instantly aflame. Pleasure pervaded her limbs, curled her toes, till her arms and legs ached, so she wrapped them around him. Henry held her arching hips in his big hands. Naked, dominant, unholy in his pagan beauty, he stopped the breath in her lungs. He told her to touch him, placed her hand where he needed it most, then said her name through gritted teeth. Verdant shadows tangled in his eyes, causing them to gleam with their own illumination as he threw back his head, shuddering when she raked her nails down his massive length. His fingers came to the delicate structure of her jaw and tilted her chin. His thumb stroked her lower lip, and he leaned down to brush a half open mouthed kiss to the place where he touched. Velvet stared up at his face and felt weak all over—a creature of shadows and mesmerizing light—he was sensuality incarnate.

Henry bit the curve of her neck and trailed kisses down her chest so he could take the tip of her breast in his burning mouth. His fingers stroked her stomach, hips, lower, lower, then that most ancient of dances began again. The pleasure went on and on, sometime during the blazing hours that flew by like disoriented minutes, when he moved fiercely inside of her, in the throes of indescribable pleasure, Velvet suspected she gave him back those three, weighty words he had given her, and thus sealed her fate.

Later Velvet sat, knees drawn up to her chin, and watched Henry sleep. Studied the way his chest moved as he peacefully breathed. Dark curls surrounded his head like a disoriented halo, softening his features and lending an air of innocence. He lay on his back, one arm crooked behind his head, the other lazily crossing his stomach. His lips were slightly parted, and she knew he dreamed by the way his eyes moved beneath their lids; Velvet wondered if he dreamed of her. She gazed at him for a time, picturing a plethora of desires, all which involved him, when she had exhausted her limited repertoire of fantasies, she turned to stare at the bloody words spattered on the ancient cave wall, just above his sleeping head.

A morbid collection of words if ever there was. Old Latin, she assumed, though the letters were hard to decipher. There had to be more to it than what this blood promise relayed. Something about it all just seemed too easy. If the love spell she had cast on the Bacchus so many nights ago had taken two lives, how much more blood would be needed to aid the transformation of beast to man? For Queenie, the second change had demanded everything.

Velvet sat, still as stone; her mind sifted through an endless myriad of possibilities, while Henry slept blissfully on. Eventually, her limbs grew stiff from remaining so long in one attitude. She stood slowly, lifting her arms above her head to stretch out the aching kinks, and twist the foot which seemed to have fallen asleep and left the rest of her body behind. Sharp pricks of stinging feeling began to attack her fingertips. Velvet raised her hand, preparing to shake it off, when she felt a presence at her back. Nothing angry or malevolent, just cold as any ice she had ever touched. Velvet suspected who it was before she spun to see a pair of bright red eyes glowing through reels of churning darkness.

"Minerva," Velvet said, on a shattered gasp. The old witch stepped from shadow into a shallow pool of aqua light. Her dark face was pale, bleached as old bones. Velvet felt a muscle in her cheek twitch, but whether it was to smile or snarl, she could not say. The visit would have surprised her, if her capacity for surprise hadn't been well and truly flattened these last months. As it was, the crimson eyes made her blood run cold.

Minerva stepped regally forward, long black hair rippling like a silken cowl to her hips, swinging arms that looked impossibly strong under the cast of multiple, distorted shadows, the inked symbols and designs that ran their length were briefly highlighted by splashes of moving light that bled from the surrounding pools. Her black gown rustled between her legs as she moved, the sound like a dozen pieces of crumpled paper blowing about in a lonely wind.

Velvet tore her gaze from Minerva's haunted face when Henry stirred, muttering a stream of nonsensical words in his Gaelic. Then he rolled onto his side, sighed deeply, and slept blissfully on. Velvet released a breath she had not been aware of holding and turned back to the forgotten goddess.

"*Your protector,*" Minerva stated, speaking in that shrill mind voice Velvet loathed.

"Can't you speak?" Velvet asked on a sigh.

"*It is as I told you. I have not uttered a word in more than a millennium, not since the night I lost what I love.*"

"Your lover," said Velvet, trying to keep her voice steady. "I saw. Your sisters showed me that night, for screaming seconds I lived in your skin." Velvet's voice dropped, and she rubbed the skin over her heart. "I felt your heart break, experienced every second of your misery."

"*I am sorry for that. My sisters have become hateful creatures.*"

"Because of you," Velvet said, "because of what you did."

Minerva lifted her chin a fraction of an inch. "*Because of what I did. Would that I had known, understood the true price of such magic. I was young and stupid, much like you.*"

Velvet swallowed. "I thank you."

Minerva ignored her, blood red eyes fixed and steady. "*It is not cruelty; I only speak truth. How I wish...but there is no use for wishing, one cannot change fixed moments in time. I know, I have tried. You would do better to leave your brother as he is. Make your peace with his loss.*"

Velvet studied the backs of her hands, and the moving patterns of reflective pool light. "Perhaps you are right," she finally said. "It's what Louie wants, but—"

"*It is not in you to do so,*" finished Minerva.

"No, it is not. To be dreadfully honest, I would rather die. I made a promise to my mother, the only thing she asked of me, her dying wish. Breaking it would break me."

Minerva smiled, the saddest of smiles. "*There is the tragedy. If I could have died that night in place of my sisters, I would have. I did not know then what such magic demands, though I was prepared to give my life that night if it would save him.*" Minerva's bloody gaze grew hazy and distant, flooded by memories. "*I knew what was in my sisters' hearts. They would have casually slit his throat and slept the better for it. He was an intruder, my beautiful sailor boy, and the night I spared his life, I broke a sacred vow. Yet, I loved him, instantly, completely. I cannot explain it, only to say, I saw him—bruised and battered, lying on the rocks jutting from the stormy sea—and I knew he was mine. My other half, the essential extension of my soul."*

Velvet's eyes drifted to Henry, and a burning thing twisted in her chest. "I understand," she said.

"You don't," Minerva said, her voice coming at Velvet from everywhere and nowhere at all. It rang like a silent bell. *"You don't fully understand, but you will. The choice and curse are yours, as they were mine. I told the same to your predecessor. She wanted freedom for her people and meant to obtain it at any cost. What was the end, the death of everyone she loved? It's how it always ends. In you and your brother she saw salvation, so she cast the die..."*

"And lost," said Velvet.

Minerva tilted her head, the red eyes flashed, and the jaw bounced like a broken puppet. Velvet shuddered. *"Perhaps, though I believe that still remains to be seen,"* said Minerva.

"No more riddles," snapped Velvet, wanting to reach up her hands and scratch the chilling voice out of her head. "Your enigmas will stay with me past the grave. Tell me what I must know!"

Minerva's head creaked back in place. *"Of course, child, it is why I am here. 'Tis a curse to be sure, yet not the only curse roaming these shores. My sister Hecate was a witch of magic's first house, taught by the elders that will never teach again. Some now say she was the first. That is not true of course, but she made her mark in darkness and the repercussions were felt for centuries. Kingdoms rose and fell at her will; old magic infused the blood in her veins. It was her magic I used that night. I am not excusing myself, but I was unprepared for her darkness. Evil, pure and unadulterated. So, I will tell you what I did not know then. To make the change, the witch who cast the spell must first sacrifice that which she truly loves. If the love is not real, the spell will not work. One life, if that life is willingly given, two, if it is forcefully taken—"*

"I know the rest," interrupted Velvet, running her hands over her face, tugging them through her damp hair. The words for her held all the unknown terror of the ocean's deep. "I pray keep silent; I fear if I hear them again, I will run mad," she finished. Her sharp tone made Henry stir. Velvet lifted her eyes to study the beloved lines of his gorgeous face.

"Can you sacrifice the life of the man you love, for the brother you once swore to save?" asked Minerva, but it was the old witch's last words which truly lingered. *"Will you be able to live with yourself, whatever you choose?"*

Velvet turned away from her study of Henry, meaning to give Minerva her very best scowl. Minerva was gone, yet when Velvet blinked and rubbed her eyes, she thought a few remnants of the witch's murky shadow remained. Velvet sat back down, numb with dread and terrified grief. She stared again at Henry, unblinking, until her eyes teared and burned. It was a choice she could not make.

"Who did you kill for me, Queenie, and why did you love them?" Velvet whispered and knew the silence would not answer. Faces of those she had loved flashed quickly through her mind, her mother, her father, Fluer, her nursemaid, who had adored her, all of them dead. There were more faces, Nora, Devon...and Henry. She loved him most of all. His would be the life the blood magic would demand. Velvet wanted to stand and scream, tear at her hair, curse Queenie and her insane plan to wallow in the deepest parts of hell. She did nothing. Time passed, and she gave it no heed. There was only the choice. She could not sacrifice herself, and she thought she would probably die the second Henry took his last breath. Never, she could never hurt him. Not for anything, not even to fulfill a vow and save her brother. What was worse...she could never let him know, if he knew...the villain was stubborn enough to take the choice out of her hands and place it with fate.

Tears streamed from her eyes, and still she sat unmoving. To come so far and fail so miserably made her feel gutted as a fisherman's prize. Would her decision be different if this choice had been presented to her two months ago? Velvet doubted it. Even without remembering how much her childish self had once loved him, the invisible chain binding them had been unbreakable. Life without him would be life without a soul. Rescuer, betrayer, villain to his core, dark passion in his kiss, and a touch that could summon fire. She longed for the simple days where her only worries were where to fly and what to hunt. The bliss of forgetfulness was the positive of her memory loss. The price of its return was high, and she clearly remembered everything that had been taken from her. She was not prepared to lose another life she treasured.

All this while, running, fighting, plotting, she hadn't dared look back. Now she did, inspected each action, dissected each choice she had made. She had reached the X on the treasure map, only to discover the price of claiming it was far too high. It was all for nothing. The pain, the death she had caused, it had all been for nothing. If there had been anything in her stomach, Velvet felt it may have come rushing up when that happy realization struck.

~

To Velvet, it seemed she had sat—chin resting again on her knees, tear-stained eyes staring at the man she loved—since time immemorial, and it was not long enough.

Henry came slowly awake, yawning and stretching his arms over his head, his body a study in rippling pectorals, all aquamarine light, and undulating shadows. The hard lines of his face instantly softened when his sleep hazed eyes found hers. He flashed her a tender smile that cracked the heart in Velvet's chest. She made a thick, unintentional sound at the sudden sharpness of the pain.

"Come here," he murmured, his voice husky and compelling.

Velvet stood, moving like a sleepwalker as she obeyed.

"We have unfinished business," Henry told her, tugging her

down beside him and in his arms. He touched her cheek. "What is it, Marie?" He cast his eyes around the space enclosing them and found only empty shadows. "Are you well?"

"Ye...s." Her voice cracked badly over the simple word. "Why do you ask?"

Because your eyes are swollen, and there is a pretty pattern of tear stains on your cheeks. Have you been crying, angel?"

"No," she lied, quickly dropping her eyes.

Henry laughed. "I think you are actually getting worse."

Velvet's head snapped back up. "At what?"

"Lying, my darling."

"My thoughts are sad, 'tis all. I am worried about the others, Napoleon—" She broke off at a sudden rush of guilt. In the time they had been together, she had thought of nothing but him. "The fighting was fierce; we don't even know the fate of our friends. We should not linger," she finished lamely, hesitation and regret heavy in her voice. She wanted to stay here with him forever.

Henry's eyes grew wide as her last word fell, shining against his swarthy skin like two blue chips of impenetrable ice. "I see," he said, the statement a bare breath of sound. His fingers tightened on her jaw. Velvet reveled in the small pain as it distracted her from the roiling pit of agony inside. "What was sipped in shades of night loses its taste in daylight? Is that it?" he asked.

Velvet swallowed hard. She had to lie now, and for once in her life she had to do it perfectly. She looked everywhere save his eyes. "It's not that, Henry. It was—you were...are...everything a girl could dream. A living fantasy, truly, but the night is done. The bargain met. I think we would do well to collect our wayward feelings and go our separate ways."

"Do you, now?" On her jaw, Henry's fingers tightened further until her head was tilted back at an unnatural angle so her eyes were forced to crash into his. "Please tell me this is some insane jest," he said. Against her hot cheek, his hand trembled, and Velvet felt like she was burning on a pyre. The look in his eyes was undiluted misery. His brows drew together at her silence. "Why, Marie, can you tell me that? If I frightened you, I'm sorry, it killed me to cause you pain, but I did not lie, it only hurts the first time...if I was too fast, too rough—" He kissed her brow between words that tumbled atop each other.

"It was not that," she whispered, but he carried on like he had not heard her.

"I can still hear the echo of you screaming my name. I felt your desire, wet and hot, squeezing me until I wondered if one could die from pleasure. Marie, I looked in your eyes and felt you. I know you don't have much experience in this, but what passed between you and me is astoundingly rare. Some people will go their whole lives never knowing how it feels to have and be had like that. Before you, I assumed such passion was myth."

"It's just this place, this moment...if..." she tried.

"It was us," Henry said. He brushed his lips over hers, the touch so light Velvet feared she may have imagined it. "You and me, together, like it could have been, should have been, if your life had not been stolen. You were mine when we were children. You knew it when you kissed me that day. You are mine now. In every way. My wife, the duchess of Newcastle—" He stared at her lips, then his head lowered, dangerously.

"No...Henry..." Velvet cried, wrenching her head away from his touch, his kiss. "I do not want you. I gave you one night. My debt to you is paid in full."

"And that is all I am to you? A means to an end, a weapon to be used and discarded."

"If you want to expose the guts of it, then yes. You were a means to an end, Henry," she lied, motioning to the bloody words on the wall. "We have reached the end, and I have no further need of you," she finished sharply. Henry flinched like she had stuck him with a dagger, yet inside she was the one who bled. If there was any hope of saving her brother, she needed to get as far away from this man as possible, and somehow find a way to forget how desperately she loved him.

"If I give in to what you want, and walk away, what will you do?" Henry asked, his voice threadbare.

Velvet shook her head, closed her eyes so traitor tears would not fall. "My life is my own," she finally whispered. "Perhaps I will trade it to Napoleon for a throne."

"The girl I know, and love would have hacked off her own limb before submitting to that man."

"That girl drowned in a bottomless pool."

"I don't much care for the stranger who has taken her place," Henry said.

A single tear escaped Velvet's lash and rolled slowly down her cheek. Velvet opened her eyes and found his. "Nor I," she said. It wasn't enough, but she would give him what truth she could.

"Last night you said you loved me, showed me your heart, and I told you what was in mine. In all my life I have never said those three words to a woman, besides my dead mother and sister, I gave them to you."

Most of Velvet's memories of last night were vague, distorted by whatever black magic he wielded with his mouth and hands, but that moment in time was crystal clear. "I didn't want or ask for such a gift. You cannot turn this back on me, for last night I didn't know what I was saying," she finished. Neither of them believed her.

"I want you to be my wife, Marie," Henry said, impassioned, touching her cheek like she was made of fragile porcelain. Velvet wondered if the internal battle to resist him would be her death. She could feel heat rising in her cheeks. Her racing heart wanted to tear free of her chest and run to a place void of this soul torching pain.

"I can't...I..."

"I want you to be my wife," he repeated, voice rising on each word. "I want to take you home, make love to you in my bed, spread your hair over my body and bathe in your splendor. I want to make you a duchess and give you everything the Revolution took away. I want to take you to all the beautiful places in the world I've seen, show you what there is to love. If England is not to your taste, we will go to France, or the Caribbean. If you hate them all, I will buy you an island to call your own. A haven for us, for our children. If you want to be queen, I will do everything in my power to give that to you, then stand proudly at your side while you make a better world."

Velvet started to cry. She couldn't help it. The animal kingdom was fierce, cruel even, but this was much worse. His words burned in her chest. She could not sacrifice Henry for any prize, so her brother would fade from existence. The spell would settle, and he would remain a beast, lost to her forever. What would become of her love then? Better to sever the ties that bound her to this sinful duke before they grew so strong that severing them would cause a hemorrhage in her heart which would never mend.

On the heels of that thought, Velvet decided to tell the most unconscionable lie of all. She parted her lips and said words she could never take back. "I do not love you, Henry. Whatever I said was torn from me in the heat of the moment. You are right, I know nothing of such things, but I remember the talk at court. Even back then, you had the makings of a legendary lover. 'Twas rumored you slept with half of France after I gave you that kiss. It would figure that you are skilled at what we did. You hypnotized me with your hands, that's all. I think I would have said anything. Perhaps, I am a whore like my mother was reputed to be, it's possible I would have responded that way to any man," she finished, twisting the knife.

Velvet struck true; Henry's eyelids shuddered closed. He moved away from her, sitting back on his heels and, for a wild moment, she feared he would slap her. Velvet waited for the blow. It was no more than she deserved. When it did not fall, she lifted her head, and looked full into his pain ravaged face. He said nothing, only stood, moving like his body had aged decades in minutes. "I don't understand…"

"Your understanding is not a requirement for my freedom," whispered Velvet.

Henry lifted his trousers off the damp cave floor, he yanked them angrily on, and tied off the laces with unsteady hands. Preoccupied with his task, Velvet soaked up the sight of him. The way the haunting light of the numerous pools sculpted the straining muscles in his back that flexed as he presented it to her. "You sure this is what you want?" he asked.

Had she not been sitting Velvet would have fallen to her knees. It was not what she wanted at all. She wanted the life he had proposed, a life of passion, friendship, and adventure—a life with him, but fate had decreed she chose between the man she loved and the brother she treasured, so she was choosing to walk away from them both. "Yes, it is," she breathed, and wondered if the heavens would strike her down for such an unholy lie.

"As you wish," Henry said, not bothering to hide the way his voice broke over the words. Slowly, he moved to the pool's edge, stopping when the water lapped over his toes. He was drenched in the glow. Velvet knew he meant to dive in, to leave as was her wish. Her chest and throat burned like she had downed a draft of uncut whisky. Her red eyes streamed broken hearted tears, and if he turned to look at her for even one second, he would know.

"Water, beautiful, powerful and strange," he mused, turning slightly so his profile was rimmed in delicate light. "It is really a mirror, you know. Mirrors are a deep and powerful magic most people don't understand. The reflection it gives is often a juxtaposition to what one feels on the inside. We see ourselves the way others see us. At times, we see all that we try to hide right there in the open, staring back at us in the face. What will you see, I wonder, the next time you look? I think you will see a liar, and a girl who refused to trust the man who adored her."

"Henry," Velvet breathed, not knowing if she said the word aloud.

Henry paused for a moment like he heard her, then he straightened his shoulders, turned his back to her with cold finality, and dove. His body shattered the surface like glass. Velvet stayed where he left her and cried till all her tears were gone. Perhaps tears were like stars, or tiny shattered pieces of the soul. If the amount of tears detailed the level of sorrow, as once she had supposed, Velvet believed she cried a galaxy.

CHAPTER 3

WHAT IS TIME WHEN IT IS GONE?

April 8th, 1801

*V*elvet cried till every tear she had was gone. She struggled to her feet, swayed like she stood on a ship's rocking deck. In a damp heap, her dress lay where Henry had taken her that first time. Pain and pleasure you could die from, he had promised, and unlike her, he had not lied.

Quick, angry movements saw Velvet yanking the gown over her head, and she shivered when the wet, chilled material touched her bare skin. For time unknown, she stared up at the wall, committing each symbol and line of the ancient spell to memory. After that, there was not much to be done unless she wished to remain down in this world of lovers...all alone. She would touch none of Minerva's things, except Velvet hesitated, then grabbed the crimson cloak from where it lay. The material was the finest Velvet had ever felt. She tossed it around her shoulders. shoulders. It flared out, mimicking a shimmering shroud. It certainly seemed like such, having once belonged to the woman who tried to save someone, and ended up cursing them all.

"Be brave, Velvet," she admonished aloud. Strange to hear her voice echoing back at her from all sides. "You are being stupid. Don't let your heart break. You can go above, tell him why you sent him away, take the stones from him, hold them tight, say goodbye to Louis. Then, you can sell yourself to Napoleon, beg him to take you to France, find your mother's grave, then fall on your knees and beg her to forgive you for breaking your vow —well!"

Velvet kicked a smooth rock underfoot; it struck the wall with a clang. "If that isn't the most heartbreaking sequence of events —par for the damn course, better if Queenie had left me to the gentle care of the French dungeons, and the honor of the republic." Toes edging the largest, closest pool, which she believed was the one from which she had emerged. She prayed to all the goddesses above, that it would lead to the world she knew, the world with Henry. She flexed her legs preparing to take the plunge, when Velvet noticed she was sore in just about every joint, though the pain was rather delicious, because it meant she had, even for a brief time, been his. Still, a good soak in cool water would harm no one. The idea of washing Henry away made Velvet want to linger in the cave a while longer. Lonely, because it still smelled like him, like them.

Remnants in the air of what they had done, memories of how it felt when he moved inside her, what it had meant to be so tightly held in those powerful, capable arms. She would be fine, she was brave and resourceful, she would survive like she always did, but damn if it didn't hurt, didn't break every one of her bones to refuse all she wanted in the world—it hurt like the flames of a furnace heated for sinners.

Velvet gasped in a gulp of enchanted air, then dove headfirst into the pool. The water was bracing cold, and without the stones, it was a long, hard swim with no air. Velvet kicked her legs and struck out on the arduous journey back to reality. Her lungs were churning balls of fire in her chest when she finally saw a flicker of muted light swaying over her head. She kicked furiously, and dragged in huge drafts of night air, when her head broke the surface. Velvet felt like she had just emerged from an upside-down world. Trembling uncontrollably, she crawled over the rocks, dragging her feet out of the water, then she collapsed, lay where she fell for a moment and tried to catch her wheezing breath, cough, and spit excess water from her lungs.

Fragmented chains glittered near her head, touched by moonlight and dirt. The moonlight she understood, considering the giant orb bobbing overhead, but the coating of grey, chalky dirt made no sense at all. The way Henry kissed her before he locked her in those was prevalent in her mind. Thinking of his kiss hauled her mind back to the cave where danced hosts of memories.

Velvet stood and kicked the chains aside, with a touch of spite, then made her way to the base of the cliff. She stood in the spot where Zoe would have landed, had she not sprouted wings. The rope hung where she she had left it the night before, only it wasn't the same rope. This one was thick and braided, where the other had been a slender twine. The sounds of battle had gone quiet, and in the air was none of the smoke that proceeded a battle. Velvet well remembered the black cloud of smoky death after the redcoats had rained fire on Queenie's camp.

Mentally preparing herself for another physical exertion, wishing she could sprout wings at will, Velvet gripped the rope tight, which was rough against her sweaty palms, and chaffed badly. Well, on the bright side, if Velvet thought, she was sore right now, a hundred-foot climb would certainly put things in perspective. On that happy thought, Velvet tucked her skirts between her legs and started the upward trek.

Absent Henry's indomitable strength, the muscles in her arms cramped badly halfway through the perilous climb, and the tendons in her legs began to spasm. The possible futility of her venture and probable plummet to her death, nearly thwarted her resolve, but the urge to see what had come from the battle with Napoleon and William Pitt's red coats made Velvet grit her teeth and keep struggling up, up, up. For a time, there was only sweat dripping in her eyes, the sound of her battling breaths. Fading night made its own noise. The island was alive and loud.

Bright orange sun was cresting the watery horizon, painting silver on the bases of the clouds, those thick and traveling. Sweat slicked Velvet's palms. She squeezed the rope tighter in her trembling hands and ignored the burning pain streaking from her fingertips through the laboring muscles in her shoulders.When she reached the summit, Velvet hauled her quaking body over the jagged rocks, scraping her stomach, not caring at all. Her muscles gave out. Her body plummeted, and her cheek hit the wet grass. Again, Velvet lay where she fell, and was instantly greeted with a sideways view of the grassy knoll free of war and its implements. No bodies or cannon shells, no dying screams or black smoke in the air. Just the women of Sainte-Marie calmly going about their lives, fruit baskets on their heads, little ones tugging at the flowered hems of their island dresses.

Taking care, Velvet stood, and brushed her hair back from her face. The morning light was bright and burning. Velvet shaded her eyes and tried to see past the shore to the ships bobbing beyond. All she saw were thick mists eating the last of night's shadows that hovered over the choppy waves. The miles of white sand was peopled with sailors dragging nets, and pirates unloading cargo. Soldiers sitting at their leisure or starting a brawl in the old tavern at the base of the hill. None of it made sense, the new rope, the decided lack of battle fog or cannon residue in the air, and all the people going about their regular lives as if nothing had happened, as if Napoleon and his killers had never darkened these shores.

Velvet started to walk, rubbing her smarting palms on the soft underside of her skirts. Her feet took her to the tree where two nights ago, Henry had kissed, tricked, and chained her. Knees still knocking from the climb, Velvet crumpled down to the soft earth, in a chilled spot just beneath the tree's leafy shade, and from there, she watched the sunrise. It didn't take much to realize she was exhausted all the way to the marrow of her bones. Her body brought to its limit; her mental endurance tested to the maximum. In the back of her drifting mind, Velvet wondered when last she slept, or properly ate for that matter. Her eyes blinked, she struggled them open, they blinked again and stayed closed, Velvet slept then, perchance she dreamed.

Velvet's dreams ended as all dreams must. Waking with a soul-jolting start, it took a moment to adjust to her surroundings. Green and gold blades of grass waving in the twilight wind. Beached ships bobbing on the moon tide, surrounding black cliffs, a single volcanic peak at sea belching clouds, wild sunset colors brushing the sky, vibrant and gothic, brightening the glow of the fireflies. Velvet realized she had slept the day away. She felt sticky, dry-mouthed, hungrier, and even more miserable. The ache in her chest throbbed with unerring persistence. She tried to stand but stayed on her knees and held her head while it swam in dizzy circles.

"Velvet!"

he sharp, clear sound of her name being called made her head snap up. She searched the horizon. Black clouds gathered, the waves were white capped, crashing against the shore. There, in the space between sand and grass, harshly backlit by all the vibrant colors of faded day, stood a slender man, pale and ghostly as a mirage. Velvet blinked again to make sure the hazy image wasn't a figment of her imagination. The man lifted his hand, tossed her a wave, then called her name again, and moved toward her, his walk seeming too sprightly for his pallor. It was the wave, the tilting head, and the jaunty skip in the otherwise weak steps he took as he moved toward her that told Velvet exactly who he was. Velvet was on her feet, running, tears misting her eyes as she threw herself with happy abandon in Devon's open arms.

"Velvet," he mumbled into her hair, kissing her forehead as her long locks got caught up in the breeze, blew across their faces.

"You look like warm death," Velvet said, sniffing, wiping her nose on her knuckles. "I thought...I heard all the fighting, and I wondered if I would ever see you again, any of you."

Devon held her at arms-length and smiled down into her eyes.

"Oh death, where is thy sting, oh grave, where is thy victory?" he quoted. The spark in his eyes had him looking remarkably like his old self.

"If you hold that stone much longer, death will be the most victorious bastard of all."

Devon shook his head, wind tousled his boyish hair, his smile showed a deep dimple. "Cursed or blessed fortune has deemed I find no other as fair," he said, impassioned. His eyes dropped to the amethyst in his wounded hand. "I cannot let her go, no matter the price. So," he lifted his chin, "I have decided to soldier through and seize the day."

Velvet started to smile, but it died on her lips as he moved, and she saw what the shadows had hidden. "Goddess, Devon," cried Velvet. She reached up and pressed her fingers lightly against the bright red, jagged scar, running from the tip of his right ear to the base of his strong chin. Thick, angry, but healing. "What in the name of all—"

"This," Devon fingered the scar. "I got in the way of a French man's blade who was busy slicing throats and put a target on mine." He smiled broadly. "It was a near thing, Katie saved me."

"How?" Velvet gasped.

"The little sprite flew at the man, screaming, trying to scratch out his eyes. She was nothing more than a brush of wind on his face, but he stumbled, and it threw off his aim, just enough to save my life."

"The battle, William Pitt, Napoleon, the men? I heard ship cannons, clashing swords, the screams. What happened to everything? Where are the bullets, the bodies?"

Devon didn't answer right away. He reached out and touched his finger to the tip of her nose. Velvet gave him a questioning look that turned to outrage when he pinched it. She smacked his hand, hard. "Ouch! What was that for?"

"Just making sure you are alive," he said happily. "I never know these days."

Velvet stumbled back a step. "Of course, I'm alive! Aren't I?"

"I believe so, yes, though the subject has been a topic of extensive and, at times, physical debate. The battle with Napoleon, or as the natives call it, Red Sand massacre, happened four months ago." Devon cocked his head. "Or was it five? I believe it was five. The days do tend to blend."

Velvet felt the blood drain from her face. She opened her mouth to speak, but no words escaped the barrier of dumbfounded silence. "Impossible," she finally breathed. "It hasn't been more than two days...has it?" Her voice dropped away as she asked herself how long had she been trapped in that brilliant, forbidden ecstasy?

"Yes," said Devon over a yawn. "Forgive me for not dredging up the appropriate amount of shock. However, I had a similar conversation with Henry, not thirty days ago. He wore the same flummoxed expression painting your own face, my dear. In my quiet moments I think I will find great comedy in it all, for now." He threw up his hands in a show of surrender. "Color me all the shades of bemusement."

"Henry?" Velvet whispered.

"Yes, you remember him, don't you, my dear? Tall, dark, angry as Lucifer falling from heaven. Said a host of insane things, but I spend my days holding an enchanted stone and kissing a dead girl, so I'm in no position to judge."

Velvet sat or fell down—there was no real way to be sure—

and held up her hands to him in defense. "Wait, I beg you, go back to the beginning."

"The night Henry clapped you in irons and you went with him over the edge of those rocks there. Into the unknown, I assume. Napoleon attacked with three hundred men, on some trumped up charge, stolen documents, if I recall.

He, and William Pitt came for you. That much was obvious to us all. He wants you, my dear, wants to sit you on a throne—"

"And make me his puppet," said Velvet, cutting across his words, thinking of the ones she had thrown at Henry, trying to hurt him, breaking herself in the process.

Devon nodded, pensive. "Well said. Nora rallied her men, paid others, even the women fought for her. We had the crew of the Siren. The fighting was fierce. Nora—glowing bright from the light of your brother—called a cease fire alongside Napoleon. We waited; they came to terms. This island is hers now, by his decree." Devon smiled. "Surprised party of no one, I know. I wager the woman could bend kings to her will with a single word."

"Five months," Velvet said, lifting her gaze and glaring at the world with new eyes.

Devon studied her face. "One hundred and fifty-two days. Henry's been back for thirty of them, and every one of them has been spent searching for you. It's safe to say he is obsessed. Please don't tell me you cast another spell on the poor man."

"If a spell was cast, it was on the both of us, but why was he searching? He knew where I was."

Devon shook his head. "He says the way is closed to him."

"Has he destroyed the stones?"

"No. He has tried them all, even that strange black one that cloaks him in storm clouds. His mood has grown progressively foul with each of his failed attempts." Devon sat down beside her, plucked a long stalk of grass, thoughtfully chewed on it, regarding her from bloodshot eyes with a searching stare that made Velvet want to drop her own. "Said you sent him away, none too kindly. I think I know, but may I ask why?"

Velvet closed her eyes, twitching from the effort it took to take a breath over the stabbing pain in her chest.

"I've known Henry most my life. He used to be happy, laughed all the time as a child, then his mother and sister—" Devon made a solemn sound, spit the grass, and cleared his throat. "He locked a part of himself away, until at times I thought it had died. Killing for the crown meant nothing to him. The part of him that should care was gone. Emotion, attachment, love? They were weaknesses to him. Women were beautiful toys, used only after dark. He has a will of steel, and none of the flounced skirts got him to bend, much less break. With you, all the rules are broken. He loves you, Velvet."

Velvet saw only friendship and understanding in Devon's eyes. "I love him," she haltingly admitted.

"Then, why?"

Velvet broke their stare to gaze at the backs of her hands, the rope burns crisscrossing her palms. "I will tell you this, but you must swear on your life that you will not tell another soul."

"I swear it," he said instantly.

Velvet gnawed on her lower lip, hesitating. "While we were in that cave, ghosting through time, I found the spell that will turn my brother human, and I learned the cost. To make the change, I must kill the person I love most in the world."

"Henry," Devon stated. No question.

Velvet nodded miserably. "A life for a life, blood for blood."

A frown creased Devon's forehead, but his eyes glittered with amusement. "If Henry finds out, you think he might go all noble on you and sacrifice himself?"

"Yes. I am afraid of what he will do."

Devon laughed. "Well, to use Zoe's eloquent words, aren't you in a right pickle?"

Velvet groaned; her head fell into her hands. "A sage observation, Devon, illuminating as always."

"Comedy and wisdom dear, that's my game," he said, laughing. Standing, he hauled Velvet to her feet, strong-arming any show of resistance on her part. He linked her arm through his own, then pulled her along, down toward the base of the hill and tavern beyond. When Velvet was begrudgingly trudging beside him, he was suddenly all innocence, his boyish charm returning, his deep dimples coming out to play. "What's that, my dear? Oh, I'd love to walk with you. Thought you'd never ask."

Velvet rolled her eyes. "You're incorrigible."

"Guilty, I'm afraid," Devon said, his step turned to a skip, and Velvet struggled to keep up. "Charming as you are, I cannot keep you all to myself. Besides, I can't wait much longer to see the look on Henry's face when I walk you through the door."

"I don't want to see him," Velvet said, her voice unsteady. In a flash, she remembered their naked bodies twisting together, the burning, blinding pleasure that had changed her in a million indefinable ways.

"Funny," Devon said, then he glanced at the sky, eyes locked to the silver moon. "I think seeing him right now is the thing you want most in the world, including changing your brother. It scares you because you know it, too."

Velvet struggled in his hold. Devon paused, hand over hers, not releasing her. His brow raised in a deep arch. "We both know you will never give yourself over to Little Boots," he said bluntly. Velvet stiffened. Devon laid a hand on her cheek, and his voice softened. His hand was ice cold, but his eyes were warm. "Be honest, you regretted sending Henry away the moment he left. I can see it written all over your face. We have all lost much, so don't let your love be another causality. Blood isn't always the only way. There is often another path, another choice."

"Says the man who holds death in his hands."

"A choice I willingly make each day. Speak with him, hug Nora. If you still wish to talk with Napoleon, I will escort you myself. I give you, my word. You are no coward, princess. You have it in you to face the man you love." When he saw her refusal flashing in her eyes, Devon took a long breath, and let it out in a groan. "Very well, if you will not do it for him, or yourself, then do it for the rest of us. His misery and rage over you have brought us all to the brink of sanity. Ritchie and the others have been planning a mutiny for weeks."

"You jest," said Velvet, slapping his arm, none too gently.

"Never think it, my dear. Mutiny was my suggestion, after all. A quick crack to the back of the head when he isn't looking, maybe repurpose those chains he used on you, hang him from the rafters till his scowl turns to tears."

"Sneaking up on Henry sounds highly unlikely in any scenario."

Devon flipped his hair, looking inordinately pleased with himself. "A number of ideas were thrown around. Everyone had their own plan of how the attack should go down. The knock on the head was the one that got the biggest laugh from me. Thought I would share it with you. Think it was Martin's plan, or Ritchie, hard to say. Everyone had a suggestion." Devon chucked her under the chin. "I'd wager you have a few of your own."

Velvet was expressionless. "I fear you do far too much wagering, Devon," she said, lifting her voice as the surrounding noises rose. Two women stopped to stare openly at her, and Velvet wondered at the sight she must make, a beached mermaid walking on unsteady legs, victim of the spell which had let her walk on land.

Despite all her denials, fear, and stubbornness, she could not help feeling that Henry was hers. It had only been hours since her last sight of him, yet Velvet felt like a thousand years had transpired.

Devon turned to favor her with a charming smile. "Then do not think of us at all. I hate to be the one to say it—" he passed a haughty hand before his nose, "but a bath might be just the ticket for you."

Irritated beyond baring, Velvet wrested her arm from his hold and stepped up on the cobbled sidewalk, brushing past a huddled group of men in French regalia, drinking dark liquid from a dirty wooden barrel. They greeted her loudly while one made a swipe at the hem of her skirt. Another whistled. There was a sword in Devon's hand before Velvet could blink. She was back in his arms, the blade crossed protectively over her midsection. He struck out at the man who had dared to touch her. The man made a shocked, angry noise when he saw Devon's well aimed blade flashing, bathed in moonlight. He stumbled back from his squat and fell hard on his seat. Devon growled at the others, then stepped past her, and kicked open the tavern door with such force that the wood squeaked and cracked in places. Looking ahead, Devon clutched her hand, then dragged her inside.

Velvet blinked against the darkness. The interior had drastically changed. Gone were the cloistered tables, and bubbling jugs of ale. The sand and sawdust once covering the floor had been swept clean, the dark, wooden slats beneath gleamed with fresh polish. Thick satin drapes stained with blueberry dye strung the windows and the ratty shutters had been torn away. The rest of the décor resembled a boudoir from a forbidden romance. Slouched red divans, velvet pillows, and long, low tables slathered in all kinds of island delicacies. Puff pastry cakes cut to perfection surrounded towers of cookies full of thick, chocolate chips. Velvet's stomach roared, and she put a hand to her midriff to keep it silent.

Pirates, sailors, and soldiers brushed shoulders. A woman, strawberry hair hanging past her hips, sang a Celtic song on a lute inlaid with mother-of-pearl. Nora sat on a small dais in a high-backed armchair, presiding over it, queen of all the eye could see.

Beside her, Henry relaxed in his seat with deceptive casualness, his booted feet propped up on a thick cushion. Velvet's eyes went to his face. It was a cold mask, austere and beautiful in the muted candle glow, every bit the dark duke of fantasy, somehow belonging to this storied setting as nothing else could.

His savage eyes lifted to hers like he sensed her presence, felt it, the way she could always feel his. Their gazes clashed, tangled, burned. In his dark, endless eyes, she saw his soul and all that roiled there. Murderous fury, relief, breathless desperation, and something that looked like joy. He came to his feet in a rush. The crowd fell instantly silent. Familiar faces, strangers, Nora, Abigail, Zoe, they all just stared. Sudden pallor defusing blushes. Mouths wide, dropped in shock.

Nora was the first to break. She let out a harsh, astonished cry. Both hands flew to her parted lips to hold back another. Her gown was pure gold, a twined filigree of the same delicate shade sat atop her shoulders like a crown, framing the slender arch of her neck. Her red hair was gathered in a braid that ran down her back, and if Devon had not fully convinced her of the time she lost in the lover's cave, Nora's swollen body was proof positive. She looked ready to burst.

Velvet started to run toward her friend. Rhee caught her hand as she flashed past him. Velvet blew a kiss in his direction. Zoe hauled her into a tight hug. "I can't believe you're alive," he whispered, and she pressed her lips lightly to his cheek. No idea what to say, for him it had been five months, for her—two days. Ritchie and Martin touched her hand, others brushed their fingers over locks of her wild hair, giving Velvet a sense of reality, of home.

CHAPTER 4

ALL ILLUSIONS FADE COME MORNING

*D*espite her vivid excitement, Nora exercised caution as she descended the dais one step at a time. Her baring was regal as a queen. Every drop of her royal blood evident in her poise. Even knowing what she was capable of since childhood, Henry was initially surprised with how expertly his ballroom darling had taken to the role of pirate queen. A far cry from the wild girl who ran amok through the Newcastle estates, making endless yards of daisy chains, and preferred to bed down with Katie in the stables, to the woman who stood before him, decked in jewels and pirate gold, commanding all she saw with a look. The women, his women, laughed and cried, sighing as they collapsed in each other's arms. Abigale burst from the shadows seeping beneath the lower curtain that hung behind Nora's throne. She fell upon the noisy pair and added her own welcoming ruckus.

Henry watched the teary scene, struggling to breathe. She was alive. Relief was crushing, powerful enough to sap the strength from his limbs. Thirty-one endless days of searching, thirty-two cold nights. Always their hateful, parting words ringing in his ears. Every moment wishing for her, aching to touch her, hold her. He was enraged with her, and she wasn't going to be spared the biting lash of his fury, but now he wanted her. Wanted to rip her from Nora and crush her in his arms. Kiss her, take her until this madness left him. He needed to touch her, assure himself of her reality.

Henry watched Nora lay her head on Velvet's shoulder as Velvet locked her arms around her waist. Velvet's eyes flicked open, and she searched for him over Nora's bright hair. Blush stained her cheeks as their eyes met. Henry knew the hot look in his gaze shouted his thoughts. He understood to some extent how she felt—the same had happened to him. The strange, unexplainable shift in time. It was a confusing madness which had befallen both of them.

In her mind, she had seen him yesterday, threatened him with Napoleon, and sent him away from her. Heartbreak made him leave, and he regretted it the moment his head broke water on the other side. He had returned only the find the cliff would not respond. The symbols stayed unlit and dormant, no matter how many enchanted stones he toted before them. The way was closed to him, a man. He understood now; it had opened for him once, but it had been by her power all along. The magic was Velvet, as he had always suspected.

He loved her unreservedly, passionately, frantically, with all his being. She was his only star in a sky of night, and he was nothing more to her than a weapon. An inconvenience.

He had always known he was obsessed with the chit. Even in his worst rages he had treasured her, losing her for these last thirty days had taught him that what he felt went beyond obsession, past the pale word humans had for love. Nora said some teary thing, and Velvet ripped her gaze away from his. Henry felt freezing without it.

"I knew you weren't dead," Henry heard Nora remark.

"Not at all dead," Velvet said. "I only saw you a few nights ago. Your waistline was smaller," she finished, smiling slightly.

Nora drew back her shoulders, proudly thrusting out her huge stomach. "Isn't it fabulous?" Her hands curved protectively around the bump. "She's a kicker. Strong, so strong. She keeps me awake constantly," she said, fairly glowing.

Velvet reached out, shyly touched Nora's hand, then let her fingers rove over the taut material of Nora's gown. "She wants to be born, I think," Velvet said. Her body twitching adorably when the child kicked her hand. A tender, unbidden smile curved her lips.

Henry noted the rosy flush of her cheeks, the gleam of happiness in her eyes. Her face was soft as he had ever seen it, the scheming, desperate wench was gone. In her place was the girlish, sincere princesses he had fallen in love with all those years ago. Both of them children in a French castle with no idea what life would bring.

"I have so much to tell you," Nora gushed. She waved a hand, instantly the revelry commenced, the lady and her lute continued their song. Laugher and gossips rang off the walls. Henry sat very still and watched his men crowd her. Zoe grabbed Velvet's hand and held it to his chest, not letting go when the others threw their arms around her and kissed her cheeks. His princess hardly said a word, as the crew of the Bacchus rushed her to deliver similar treatment. She glowed under their kind words and touches. Henry wanted to bare his teeth, draw his sword, fight his way through the debris of his men, lift her in his arms and carry her away from this, from everything. He wanted her to raise her eyes and look at him again. He knew she could feel him watching her, the small, raised hairs on her bare forearms told him so.

Minutes passed like years as he waited, just a glance, a single glare, would assuage the savage inside him. Nora drew her away and pressed a glass of crimson wine in Velvet's hands. Velvet went with her, and she did not look back.

Ritchie, smiling like Satan with a plan, came and clapped him on the back. Henry braced for the hit, still it smarted. "You look like a wolf in a henhouse," Ritchie observed, staring after Velvet's retreating back. Henry grunted a response and his first mate continued to ramble while Henry watched Velvet touch Nora's cheek, laugh and hug Abigale. She wore the purple cloak from the cave, and beneath it was the same dress he had peeled her out of thirty-two nights ago. He remembered the way her flushed nipples had popped free of the soft material, the way they had tasted between his teeth. Henry closed his eyes so he would not groan aloud. People moved and conversed around him, nothing registered besides her. Why wouldn't she look at him? Henry took the rum Devon pressed in his hand, then drained it in a single gulp. Devon handed him another. Henry turned and focused his attention on his friend's face, still watching her from the corner of his eye. "Where the devil did you find her?" Henry choked, while uncut, black rum burned a path of fire down his throat.

"Beneath the tree where you chained her, looking confused as a newborn bird just fallen from the nest. Like you, she had no idea about the time leap," Devon said, sipping his ale.

Henry wiped the rum from his lips on the back of his hand. "She was just standing there?"

"Yes, well, sleeping actually," Devon said, and took a step back to a safe space free of Henry's enraged aura, and the ever-present cloud of black mists he wore like a second skin. "She loves you, Henry," Devon stated softly. "You would do well to remember that in the coming days."

"Does she, really?" Henry rasped. "She has a dastardly way of showing it." Velvet titled back her head and laughed again; the sound was vinegar poured on the wound of his emotions. Devon opened his mouth to speak, but men cut between them. Additional back slaps were administered, more cups of rum shoved in his hands. Henry consumed them all, draining one after another.

She was alive, and well. He could finally relax, set down his eternal guard, and get blasted drunk, and that was just what he intended to do. He tried to focus on the conversations between his men, tried to wrangle his thoughts away from her. It was impossible. Her smell was in the air, roses and rain, the bell of her breathless laugh rang in his ears, again and again. He wanted all her laughs, all her smiles. She was a siren in his soul, and Henry knew he was drowning in her song.

~

Velvet knew he watched her. She held Nora's hand, listened to tales of what transpired while she had been beneath the water, locked in Henry's arms, or curled into herself on the cold cave floor trying to forget how wonderful they felt wrapped around her. Velvet laughed at Nora's stories of Napoleon, her vivid description of his tiny size, and massive nose, but the laugh felt forced and dry. She nodded approvingly and said all the right things as Nora described the mansion she was building on the island, while Abigale spilled fantastical stories of Nora in battle, painting her to be a veritable Joan of Arc. Nora preened and glowed under the elaborate praise.

Velvet answered when asked a direct question, but her mind and heart were not in it. Everything in her considerable power was focused on not turning around and giving Henry a taste of his hot regard. The men asked him questions, and she listened for his curt responses. Goddess, how she wanted to run to him, wildly kiss the frown off his sensual lips.

Nora took Velvet's hand, squeezed it hard, demanding her attention. "I'm sure you are struggling to make sense of all this, just as we were," Nora said, patting Velvet's hand. "Devon, your brother, and I have some theories, but I won't bore you with them now." Nora stroked her fingertips down Velvet's cheek. "Poor princess. You need a bath and a new gown, or a pair of trousers if you prefer. You could borrow one of mine. None of them fit me anymore," she admitted mournfully.

"Thank you," Velvet said, deeply glad for the chance to escape. "A bath would be just the thing; I've near forgotten what soap feels like on my skin."

Nora stood slowly, hand clutching her lower back. "Come, I

will show you where you can sleep. Rhee and Zoe will bring heated water. I am sure you want to be anywhere but here. You must feel quite overwhelmed. Besides," Nora sighed, "if Henry stares at you like that much longer, I fear we may all catch fire. He searched every day for you, spent endless hours in that pool."

"So, I have been informed," Velvet muttered, then dared to cast a furtive glance at Henry from the cover of her thick lashes. He was impossible to miss the way his dark head towered over them all. His austere face wore an unreadable mask. He was clutching a cup of rum in a white knuckled grip. Martin and Zoe were speaking animatedly to him, Zoe waving his thin arms in front of Henry's face. Velvet doubted he heard a word. Her eyes stayed on him while Nora led her to the south side of the room where a small marble table sat, decorated with a jug of wine and an assortment of glasses. They were, for the most part, alone. Nora pressed Velvet into a black, satin seat with wide armrests, a soft pillow crushed behind her head. Velvet sighed at the comfort. "Leave it to you to transform a musty tavern into a den of luxury."

"A queen must have a court," Nora declared cheerfully, then her expression sobered, her hands went to her generous hips, while her brow knitted in consternation. "Was the news truly that wretched?" Nora asked, lowering her voice for Velvet's ears alone.

"I don't know what you mean," Velvet whispered.

Nora snorted a loud and unladylike sound, and a few heads snapped in their direction. "Please," Nora murmured, her face soft and sympathetic, "the horror of whatever transpired is written all over you. Even now, you can hardly meet my eyes."

Velvet smiled up at Nora. Nora's mouth turned down in a line of frustrated distress. "I have no idea what the devil is going on, but I am sure it is nothing to smile about."

"I'm smiling because I adore you, Nora," Velvet said, looking directly into her friend's piercing, intelligent eyes. "I love that you know me so well. No matter where we are in the world, I am never an outsider with you. I think I could tell you anything, and you would like me just the same. It is a wonderful thing."

Nora's eyes sparkled, but sternly she said, "Flattery will not divert me, so tell me what you learned about the spell."

"There was nothing. It was all worthless. The spell itself was old and written in blood. The words could be Latin, very ancient of course, but I think not. Gibberish to me, and not well preserved. I cannot give my own life, and I do not have Queenie's powers, whatever they were," Velvet said dejectedly, meaning to speak truth best as she could. "Alfonso is right. The stones should be destroyed, the way to the cave hidden forever. It was a place of death and pain. Using the stones in any way will only bring more of the same."

Nora's blue eyes darkened; her arched brows rose high. "I don't believe you are telling me the full truth."

"I'm not," Velvet readily admitted. "Just trust me when I say there is no way."

Nora snorted again. "There is always a way," she said calmly, before an expression of sorrow and anxiety overtook her pretty face. "I can't lose him, Velvet. Louie is everything to me."

"Me too," Velvet said bleakly.

Nora fell silent. Velvet could almost see the wheels in her quick mind spinning as she sifted through various possibilities. She went quite pale for a moment, then snorted again, the loudest of them all. "No! Poppycock!" she exclaimed, clapping her hands together with a fantastic bang, startling them both as Velvet had once done in another tavern, time, and worlds away. They both simultaneously recalled the event and laughed but sobered quickly. Nora sat on the arm of the chair and wrapped her arms around Velvet's shoulders. "I don't know why I'm laughing when I feel like crying. I'm sure you do as well. Let's go upstairs. We'll get you in a bath, then we can cry together."

Velvet nodded, knowing Nora's inquisition had not yet reached a verdict; more questions would definitely be asked. Nora could pry and dig down to the truth of a thing like no other

—yet Velvet was glad for the moment of reprieve, as she was currently uncertain of how to go on without spilling all her secrets. Saying what the spell required would only drag Nora into her agony. Giving her the painful knowledge of such a dreadful choice was a thing Velvet could not do. It was too horrible a price. She loved Nora too much to even let her contemplate it, would not allow the darkness of it to touch her, touch any of them.

Nora captured both Velvet's cold hands and tugged her up. Velvet shot a final, secretive glance at Henry. What she saw was a dark-skinned woman, with lush red lips, and a delicate bone structure standing beside him, her slender arm draped around his waist. A transparent scarf wrapped her otherwise naked hips. The girl wore nothing else. Strings of seashells and tiny bones dangled around her neck, hanging in the deep valley between her ample breasts. Under the touch of firelight falling from the numerous candles, her dark skin glowed like warm honey. Henry did not lean into the beautiful woman's advances, but Velvet saw he did not pull away.

Velvet's insides roiled like she had drunk poison as the girl's knowing hands caressed the taut muscles of Henry's stomach, through the thin linen of his shirt. She half walked, half twirled her fingers up the strong plains of his chest, found the buttons at his throat, undid them with nimble fingers. Velvet wanted to scream, bare her teeth and tear the woman's wandering hand from her pretty arm.

Henry glanced up, no doubt feeling the heat of Velvet's furious regard, but Velvet had already averted her eyes. Nora gave Velvet's hand a hard tug, and Velvet trailed her up a set of spiral stairs, where the decorative, twirling banister had been polished to show the rich mahogany.

Somewhere behind them, Velvet heard Henry's deep voice, too garbled by all the varied sounds, for her to make out his words. She thought he called her name but did not pause to find out. She was sure, however, that his eyes tracked every step that took her from his sight.

At the top of the stairs, Nora lifted a lantern with an orange flame, jumping behind the dusky glass from a brass knob on the wall. Hoisting it high, she used the shedding halo of light to guide them down the slender passage. The balmy air from the open windows seemed to penetrate every inch of her skin beneath the stolen cloak. Dark curtains blew wide, flying out into the night, waving over the noisy street below.

Nora came to a stop before the third door on the right. This door had a far more eloquent design than the others. Velvet glanced quickly over her shoulder at the way they had come, the weak light from the fireplace at the end of the hall, and flickering lanterns could not combat the thick darkness, the effect turned the scene ghostly. Velvet shuddered as a chill slid down her spine. Nora turned the brass handle and threw open the door. Velvet rushed inside the room, then closed the door firmly behind them both, feeling those screaming black wraiths were back and nipping at her heels.

Nora walked ahead into the darkness, set the lantern on a circular table, lifted a book of matches, and lit the short wick of another; a warm glow fell around them. Velvet saw that the room they were in was wide and oval in structure, it contained a large bed draped in a heavy canopy, shining rosy gold, and champagne silk. A thick shag carpet lay at the foot of the bed, mimicking the shape of the room. A silver-tinted writing desk sat in front of an arched window, thrown open to show the indigo sky, and iridescent moon, letting in wafts of warm wind and the smells of the island at night. A clawed tub sat behind a sheer curtain, the perfect complement to a high, French armoire, complete with a floor length looking glass. Velvet's reflection terrified her. Tangled hair framing, crazed, red-rimmed eyes. The cloak seemed like a slice of violet night, changing colors when she moved.

"Yes," Nora said, looking over Velvet's shoulder, meeting her eyes in the mirror, "you do look a fright." Nora shook her head, smiling. "Five months, Christ. At times I almost gave in to the terror and believed you both dead, done in by the very spell you retrieved to save us. I am inordinately pleased that was not the case. When I found Henry stumbling around the island, I scared him by promptly hugging him, and crying my eyes out. Man's a right bastard at times, but I can't help loving him. He's always been the best of brothers to me, ever there when I needed." Nora captured Velvet's owl-eyed gaze with a meaningful stare. "You love him too, don't you?"

"It's like you said, I can't help it," Velvet said, dropping her gaze to the polished wooden slats shining under her dirty boots. Nora's hands went to Velvet's throat, and she undid the silken bow there. The cloak slid to the floor, then she went to work on the small buttons running down the back of Velvet's dirty white dress. Velvet had nothing but a sheer chemise beneath, torn in places by Henry's hands and teeth, and she flushed brightly as the dress dropped in a heap.

Nora noted the condition of Velvet's undergarments, and said nothing, but Velvet saw her knowing smile in the looking glass. The smile faded when Nora saw the red marks on Velvet's neck and shoulders. She clicked her tongue loudly against the roof of her mouth. "He's wanted you so long, I suppose it wasn't in him to be gentle," Nora observed.

Velvet's blush reddened the tips of her ears. "He was divine," Velvet said.

Nora laughed. "I guess he must have been. Sometimes gentle isn't exactly what women want, is it?"

Velvet closed her eyes so she would not see the twinkling light in Nora's. Laughing, Nora walked past Velvet and threw open the armoire. She took a fluffy white towel from the bottom shelf, and a long white cambric nightgown off a swinging hanger. "The nightgown is mine; I've been sleeping in here since I gave Henry the master suite, but tonight he can bed down with the horses. The room is rightfully mine, and I give it to you."

"Because Napoleon gave you this island?"

"Because I demanded it," said Nora. "He is a cad. I suspect

that preposterous man does not have much longer in this life.. He would do well to make better use of the time he has, instead of running around trying to conquer the civilized world. I could have beaten him the night he attacked. We both knew it. I didn't want to lose another life, and he didn't want to lose, period. It was how we reached our amicable accord. He is not an amicable man. Remember that when you plan your next move." Nora walked to lay the nightgown at the foot of the bed, smoothing the wrinkles in the cloth. "Be careful, Velvet," she finally said, "that is all I ask."

Velvet almost smiled. "How is it that you've always been able to see me exactly as I am?"

"Oh, I wouldn't make that claim," Nora said, walking back to Velvet and wrapping the towel around her shaking frame. "Now you stand here, shiver, and contemplate the wisdom of your actions. I will have the lads fetch water for your bath." Nora leaned in so she could kiss Velvet on her cheek. Her skin felt chilled despite the warm, island wind sweeping through the room. Nora stood unmoving. Velvet's hand caught between hers as she studied Velvet's face with bright blue eyes. "You have friends," she finally said, her voice earnest. "The best, really. Depend on us."

Velvet nodded, wondering if Nora could read minds, if she knew Velvet meant to run from them all.

The bath was hot and divine. Velvet rested her head against the lip of the tub and closed her eyes. She had washed her hair three times, using the lavender soap Nora had ordered from France. The soap was soft, filling the room with its heady scent and pulled the tension from her aching joints. She scrubbed until her skin was rosy and glistening, and she felt at least a modicum of her old self return.

For years, she had been a solitary creature, caring for no one but her brother, and Queenie at times; everyone else she had loved was dead. Then, one terrifying night, she wasn't alone anymore. Instead, Velvet was surrounded by people, with lives, emotions, and dreams which they all put on hold for her. Suddenly, she found that their incredible lives were somehow resting in her unworthy hands. Velvet could barely admit it, even to herself, but she was tired of trying and failing, repeatedly gaining then losing the same ground.

Pensive, she stood and let the golden water drops run down her naked body to splash on the floor. Velvet wrapped the towel around herself with absent, clumsy movements while she stared out the window to the night beyond, listening to the surf crash against the white shore. "My goddess, what have I done?" she whispered. She should never have let any of them accompany her on this insane, perilous quest. She should have tried harder to escape—escape Alfonso, Henry, Nora. The truth was, she had not wanted to. Friends were a rare and strange treasure, and she was loathe to lose the few that fate had given her. Velvet decided then that she was a stupid, selfish girl and deserved whatever misfortune came her way. If only she could have given her own life and made some small atonement for all she had done.

Velvet sighed and stepped from behind the screen, her mind lost in turbulent thoughts, her eyes seeing everything and nothing. She could see a few twinkling stars through the reaching branches of the baobab tree swaying outside the widow. From the corner of her eye, Velvet saw the flash of a dark figure moving on the bed. She shrieked, dropping down to a crouch, one hand clutched the towel, the other held out in front of her face to ward off the menace. Badly startled, heart racing, Velvet could only stare, her mind wiped clean with alarm. The man stood, the shadows crisscrossing his form resolved. There was a tautness about his face, a banked glow in his hungry eyes.

"Henry," she gasped, straightening quickly, and took an unsteady step toward him before she could stop herself. Velvet's feet tangled in the hem of the long towel. Her arms flailed, then she pitched forward at an incredible velocity, and crashed into his waiting arms.

Velvet heard his mocking chuckle, felt it like lash on her bare skin. "Now, now my love, it's clear my charms are too much for you to resist, but there is no reason to throw yourself at me. All you have to do is ask."

"Let go of me, Henry," she said, her voice deceptively calm. "I don't like it when you hold me like this. It makes me feel...just let go."

"No," he replied with jeering softness. "You don't have a choice, madam, you are mine. I believe by rights I can hold you however, and whenever I desire." His hands coasted over her shoulders. Velvet stiffened.

"Are we really back to that?" Velvet sighed. "A couple hours, or thirty days ago, depending on your perspective, you walked away from me. Please do so again. We have said everything there is to say."

"Thirty-two days," Henry corrected. "And there is much more to be said, I'm afraid."

Velvet lifted her chin, trying not to feel the iron body against hers. The rigid proof of his desire pressed hard against her abdomen, burning like a flame between them. "Damn you, I missed you," he said, his voice guttural. Velvet closed her eyes. Henry held her at arm's length and shook her. "Tell me you did not miss me, crave what we had."

"It was no more than a few hours for me," she protested, leaning back to look at his blazing eyes. A lock of dark hair fell over his forehead, and her fingertips ached to brush it away.

He was breathing hard, staring at her with blind, naked yearning. She could smell the rum on his breath, the scent of a woman's sweet perfume on his clothes. The laces of his boots untied; the top three buttons of his shirt undone. He was rumpled, raw perfection. Velvet could see the bronze skin beneath his open collar, and her eyes traveled down his body before they flicked back to his face. He looked like a pillaging savage, some ancient, warring god. She damned the sudden awakening of her senses.

"I wanted you again the second I left you," he rasped, hands wrapping her waist as he crushed their bodies together, and rocked his hips, once, twice. Velvet shuddered. "Tell me you don't want this," Henry demanded, moving against her with maddening rhythm. "Tell you don't need me as much as I need you. Tell me how bad you want your freedom while you melt in my arms."

Velvet's body flushed with heat, nerveless and weak. Her hands came to his head, her fingers tangling in his wild hair. It would be so easy to surrender to the pleasure of his hands and mouth. There had never been temptation like this, but she would not give in to the self-destructive urge. It would be disastrous. If only her mind could control her traitorous body.

Henry snarled at her silence before his lips crashed down on hers. Thoughts of resistance instantly burned to wispy embers. The heat of his lips and tongue robbed her of breath. His arms were hard as they closed tightly around her. His hands gripped her hips as he lifted her, and Velvet's legs linked his waist of their own volition. While her body strained desperately against his, her hands clutching the back of his head, holding him tight as his tongue stroked and swirled, setting every part of her aflame.

He grabbed her towel in one fist, ripped it away, and threw it into the corner of the room. Velvet followed his mouth with blind yearning. He lifted his head a few inches, and she met his eyes, near black with drink and passion. "I'll never let anything take you from me, not even you. What we have is magic in its purest form."

He was right. Velvet knew it in her bones, that she would never find this with anyone else. It was a terrible truth. She must not let herself love him, must not let herself fall any further. This would be more than possession, this man, of dark silk and fire, would own her very soul. Velvet struggled hard against him. Henry said something foul beneath his breath and set her on her feet. "The dark side is not worth the light," she snapped. "What if it's you? Dominating villain that you are. Maybe you are such a terrifying, treacherous man, I don't want to love you, I don't want to need you."

Henry colored with fury. "I know we belong together. Damn you, Marie, can you not trust me? Just this once? Let me help you, no bargains, or battles between us."

Through the blur of her wet lashes, she stared at him, his furious gaze promising erotic fantasies. His hand was unsteady as he brushed her long hair to the side, kissed her bare shoulder. "I need you, my love, in ways I can hardly fathom."

Velvet crossed her arms over her breasts. "One would think you would be satisfied after last night," she stated breathlessly.

Henry dragged her back to him, pressed his lips against her brow. "Last night for you, thirty-two nights for me, I have wanted you for all of them. Lay in bed at night plagued by visions of you, dancing through my mind like a nymph, toying with the delicate threads of my sanity." He pulled her close, their bodies touched, burned. "I can't stop remembering, desiring. You are a fever in my blood, the sum of all my desires."

Velvet's breath caught; her heart hammered in a furious rhythm of need. "I don't love you, Henry, and I will leave you."

Staring at the small, unyielding stranger before him, Henry balled his hands into fists. He stepped back to look at her, face set, cheeks flushed, lips swollen, and beautiful eyes slanted like a cat. Naked, proud, glorious. "I cannot live without you," he said, raking a trembling hand through his hair. "The devil knows I have tried. I missed something in that cave, some vital piece of information that made you turn on me. Whatever it is, we can face it together—"

"We can do nothing," she cried, tears filling her eyes. "It is over. There is nothing left for me, save to try and live for some purpose, forget my brother, forget the things I've done." She closed her eyes and took a shallow breath. "Forget you."

"Why?" Henry demanded, enraged at the tremors he saw rushing through her. "Why, tell me why?"

"No! I will not speak to you like this, drenched in another woman's perfume, reeking of rum. You're drunk! Indecent."

"Drunk, madam? Not yet, indecent? Most assuredly," he said, "I would like to devour you, lick you till you screamed, stroke my fingers inside of you until you were wet and shaking, then make you take me in a thousand different ways—"

His voice broke, and they stood, panting, and exchanged a challenging glare. Then he felt himself smile, mocking the situation, mocking her and the lies she told. Slowly his eyes fell to the fire-lit drops of water glittering on her arms, shining in the hollow of her throat.

Her hands struggled to cover her lush breasts, only succeeding in pushing them together deliciously. Errant drops trickled over her stomach; his eyes tracked their downward path to the golden curls between her thighs. The tantalizing, teasing slide of the tiny drops was Henry's undoing. Velvet resisted as he linked his arm around her waist and hauled her against him, not caring that she kicked and spat at him like a wild cat. His knee pushed between her bare thighs; he dragged her up his body and fastened his mouth to hers.

～

Velvet was drowning in sensation, desperate for what she had forbidden herself. He overpowered her struggles with humiliating ease, carried her to the giant bed and threw her down none too gently. He leaned back, resting one knee on the edge of the bed, and ripped off his shirt. His caressing gaze swept over her, then he gathered her close and Velvet reveled in the feeling of his scalding body against hers.

His husky whisper fell hot against her throat. "Don't fight me, love, I need to be inside you. Now." His eyes were ferocious as his tone. Thoughts of rage, terror and resistance were banished from her mind as he took her face between his hands and kissed her again, gently. Slow, drugging. Sweltering minutes passed, and Velvet knew she had surrendered the moment she stepped into the tavern and met his eyes across the crowd. What was one more night? He had already taken her innocence; the damage was done. One more night to say goodbye to the man she loved.

Henry felt her surrender in the softening of her body. He kissed the corner of her mouth lightly, in love with the petal soft skin of her flushed cheeks, brow, the fluttering lids of her eyes. Her body was silk and satin under his hands, her lush, perfect hips, slender, flared waist, and long shapely legs seemed made exactly for him. He peeled her fingers from her breasts. "Don't cover yourself, I want to see all of you, need to," his voice broke, "need you." He captured her wrists in his right hand, lay her back on the bed, then locked them above her head. Her back arched under his hold, so the taut tips of her breasts brushed his chest. He leaned down and sucked one into his mouth.

Velvet gasped his name. *He was pleasure personified, the devil incarnate,* she thought as the sensations he invoked made her twist and writhe. "I love the feel of you, so soft and perfect, Marie, I love you," she heard him rasp, his raw voice muffled in her hair, flowing over her shoulder, pooling between them.

Velvet's body was flushed with heat, nerveless and weak. She struggled against his hold on her wrists—she wanted to touch him. Lock her hands in his hair, anchor him closer, as his tongue stroked and swirled. Ecstasy spiked her blood, words rushed from her heart unbidden, poured from her lips. "Love you, Henry," she heard herself rasp, "missed you every second, wanted you...wanted this..."

"Then touch me," he grated, the green in his eyes unfathomably dark. He released her captured wrists, took her small hand, and dragged it down his body, and closed her fingers around him. He was too big for her hand, and she struggled to make her fingers meet.

~

Henry sucked a breath between his teeth, feeling his blood rush madly to the place she touched. Her exploration of him was timid, gentle at first as she skimmed her nails slowly down his length. He made another husky sound, and she looked up at him through her thick fan of lashes, stared directly in his eyes as she stroked him from base to scalding tip. Henry almost spilled in her hand. He uttered a harsh, guttural groan, perchance some garbled version of her name. Velvet snatched her hand back, her cheeks turning scarlet. "I'm sorry, I didn't mean to hurt you," she whispered, sounding embarrassed and contrite.

"Then, do it again," be breathed.

"I...are you sure?"

"Yes, dear god, Marie, again," he demanded. Her brows drew together in consternation, front teeth worrying at her lower lip, then she reached for him once more. Henry closed his eyes, pure ecstasy lived in her touch, Henry knew, long as he lived, he would never want any other woman but her.

"I don't know how to touch a man," she breathed. He opened his eyes to find her gaze still locked to his face. "Will you show me?"

Henry prayed for control, wrapped his hand over hers, did as she asked, and watched her stare at him through slitted eyes, her hips unintentionally rocking to the rhythm of her hand, giving what he demanded.

~

Henry was hard and hot as blazing iron, so large he overflowed the confines of her grasping fingers. She felt his pulse throbbing wildly against her palm, watched him tremble from her touch in awe of the power she had over him. Sweat misted his golden skin as his breathing became labored. His hands swept up her back, came around to cup her breast and he spoke against the curve of her neck. "I can't take any more. I must have you now."

"I am yours," she said, and for the moment, it was the truth. Henry held her close and tumbled them to the silky bedspread. Rolling on his back, he took hold of her hips and pulled her atop him, so she straddled his thighs. He wrapped a hand in her long hair, used it to tug her down to his mouth.

His words were hot against her parted lips. "Are you? Show me, ride me, Marie."

Henry's hands rested lightly on each of Velvet's knees, his fingers drawing patterns on her skin. Their gazes tangled as he waited. Velvet felt like she should stammer out a reply, but the thought of what he was asking her to do made her tremble. His fingers stroked her inner thighs, slid between her legs, pressed inside her. Velvet bit down on the back of her hand so those below would not hear her scream.

"I've imagined you like this so many times," Henry rasped, moving his fingers with soul-rending skill until she was warm and trembling all over, calling his name. The pleasure was coming, that sparking white-hot place he had let her touch before. Velvet's legs began to stiffen. His fingers withdrew. Velvet moaned in denial. He reached between their bodies, grasped her hips, lifted her high, then let her drop down hard. Henry locked his teeth, and she took every inch of him in a slow, aching glide. Velvet laid her palms flat on his chest and let out a long, trembling sigh. Henry propped his body on his elbows and licked at the tips of her breasts, pressed more kisses to her throat.

Velvet remained perfectly still, adjusting to the indescribable feeling of him inside of her. His hands went to her silver-gold hair, and he ran his fingers through the locks. Velvet was mesmerized by the way he looked at her. "So gorgeous, ethereal as mist on a twilight wind," Velvet thought she heard him say. She knew they were both seeped in the sense of being outside of time.

Henry's chest rose and fell with his rapid breaths. The look on his face made her heart pound in anticipation. The satin canopy billowed around them as warm wind rushed over their bodies, full of all the darkness and mystery deeply entrenched in the old ground on which they touched.

CHAPTER 5

SPELLS AND THINGS

*H*enry watched his princess throw her head back. Ethereal. It was beauty incarnate the way her pale skin reflected the moonlight. Hungry for her, he greedily absorbed every detail. The ice-satin skin, the gentle rise of her high breasts, perfectly blushed with powder pink tips, her normally bright crystal gaze, now hazy as smoky glass. She saw him watching her and seemed to read the thoughts in his eyes as she sank her teeth in her flushed lower lip, a thing she had done the second after she kissed him when they were children. The adorable gesture made him painfully harder, if such a thing was even possible.

Velvet finally broke their heated stare, and her lashes brushed her cheek as a long, husky breath tumbled from her lips. "I don't know what to do...I don't...I..." her voice trembled.

Henry felt his smile. "I think you do."

Velvet's hands moved in a helpless flutter. He ran his fingers up her thighs. "Ride me, Marie," he begged. This time, she did.

Velvet was aware of his brutal power, knowing he could shatter her bones like eggshells, and she was shocked at his gentleness, his restraint. Apart from his roving hands stroking maddening patterns on her thighs, Henry held statue still. Under the misty island light his swarthy skin looked nearly black, the aqua light in his eyes was a startling, compelling contrast. Tentatively, Velvet rocked her hips, trying to adjust to the feel of him, huge, hot and hard as hammered steel. She made a sound of shock and need as her breath shortened. She closed her eyes, still feeling his own studying her. This was pure desire, she thought dimly, this time was more than last time; he was different, his touch, the light in his shadowed eyes darkening to look black instead of blue.

Velvet couldn't seem to control the rhythm of her lungs, and he was so huge inside her, she could barely breathe. Henry's hand came up to cup the back of her neck. She let him tug her down to him as he said her name and took her mouth in an ardent kiss. Velvet made an inarticulate sound against his lips. His large hands moved to cup both sides of her face, his fingers tangled in her hair as he deepened the kiss, skillfully seducing her mouth and mind. Her hips moved, pleasure sizzled like lightning striking in the place where their bodies linked and touched. Henry made a rumbling sound, told her how much he wanted her, how perfect she was. His words rendered her breathless. She was gasping, falling, flying.

Velvet's back arched as his hand slid up her taut stomach to cup her breast, lift it to his mouth, draw the tight tip of it between his teeth. He pinched the other, hard—wonderfully so. Finally, breath ripping between his teeth, Henry moved. Velvet thought she might die as sensations streaked through her, awoke a part of herself, a demoness she had not known existed.

Making wild sounds, she clawed at his chest, brought her hips up then slammed them down, did it again and again. A shaken sound escaped her, then a moan. Leaning on one elbow, Henry tugged her back to his mouth, his kiss deep and wet, Velvet bit down on his lip, tasted blood. His hips lifted again, meeting her thrust for thrust. Her body undulated; she felt her muscles clench around him.

"God's blood, Marie!" Henry stared up at her, wonder and raw lust imprinted on his face. His tongue flashed out to taste the drop of blood welling on his lip, the look in his eyes so hopelessly alluring that Velvet made a small sound and felt him jerk inside her.

"Wild witch," he accused, "I could devour you." He touched the hot blood blushing her cheeks, kissed the sweat on her neck. "Red Velvet, it suits you, even without the blood tipped wings, even without the shocking color your hair was when you danced on the Bacchus. How I've dreamed of you like this, legs open, hot, and begging for me."

Velvet could barely make sense of his maddening words, as he brought his fingers between their straining bodies, and stroked that place at her core made of starlight and ecstasy. That place he kissed in her dreams. His body moved like a storm, his mouth was everywhere, setting fire to her heated skin, and again between them was that exchange of souls, as his grinding hips once again branded her his for all time. It shattered then, that thing building so intensely inside her. White-hot waves, which crested and crashed again and again.

Henry kissed her, his mouth absorbing her screams. He rolled her onto her back, and, for a time, the world was twirling, turbulent blackness, glittering stars, and shimmering pulses coursing over her body. Beautiful tremors that made Velvet want to live and die in the moment. Her legs tensed 'til she thought her bones might break; against his lips, she screamed his name.

~

She was stunning like this, Henry thought, gazing down at the slender, arching form in his arms. A vision in reality, a dream to touch. He loved hearing his name, a trembling scream on her lips. Her tight body squeezed him unbearably, but Henry gritted his teeth and fought off the claws of release. He kissed the perfect skin under his hands, rubbing his lips over her flushed breast, the shell of her ear, and sloping curve of her jaw, and remained impeccably still. If he moved, it would be over, and he wanted this night to go on for a long, long time.

Whatever secrets she had learned in that cave had caused her to turn on him, lie to him, most likely she assumed in her suspicious mind that if he knew, he would do something that went against her wishes. Stubborn vixen. Let her think of this night when she thought of them. Perhaps if he touched a piece of her soul, she would find it in herself to trust him. He stared down, memorizing every inch of her, watching each of her rapid breaths, until they eventually steadied, and her luscious tremors stilled. He feathered kisses on the lids of her eyes, the enchanting column of her throat, the rosy tips of her breasts. She was a strange, exotic brew, and he was drunk on her.

Finally, her eyes flickered open as she slowly came back to the world. She looked dazed, sated, and in love. Gently, Henry withdrew from her, keeping his hands on her thighs, and her soft legs parted.

Velvet's gaze flicked down his body, and a touch of innocent confusion shimmered through her wide, blue eyes as her lips trembled. "Do you not...was I not—?"

"Not yet," he breathed, dragging his mouth across her stomach. Velvet's body tensed with a flash of fear. "No Henry, I can't, not again."

Henry smiled against her inner thigh. "You can, you will. In this, at least you must trust me."

Velvet let her head fall back on the lush pillows, felt a smile flirting with the corners of her mouth. "I do not trust you. I am too tired. What you want from me isn't possible."

"It's inevitable," he whispered, his breath falling low, heating her sensitive skin. Her hips jerked reflexively, then his scalding tongue touched, stroked, kissed, effectively proving his point. Velvet locked a hand over her mouth. In seconds, her whole body was a mess of writhing nerves aching to touch that pinnacle of brilliance she knew he could give her. Just before she tumbled over the edge of ecstasy, Henry moved back up her body and kissed her. Velvet tasted herself on his lips, and trembled. It was done, after the intimacy of this night, there was no going back. This man truly owned her, body, mind and soul. The kiss was slow, gentle, exquisite, and he licked and tortured her lips until she was begging for him, digging her nails in his skin, every ounce of inhibition burned to ash.

"Wanton witch," he murmured, making the last word a caress. The accusation was true. She wanted him; she would never be able to live without this, and she suspected he knew it well as her.

Henry flipped Velvet onto her stomach, spread her legs, drove inside her, and gave her what she begged for. The pleasure blazed, swaying through her in blistering jolts that rocked them both.

In the weeks and months that came, Velvet knew she would discover all the ways this night had changed her. All she knew now was that when she walked away, she would leave her heart in his hands.

Henry held her fiercely, and finally found his own release, growling against the side of her neck, his body taut and shaking, hot voice telling her how perfect she was, swearing he loved her, would love her till he died. Trembling against him, Velvet returned the words. Let him remember this night when she was gone, and perhaps he would know that for a time she had truly been his.

Henry didn't let her go when it was finished. He pulled her close, wrapped his arms around her in an unbreakable, wonderful vise, dropped a kiss on her bare shoulder, then buried his face in her hair, and promptly fell asleep. Velvet twined her legs through his, fiercely reluctant to let the intimacy end, then rested her fingers lightly on his forearm, holding him to her. Letting the afterglow shimmer around them, Velvet stared up at the slatted roof. When she heard Henry's deep, sleeping breaths, Velvet started to cry. Huge hot tears slipping silently down her cheeks. There was no help for it; she loved her brother, had loved him since the day he drew his first breath, but leaving Henry was going to be the hardest thing she had ever done in her life.

Her body tightened around him. Tears continued to stream, her eyelids trembled closed, until eventually she fell into fitful sleep, and dreamed.

In her dreams she ran flat out over a grassy knoll, the tree, her, and Henry's huge swaying Baobab stood in front of her, orange smoke and cannon fire painted the sky at her back. The tree wavered and changed; it became a golden throne studded with all the stones that had cursed her. The stone of Tamora sitting proudly at the pinnacle of the gilded chair. The high back was shaped like a crown, the crown was dipped in blood, blood ran over the armrest and dripped to the grass. Not a crown, she realized, antlers. Tall, and forked, made of pure white bone. Bleeding bones, blood soaked the cushioned seat, pooled, rippled, and ran toward her. Blood drenched the moon in the sky, and there was blood all over her hands. Velvet looked down at her crimson palms, bright red and glistening, and she started to scream.

Velvet woke with a jolt, heart racing, perspiration dewing her skin, filled so full of longing and loneliness that it nearly drove her to instant despair. Terrified, she raised her hands and stared at them, trying to see through the darkness. Instant relief made her dizzy—no blood. Her hands were pale and sweaty. She let her pounding heart calm, cradled her hands to her chest, and lay that way for nearly an hour, still as stone, listening to Henry breathe, hypnotized by the heavy, steady beat of his heart.

Sleep ran from her, and why should it not? Her mind was busy plotting, and all plotters deserved their restlessness. As she lay, one problem grew foremost in her mind, until it overshadowed all other thought: her growling stomach. It roared incessantly, sounding for all the world like she had swallowed a bear with his foot caught in the metal teeth of a trap. Velvet truly feared the next atrocious noise would wake Henry. The quest for food would be a challenging one. She had no idea where the kitchens were, and no desire to wake her sleeping friends. Perhaps someone would be awake below stairs who could aid her. Willing her limbs to cooperate, Velvet turned her body to the side with careful, tiny moves, terrified to jostle Henry. If he woke, he would kiss and touch her, and she knew if that happened it would be hours before she thought of food again. Slowly, not even daring to breathe, she slid down beneath the curve of his arm. Henry stirred and muttered some deep, Gaelic words. Velvet froze. Henry tossed his head and mouthed her name.

Velvet's heart twisted as she ducked to finish her perilous maneuver. When she was on her knees beside him, she dared to lean in and press the lightest kiss to his lips, then she stood. Touching her bare thighs, she sighed, wishing for her daggers, lost somewhere in the lovers' cave.

Velvet stepped lightly from the bed, her toes curling in the soft, plush rug. She lifted the cambric nightgown off the ground from the spot it had fallen when Henry kicked it off the bed. Smiling at memories, she fitted it over her head, shoved her arms through the crisp, clean sleeves. Minerva's cloak lay where Velvet had left it, folded over the back of the silver chair sitting in front of the pretty writing desk. Staring out the window to the flickering lights of the docked ships, listening to the crashing surf, Velvet closed her eyes, allowing herself to exist for a few moments, the future was dark, but with Henry sleeping a few feet from her and the sounds of the island all around, the present was beautiful. Waves beat and battered the rocks. The ocean was still foreign sounding to her, soothing and simultaneously terrifying. Having spent so much time flying in the sky, Velvet had the good sense to be wary of the creatures lurking in the deep. She wrapped the cloak around her shoulders, watched the way the material shivered and glowed as it fell down her body.

Velvet kept her steps light as she moved toward the door. She gave her dirty boots a disdainful glare and decided to take her chances barefoot. Henry's clothes were strewn across the floor, a leather jerkin, a white silk shirt, trousers with one pant leg turned inside out, and his weapons belt, lay askew having been discarded in haste. The belt held two pouches, a silver revolver, snapped in its holster, and a wicked looking knife. One of the pouches had opened during the fall, Velvet saw the black bag that held all the stones, just lying there in the open, almost begging for her to take them.

She stared off into negative space for a long moment, her eyes continually drifting to the stones. Her fingers tingled with remembered power, but that sick feeling twisting her insides was there too. Velvet bent, tearing her eyes away from the stones. She plucked apart the snap on the holster and lifted the revolver, then slid it deep in a hidden pocket of her cloak. Pausing before the door, she tried to wrap her long hair in a knot atop her head, but curls, mussed by Henry's hands, resisted, and ran wild. Sighing, Velvet rested her hand on the silver doorknob and cast a final, furtive glance at Henry, still sleeping blissfully on. She felt her eyes roll, wondering why she was bothering to be so quiet; the man was lost to the world. She doubted the horn of Jericho could have woken him.

Velvet opened the door and stepped beneath the gilded frame, still smelling of fresh paint. Idly, she wondered how much it had cost Nora to restore this place. Silently, she closed the door behind her. The lanterns in the hall had gutted hours ago. Darkness was a thick, moving thing; the fire that blazed in the hearth had turned to cold ashes. Velvet moved forward like a wraith, rushing past the closed doors and open windows. Wind moaned, and rattled the wide shutters, curtains flapped and gusted through the hall, looking for all the world like tilted ball gowns.

Velvet moved in the direction she believed the kitchens lurked, hustling down the stairs, keeping her back to the railing and walls. She started at two dark shapes, one which turned out to be a toppled chair, the other, a floor length earthenware jug that smelled like poisoned bog water. The slender foyer opened to a wide room with arched ceilings and floor length mirrors framing the chair Nora had used as a throne. Men slumbered here, heads on tables buried in their folded arms, a few others found their rest on the ground in sticky puddles of drying ale. Henry's words in the cave came back to her. *What was sipped in shades of night loses its taste in daylight.*

Velvet passed through their snoring midst without incident. The common room lead to a spiral staircase that wound into a long, dark corridor with a low ceiling. She moved quickly, not caring over much for the clinging dark, so thick her hand was practically invisible when she held it only inches from her face. An orange spill of soft light finally showed in the distance. Velvet breathed a heartfelt sigh of relief and ran toward it, her bare feet slapping against the ground.

Suddenly, the stifling hall fell into two sharp steps, then opened to a wide brick room that smelled like heaven. Pepper, apples, bread, meat, jam, honey. Lanterns burned everywhere, and the warm light gave the kitchen a homey feel, making her yearn for something she never had. Instantly, her eyes searched out the source of the smells, making her stomach roar. Baskets of apples and bread sat on the brick island standing proud in the center of the room. Strewn in haphazard perfection were small, puff pastries leaking sticky peach filling, cuts of cold meat and a plate of bright red berries.

Velvet scooped up a handful of berries, lifted a small, slightly stale cut of bread then stuffed it all in her mouth. She chewed vigorously, shoving in more food before the first mouthful went down. Slices of cold, mystery meat followed more berries, a slice of pastry the peach filling so sweet it made her shudder to swallow. More meat, another pastry, two giant bites of bread.

"Bonsoir mademoiselle," said a deep voice just over her right shoulder.

Velvet jumped and spun toward the intruding sound. Mouth

full to the brim, a half-eaten item of food in each hand and a deep blush on her cheeks.

The man was tall, excessively so. His face long and serpentine, a badly trimmed mustache marred his thin lips, his white skin was mottled as clotted cream and his eyes were shot through with blood. He stood a few inches away, swaying on his feet, the laces of his boots undone, cravat askew. She saw the royal coat of arms on the sleeve of his dark coat. He was a French soldier, far from home.

Velvet cleared her throat, a piece of dry bread flew from her mouth and soared across the room. "Good evening, sir." She swallowed hard, the food going down like a gulp of sawdust. "Excuse the spectacle, for I was starving," she blurted. The sudden twisting of her stomach made her feel as if she would never be hungry again.

The man said nothing. His dizzy eyes streaked down her body in appreciative perusal. He whistled between his teeth and brought his gaze back to her face. When she saw what was sparking in his eyes, her whole body went numb. Uneaten food fell in slow motion from her cold hands.

He smiled, then dropped in a slow, clumsy bow. "I woke from a rum dream and followed a strange noise. Who knew it would lead to such a beautiful prize?" He took a step closer, the smell of his sour, liquor-soaked breath saturated the air between them. Velvet tried to take a scrambling step away from him. The hard edge of the brick island slammed into the backs of her legs. Her heartbeat sounded erratic and loud in the silence. It was the thought of the hidden revolver that stopped her chattering teeth. The intent of what he meant to do was clear on his face. His breathing was ragged. "I feel my brain is so addled by drink it has turned a common maid to a princess."

Velvet suddenly found her voice. "Addled as it is, your eyes do not deceive you. I am a princess; I am afraid if you touch me, you will die."

He laughed, a wet, rasping sound that grated over her frayed nerves. He reached out and took a lock of her hair and rubbed it between his grimy fingers. Velvet's head snapped back; she ripped the strand away. "Step back, sir," she commanded, her voice glacial.

"You won't mind as it's clear you've already been plucked. What is one more man to a girl like you?"

"I assure you, I am at capacity with the man I have."

The man ignored her commands, only leaned in, and took a long sniff of her hair. Revulsion made her skin crawl. "You smell like an angel." His fingers touched and circled her throat, "Si délicat, si beau."

Velvet's back went ramrod straight. "I am not at all delicate, sir!" she shouted and shoved at his chest. "And there are no angels, only desperate women."

He seemed not to hear her and his hands slipped behind her, pulling her hard against him. "Ah, mon chéri, the feel of you could drive a man to madness."

Velvet groaned at the horrid contact of bodies and spoke through her teeth. "So, I've been told. Now, please, I—"

He moved quickly, his jaw fell slack, then he opened his mouth and pressed a sloppy, wet kiss on her horrified lips. Velvet drew back her hand and slapped his intruding face with all her strength. He jumped, shock and pain clearly dispelling the drunken haze in his eyes.

Velvet's heart was hammering so wildly, she could barely find her breath. She lifted her nose in a haughty, imperious tilt, which would have made Nora proud. "Sir, I demand you unhand me this instant!" The corners of her lips lifted in a sneer. "I can't say I've enjoyed your scintillating company; I am leaving. Remove yourself from my path."

The man just stared at her, fingering his reddening cheek, then he laughed. "Ah chéri, I'm afraid you are not going anywhere."

Before she could voice another fierce rejection, he wrapped his hands around her throat and tossed her on the table. Her head hit something sharp, and hard, and pain shot a blazing light through her vision, bright stars exploded briefly, obliterating her sight.

Velvet could not believe this was happening. It was true then; misfortune really did follow her every step. Absently, she wondered what dastardly deed she committed in a past life that had a hand in cursing her to such a dreadful fate. When he pushed his big body between her legs, she heard him fumbling with his clothes, and the distinct click of a belt buckle coming undone. She felt this was happening in a nightmare, some monstrous horror she could wake from if only she had the strength. She kicked and bucked, drew in a breath for a scream. The man slapped his hand over her mouth, so Velvet was forced to choke on, or swallow her wail. The food she had hastily consumed struggled hard to come back up.

Velvet's left hand flapped and searched for the revolver, deciding she would wave it in front of his face the way she had seen Katie do, steady hands not a stitch of the desperate fear battering at the boundaries of her control. Hard hands groped at her bare thighs and tugged her nightgown high. Images of Henry hovering over her, a look beyond passion in his eyes assaulted her. The familiarity between the two acts made her ill. A terrible rage rose like a sudden inferno, so she saw everything in hazy shades of red. Felt it all touch her soul, that sick twisted nightmare that lingers.

The man freed himself from the final constraints of his clothes with one hand. The other pawed at her breast. The sharp sound of shredding cloth as her nightgown gave way was a scream in the silence. She dug her hand deep in the hidden pocket of her cloak, closed her fingers around the cold metal and felt some portion of sanity return. Inexplicably, the cloak seemed to aid her efforts in retrieving the pistol, the cloth moving and tugging away with no assistance on her part.

The man's eyes were fixed on her exposed breasts, hot sweat ran down his face, dripped onto her cheek. She took a gasping breath, then let her body relax as if she had decided to submit to his dubious charms. He nuzzled her throat; she felt his leer against her skin. "That's right, there's no need to struggle, you know you'll love it."

"I know nothing of the kind," Velvet said coolly, then pressed the mouth of the gun to the underside of his chin and cocked the hammer. The metallic click was loud and meaningful.

The man jerked backward, laughter and color draining from his face. "Careful, mon chéri, the last man who drew on me died."

"I am not *your* anything, nor could I belong to such a loathsome cad. Now, kindly get off of me, allow me to leave, and I will do my best to forget this unfortunate incident. Do not, and you will find my shaky hands will not hamper my aim."

"Such bravado from one so small, like being bitten by a butterfly."

"I assure you, sir, I am no butterfly, an owl maybe, and we bird of prey are killers to the core." Around her black smoke poured rose from the lanterns. Orange flames, jumping behind their glass barriers. Velvet could smell and feel the food squishing under her back, hear the wind howling outside the shuttered windows.

The man lifted his weight from her. Velvet felt her hold on the gun ease, as she could not kill a man for the crime of drunken lust, and mistaken identity. He began to lift his hands, that age-old sign of surrender. It worked—he would leave her in peace—the relief escorting that thought made her lightheaded.

Velvet blinked, took her eyes off him for one second, and he dove for the gun. She shrieked, and jerked her hand, her elbow smacked something sharp that made a lightening blast of pain streak up her arm. His hands made fists, and Velvet ducked as they swung toward her face. She dodged the worst of it, still his knuckles grazed her cheek and sent her reeling back. He made another grab for the revolver then, but she fought like a cornered wild cat. The man's eyes held a glazed, insane look as he wrestled to subdue her renewed struggles. Velvet kicked and bit whatever she could reach. He grabbed her swinging arm, squeezing her wrist until her numb fingers clutching tight to the gun twitched and trembled. She raked the nails of her free hand down his face, and he sunk a hard fist in her stomach.

Velvet coughed, pain made her mind white and blank. He drew back his fist and hit again, again, again. The room expanded and contracted, and the time she lived in became a sequence of agonizing layers. When he made another grab for the revolver, Velvet had lost the will to fight, breath wheezed in her lungs, and a sob broke through her wracking coughs.

She felt him snatch the barrel of the weapon, fought weakly as he tried to wrench it from her hold. Her finger instinctively tightened on the trigger. The revolver fired with a sudden, shocking bang. Velvet felt the metal jerk against her middle, she drew in a deep breath, closed her eyes, and waited for the pain. None came, her eyes flew open. The man was staggering, hand clutched to his gut, blood spewing hot and red between his splayed fingers. Velvet dropped the smoking gun, watched him stumble, sway, and fall to his knees. Shock and terror warring in his eyes.

"I didn't mean...I'm sorry...I..." Velvet's broken whisper ended in a sob. Blood soaked her hands, dripped down the finger that pulled the trigger, spatters of it stained her shredded nightgown. The man's eyes rolled, a weird moan escaped his lips as he gave her a final, hate-filled look, pitched forward, landed hard on his face, then died.

CHAPTER 6

TRADING HONOR FOR A CROWN IS A THING
THAT'S BEEN DONE BEFORE

*V*elvet's mind did a terrible thing and went blank, like it needed to shut out all to keep her delicate crystal ball of sanity from shattering in a thousand, irreparable pieces. She felt exposed, naked, like the blood soaking her hands and clothes told the dark truth of who she was and what stalked her. Death, death, and more senseless death. She had been in this body for less than eight months and she was murderess a half dozen times over. Those who got too close met the grim reaper who was her shadow. It was imperative she get away now, escape from those last few she loved before this death too was their fate. She felt herself on the brink of a terrifying self-awareness.

Velvet backed away from the expanding pool of blood. It rushed toward her bare toes with intent to tarnish all it touched. Feeling like the hounds of hell were nipping at her heels, she dashed back the way she had come, down the hall to the main room filled with sleeping men. Some lifted their dreary eyes, tracked her uneven steps. Velvet feared they all saw her for what she was, a killer to the core, the very shadow of death. None made a move toward her, as she took the winding stairs to the upper rooms two at a time, not realizing she was crying till she felt the scalding tears rushing down her cheeks. She threw open the door to the room she had shared with Henry. He was sitting up in bed, rubbing sleep from his bright eyes. "God's blood, Marie, what the hell was that sound? Did I hear a gunshot?"

Velvet's lips trembled, and she could find no words. The sight of him sleep-mussed and stunning, all hard angles and dramatic, sensual lines, nearly cracked her resolve. She gasped in a shaky breath; the tears fell faster. Desperate, miserable emotion twisted her insides, maimed her heart with red hot pokers. Time was not linear with him. She saw and felt every moment that had ever been between them in an endless, painful, repeating loop.

"Marie?" he said, coming to his feet, concern infusing his voice as he noted her pallor. Velvet waved a hand to ward him off. His flushed complexion paled as he saw the blood. Velvet couldn't give any of it another thought, as she had already wasted too many. She loved him, wanted him more than she believed imaginable, but this death that stalked her would not claim him so long as she lived. She would go far away from him, break her own heart, and run to the ends of the earth. Save him. Save them all.

Her fate as an outsider was well deserved, for she was cursed. Perhaps the curse which infected all those who carried her blood, or something else, darker. Whatever the case, the fact remained that she was a menace; she should have let the church take her head.

Henry made a move toward her as Velvet dove for the bag of gems, and her hand closed around the familiar cloth. She waited for the lightening jolt of power to rush up her arm, shuddered when it rippled through her. The sensation was terrifying.

Velvet forced herself to look up at Henry who loomed over her, stark naked, and gorgeous, that sculpture of a god from a forgotten time. His eyes, twin moonlight chips of ice were desperate as he saw her intent writ plainly on her face. He shook his head in denial, making dark curls tumble into his eyes. "Don't, Marie, I beg you." His voice dropped low, full of the husky, Gaelic tones she loved. "M'aingeal, trust me. There is nothing in the world you can say that would make me not love you, want you—" The look in his eyes, the voice, the very presence of him were nearly her undoing, if she had not just killed a man, if the spell to save her brother had required anything but his life, if, if, if...

Velvet stood slowly, not breaking the smoldering chain-links holding their eyes tethered.

"I'm so sorry, Henry." Her words were a broken sob as she lifted the bag and saw that her hand was shaking.

"I'll find you," he said in a ragged voice that decimated what remained of her heart. "From the depths of my soul, I am begging you."

"I didn't consider the implications of my words when I said I would do anything to save Louie. I know now that I was wrong. I will not sacrifice you."

Henry took hold of her arms and drew her up his naked body, hot and hard as flaming steel. "Don't take my right to choose. Allow me to prove that from now on I will always choose you. Whatever the price."

"That's what I fear," she breathed before his lips touched hers. He kissed her with an aching tenderness that made more tears pour down her cheeks. His hands came up to cradle her face, and she felt treasured, precious, and broken. He leaned back; the intensity of his gaze made her drown in the blue inferno his eyes.

"I will find you," he said again, his words filled with fire and fear. "There is nowhere in the world you can hide from me. I will never stop looking, no matter how long it takes."

"I know," she breathed, then tightened her fingers around the bag of stones. His head lowered; his lips parted to kiss her again. "Sleep," she said, putting every ounce of her pain and misery in the word.

"No, Marie, goddamn you to—" The rest of Henry's curse drifted away as his lids dropped like led over his hurt-filled eyes. He swayed, then toppled, the way a falling mountain might.

Velvet knew when his body hit the ground he was already lost in the vale of dreams.

~

It was hard to see through all the tears. Velvet swiped the back of her hand over her streaming eyes. "I'm so sorry, Henry," she whispered to his sleeping form, then dared to lean down and run her hand through his tousled hair, trail a finger over his full, drugging lips. For a moment, she wondered if it was in her to leave, if she could actually do such an unthinkable thing, then she pictured the man, probably still lying in the kitchens below, gave him Henry's face, it was Henry's blood making a scarlet pool for the rats to feast on, and the decision to go was shockingly easy. "Good by your Grace," she breathed, "it is probable I will love you till I die. If there is a god, may he be with you, for I cannot be." Then she was gone, turning her back on him, running for his life, for all their lives.

Not breathing at all steadily, Velvet descended the stairs again. She carried the bag of gems in her right hand, cradled it close to her pounding heart. In the common room she paused in the center, a frozen tableau like the wax drippings stopped in motion, clinging to the cold, gutted candles. The blood on her hands was food for her spell. Let them all sleep, give them, saints, pirates, and villains alike, a night of beautiful dreams. She had already paid the blood price.

It wasn't anything so grand as transformation, just a simple wish for gentle sleep. Velvet hoped the single life she had taken would be enough. A few of the men lifted their heads to stare at the glowing intruder in their midst. "Sleep now," she whispered. Indigo light seeped between her fingers, swirled up her arm. In that moment, Velvet knew the truth; she was the villain, the evil witch in all the fairytales as she did what she had sworn never to do again. "Sleep, and dream."

Velvet moved to the door while behind her, the men

dropped one by one. She shoved it open and ran into the night. Wind attacked her unbound hair, throwing it all about, but it had no power over Minerva's cloak. The material moved to its own tune; it flowed and rippled down her slight frame, staying close. The spell's lingering light had hidden threads in the cloth still glowing, so she cast a brilliant shadow. The warm island wind dried the tears, leaving a wealth of uneven stains on her cheeks.

Velvet knew to stay off the slender, cobbled roads and winding pathways. A plan depended on execution much as concept. There was no going back now, so she kept to the shrubs, avoiding packs of wandering pirates looking for a maid to ravish, and blazing beach fires. Keeping her body in a stiff crouch, and moving from tree to tree, she cut a steady path toward the beach, and the warships bobbing just beyond the night-lit cove. That last sight of Henry's face possessed her thoughts as she ran. She had sworn to never cast another spell on him, and she had broken her vow to save him. Now, she was on course to put herself forever out of his reach, and she knew he would never forgive her. Not this time. What was worse? He would never know just how much she loved him, that he had burst into her life like a shooting star of hope fired through a sky darkened by misery, terror, and loss. That every second away from him would be a lifetime wasted.

Would he find someone else? Of course, he would. Women for him melted on command—the visual of Henry's lips kissing another, made Velvet want to wretch and cry. She held a trembling hand over her mouth so the night would not hear her sobs. The volume of the crashing surf increased with every step she took until she felt sand squish between her toes. Her teeth were clattering, and Velvet knew she walked in fear of the violent unknown.

Sinking beneath the grassy mounds, above the horizon, climbed the imposing lines of Napoleon's famous black ship. The sixteen-gun alcyon-class brig, with its dominant figurehead standing high, the carved face of the mahogany nymph, set to catch the sun god's first touch of glow.

"Fear is a trap, I will not fall in it," she whispered aloud, made breathless by her mad dash from the tavern, the hazy splendor of pre-dawn, and the black substance twisting in her gut. She walked on further until the blue-black horizon dipped and rolled. Soon the shrubs were knee-high, and there was no more hiding. The sand underfoot seemed to stretch endlessly, edged in white-tipped breakers.

Velvet lifted the cloak's thick hood to cover her bright hair, tightened the laces beneath her chin, then continued her trek toward the ships in the distance, black shadows blending well with the night. Velvet knew—even buoyed by the adrenaline shorting her breath—she could not swim such a distance. Crescent moonlight hit the edges of high tide, but beyond the water was indigo and foreboding. Small boats bobbed just offshore, swaying as the waves surged and retreated.

The first group of men she passed crossed themselves. Her skin and cloak still glowed, and Velvet hoped they believed the rum and moonlight were playing tricks on their eyes. Velvet hurried on.

Prostitutes, pirates, deserters, and common thieves. Save the good-hearted islanders being dragged away in chains, and loaded onto ships by soulless slavers, the coast of Île Sainte-Marie was like a who's who of the world's miscreant population. At the end of it all, Velvet spied a band of French soldiers. It was impossible to tell at this distance, but she would have bet her body, they wore Napoleon's colors. She reached the men without incident, though many a strange look was tossed her way as she passed. During her childhood years at Versailles, her Nounous had forced her to walk with a stack of books balancing on her head, in an effort to make her glide like a princess. The books had always fallen, still Velvet held her head high, determined not to show an ounce of fear. Let them see the princess, she silently begged, petitioning the moon to lend her strength and glow.

The men saw her coming from a distance. All conversations ceased. Velvet wanted nothing more than to cower away from the intensity of their stares, but she straightened her spine and held the stones close. She stopped a few feet away, returned their glares with interest. One man, an older gent with an imposing posture, and bright grey eyes, gave her a courtly bow. "Mademoiselle, Marie-Thérèse Charlotte of France, I presume," he said. The smug smile on his lips said he knew exactly who she was. A low murmuring went through the men.

"I am."

"We've been searching for you," the man said, taking a step toward her.

Velvet held her ground. "How fortunate for you that you've found me. I formally request you take me to your general," she finished, infusing all the regal training she recalled into every note of her voice.

"'E' wants to see you," said another, a callow youth, all pale skin, skinny limbs, and hot pimples.

Velvet's smile was dead as old desert bones. "Then, it seems fortune smiles on us all."

CHAPTER 7

THE LITTLE CORPORAL

*I*f it wasn't for the cold threat of murder in his eyes, and the stain of blood on his hands, Napoleon would have seemed to Velvet to be some sort of whimsical creature. Nearly childlike, diminished by the rough-hewn mahogany desk that filled a good portion of the captain's cabin. Papers stacked taller than the warlord, surrounded all sides of the huge armchair where he sat, casually regarding her through tiny, close-set eyes that glittered like a rat in the dark. His thin lips were unsmiling, his cleft chin lifted high, his neck arched, like he could add to his height by sheer force of will. For a long moment, he just stared at her. Velvet bristled beneath the folds of her cloak, but the material remained deathly still, hiding her fussing. Eventually, he rested his weak chin on steepled fingers and made a thorough inspection of her person. "There is a slight glow about you, my dear," he finally said.

Velvet grimaced. "The sheen of my exertions, nothing more."

"Humm," he nodded, not looking like he believed a single word of her lie.

"Months I have been searching for you, yet here you stand, shivering on my doorstep like providence's very own gift." Napoleon stood and walked to her, the fine lines of his uniform pulled tight over his paunch, still he was a dominating figure of a man despite the fact that his height forced her to hunker down and drop her head if she wanted to meet his eyes. "Why are you here now, after running for so long? What has changed?"

Velvet sighed. "I suppose that really is the only question that matters. I want protection from England, and the Republic. I have come for my brother's throne."

Napoleon laughed, so his whole body shook like an old bowl of gruel. "You're a pleasing thing, aren't you?" Slowly he circled her, then continued speaking in a low voice, but one designed to carry. "If I acquiesce to your command? What do I get in return?"

"I'm very tired. Let's not play games, shall we?" Velvet asked gently, moving to take the seat he had vacated. It was a bold move, but Velvet felt at the moment, it served them both. She met his calculating gaze with her own unflinching glare, as her mind touched on a prescient memory of standing beside her father during a war council, peopled by powerful men and their paunches. "Take me away from here, restore my lands and my father's throne to me, and I will give you my country. I am what you will get out of this sordid arrangement. Wasn't that the plan all along?"

The light of the scattered lanterns highlighted the yellow fuzz clinging to his teeth as his face broke into a pleased smile. He clapped his hands jovially, seeming unfazed by her own dark purpose. "What an entertaining chit you are. A face like your mother's though I am sure the similarities end there. No wonder you set the Church of England on its ear." He laughed loudly, throwing back his head and displaying all the signs of genuine humor.

"My mother was a princess who grew up in a cage, married to a boy before she knew what it meant to be a woman. Much as I wish it was, otherwise, you're right, I am nothing like her. She was kind to those who were cruel, always saved the lives of her enemies. I, it seems, cannot even save the life of a friend."

"How do you treat your enemies?"

"Much the same as you, I suspect," Velvet said.

Napoleon roared his mirth again. "What of your husband? The world knows you were married by proxy to the Duke of Newcastle. Is it a true marriage?"

Velvet's mind briefly went blank, then rushing images of her and Henry in the cave filled all the empty spaces. The way he had looked in that second before he took her virginity, the spell-binding light in his eyes, the insane heat of his touch, all that soul changing hunger. "I mean to put myself forever out of his reach," Velvet said, tasting the words like acid. "I will petition Pope Pius the seventh for an annulment. He is no lover of the British monarchy, and according to my mother, he regards king George as a garden worm. Then, when the marriage is dissolved, you will find me another, one who will suit your purposes I presume."

Napoleon did not seem surprised by her bold words, only moved closer till he could rest his pudgy hands on the armrests of the chair where she sat. His jowls bobbed up and down as his paunch jiggled and shifted under his coat. "You are very brave for a girl who is offering herself up as a lamb to the slaughter."

"I am not brave. I am hungry, tired to my bone, beat down by events beyond my control and the stars under which I was born," she said on a sigh, staring past him, surreptitiously taking in her surroundings. A circular, wide room colored in shades of red wine and the deepest sepia. The ceiling had a subtle arch, giving the illusion of greater space. All of it grand by any ship's stan-dard. Stuffed full of richly appointed furniture, which dwarfed them both. She had willingly walked into the lion's jaw and was not at all afraid. If anything, she felt only numb, save the small screaming pain in her chest, which she did her best to ignore.

Napoleon straightened, and motioned to their surroundings, seeing the path of her eyes. "Impressive, is it not? The ship once belonged to the royal British navy. I relieved them of it last year. Old George was deeply disturbed, as this ship was one of his favorites. My dreams were brilliant for weeks," he said. His inane words meant nothing, his clever gaze stripped hers, and Velvet believed it was possible he understood the thoughts in her mind. He was a man who carefully weighed each decision. The depths of his clear intuition made her reevaluate her initial impression of him, an impression conjured by rumors and tall tales.

Despite his stature, or perhaps because of it, Napoleon was no mere man, he was a tactician, a warrior, a modern king, and she, rightful princess of France, his lawful sovereign, would be this man's puppet, his chattel, his slave. The man himself, the ship, this room, gave her a feeling of deep unease, like she had fallen in a trap of her own making and was even now plunging headlong into the worst decision of her life.

Napoleon smiled and clapped his hands, having for the moment finished his inspection of her. "I stand by my words, you are brave. This is not fully a compliment, for bravery is oft an attribute of stupidity. Still, you have managed to outsmart the British and French alike—"

"Out run, you mean," Velvet interrupted.

Napoleon waved her words away. "Whatever the case, you have grit, but an obvious case of nerves. I assume this demand of yours is time sensitive?"

"Yes."

"I see. Should I presently expect an enraged duke? If memory serves, that Scott is fearsome when sleeping, awake and missing his wife?" Napoleon's small eyes drew together in consternation as he seemed to recall Henry, and what he was capable of. "Perhaps I should alert my guards."

"That won't be necessary, so long as we set sail before daybreak, you lot will be safe from his wrath." As I never shall be, she thought miserably.

Napoleon began to pace rapidly, so his bobbing stomach cast bulbous shadows on the floor. "You will not seek to supplant me? You will let me rule and conquer as I will?"

"I swear I will do nothing. I only wish to find a pillow in a small, hidden place, bury my head beneath it, and live out the remainder of my days in some semblance of peace. I am tired of running, sick of blood and death. I want no more. I will surrender to all your demands.

Napoleon smiled, making his hawk nose dip low. "Very well. I will spirit you away from your unwanted husband, and the glamorous life of a fugitive. We will set sail within the hour."

Velvet's gasp made her whole-body jerk. "So soon? We have hours yet till sunrise, I—"

Napoleon's deep brows furrowed; he gave her a long, curious stare. He lifted a half-smoked cigar from a silver holder situated at the edge of the table. He took his time lighting it on the small, jumping lantern flame, sucking, and puffing on the smelly thing until huge reels of smoke curled, then dissolved in the silent space between them. "Why would I stay?" he finally asked, studying the red, crackling tip of his cigar. He tapped it twice, and ash fell to the ground as his eyes moved back to her face. "Stories of you were what drew me to the cursed island, as I'm sure you have been warned. Now that I have you, I see no purpose in tarrying over long. You are a prize princess, dead or alive."

Velvet closed her eyes. So be it. Everyone she loved would finally be safe from her, and she would return to the country that spawned her. It was the best possible outcome. She had made the right choice. Now all she had to do was convince her screaming, weeping heart.

"One hour," she said, giving Napoleon a brittle smile, one she feared might crack her face.

Napoleon stubbed out his cigar after taking a deep, final drag that made him puff out his red cheeks. "Come then, child, I shall see you fed while my men make ready to set sail. Velvet nodded and swallowed hard. She knew the huge, burning lump in her throat would turn any food to ash. Her eyes, so puzzlingly dry one moment, stung terribly in the next.

Napoleon saw her hesitation, and he captured her right hand in both of his, then tucked it in the crook of his arm. He noted the icy temperature of her skin, and a slightly paternal, almost kind light flickered through his eyes. When he spoke, his words fell like stones on her grave. "It's best now that you speak to your heart, child, there is no changing your mind."

Henry woke to a raging headache that threatened to split his skull. He sat up quickly, groaned, and held very still for a moment, battling dizzying disorientation. His body was wracked by occasional coughs as he tried to spit out the cloth that he felt sure must be lodged somewhere in his throat. The misery persisted while he struggled in pained silence to remember his own name. He remembered hers first, then whispered it like a curse, damming her to hell when it all came crashing back in sickening waves. He was on his feet without thinking to do so, the fist he put through the wall was intentional. The pain as the splintering oak panel cut through the skin stretched over his knuckles returned to him some speck of cognitive sanity.

Swaying on his feet, he stumbled to the door, flung it open, stepped into the dark hall, and shouted for Zoe in a voice that shook the rafters. Then he stumbled back into the room and made a clumsy grab for his trousers, his vision drunkenly reeling. He managed to snatch them up on the second try and struggled to unwind the tangled cloth. His mind raced in rapid circles as he put the trousers on and went searching for his shirt. She had placed another spell on him, damn her—he would bet his life that she had gone to Napoleon. Henry was going to take the man apart with his bare hands. There would be no armies and Spanish butchers between them this time. The color of anguish distorted his thoughts. She had not trusted him in the end, not even after all that had gone between them. That alone made him want to die, and throttle her, not at all in that order.

Zoe appeared a few seconds later in a knee-length nightshirt, carrying a lit candle stub that burned in a silver holder. Henry tugged his own shirt over his head. Zoe masked his unease with a quick scan of the room before his eyes went to Henry. Zoe took one look at the state of him, saw the pulsing light in his rage-crazed eyes and sighed. "So, she finally left us. I always wondered if she would really do it. At the same time, I always wondered why she stayed."

"Wake lord Eden this instant, tell him to inform Nora that I mean to be hot on Napoleon's trail in the hour. Then wake the crew and have them make the Second Song ready to set sail."

"Your Grace, H...Henry—" Zoe stuttered, his eyes like lit beacons in his flushed face. "The ship is not ready, so maybe this is best we..." Zoe's words died a rough death in his mouth as he saw the look that transformed Henry's face, from man to avenging angel.

"Go!" Henry barked, in a ragged voice that did not sound at all like his own. Zoe sighed and gave him a long, judgmental look, but kept his mouth blessedly shut. After a few beats of indecision, he rolled his big, brown eyes, then obeyed.

Henry punched another wall. From the moment he had taken that woman in his arms, some good sense within him had warned he was making a terrible mistake. That first touch, and it had been too late. The sight of her had always made his knees want to buckle, slammed his heart into his ribcage so hard it hurt. The longing, the damn naked desire that all but possessed him when he was near her, twisted in his chest, evolving into more heart-grinding spasms of disillusioned rage.

What the hell had he missed in that god forsaken cave? For a few hours down there, she had been his, truly, irrevocably. The way she had stared at him, kissed him, let him take her innocence as she begged for more had been raw, honest. He knew she had decided to forgive him, give in to the flames that seethed between them, submit to how desperately he loved. Had always loved her, broken, flawed, perfect, beautiful her. Down in the cave, he had fallen to sleep, comatose with bliss, lying next to an angel, and had woken to a stranger.

He remembered the breathy, wild sounds she had made last night as he moved over her in the dark. He had kissed every inch of her, made her scream his name, yet had been unable to touch her soul. Now she was gone, and Henry knew this time he would break the world to find her. He stalked the room until his feet took him to the black rum, which he drank straight from the bottle, sighed as it burned a fiery path to his twisting gut. God damn her! How dare she abscond with his heart and leave him half alive? Choking back grief and fire, he wiped his hand over his smarting eyes, shocked to find moisture there. He drank again, chugged until his vision blurred and every drop of the potent stuff was gone. Damn her! Damn this unreasonable pain. Why could he not separate himself from her? What magic made it impossible to let her go?

Though he wished he did not, Henry knew where she had gone. Down in their cave, she had threatened the very thing he feared. Napoleon, the man responsible for his days of torture in a Spanish hell, a man who had tried diligently to kill him once. Because of the way he loved her, had always loved her, it seemed fate meant to give *Little Boots* a second chance. So be it. Henry yanked on his leather jerkin, checked the chamber of the pistol she had fired. He could still smell the charred gunpower as he holstered it. One day, he may grow tired of chasing a chit that did not wish to be caught. Unfortunately for her, today was not that day.

CHAPTER 8

ESPIONAGE, SECRETS, AND DARK CORNERS.

*T*he gilded state room of Napoleon's war ship was wide, filled with sparkling champagne flutes, and enough food it seemed, to feed a small country. A luscious spread as she had ever seen, even during her days of opulence at Versailles, before the violent deaths of her mother and father.

On the polished tables sat pheasants stuffed from tail to beak, basted in cranberry jelly, smelling of sugar and rosemary, the skin crisped to a golden brown inlaid with spiced orange slices. There were deviled eggs whipped to perfection and sprinkled with paprika, beside small chunks of toasted garlic bread. Salmon soaking in a white wine sauce, all covered with toasted capers. Velvet was too nerve-sick to touch a single morsel. The food smells blended wrong in her nose and turned her stomach.

Slowly she moved into the room, knowing all eyes followed her every step, traced down the lines of her crimson dress. The men had gifted her with a whore's old togs, the only female items they had on board. They all leered at her when one man suggested they could stay and watch her slip into it. Velvet had slammed the door of the small room Napoleon had given her, directly in their faces.

The gown was ghastly, the bodice cut in a low V and waist cinched tight with a gaudy, black satin bow. It was not the gown of a lady by any means, but it was not the garb of the peasant. She left her blonde hair tumbling to her hips and knew she cut an exotic figure, mysterious and enticing. She had known they would all stare. Velvet lifted her chin a notch. Let them! Let them see the princess their republic had deposed.

Napoleon sat kingly at the head of it all, presiding over his court of politicians, soldiers, and assassins. She could clearly see him through the crush of decorated bodies, resting his pudgy, scarred hands on his generous paunch. Velvet looked past him; she couldn't help but search the crowd for Henry's face. When she did not find him, there was no way of knowing if the crunching feeling twisting the pit of her stomach was misery or relief. Dazed and lost in thoughts of past nights, Velvet jumped when a man caught her cold hand, only the hard arm the man slipped around her shoulders kept her from stumbling. Velvet spun, outraged, and her eyes crashed into another pair of identical blue. It was something in the man's direct gaze that kindled a spark of recognition in her own. Memories of golden halls, hot-house roses and moonlit nights, her mother holding this man's hand and laughing up at the stars.

"Paul, Paul Beauchamp?" Disbelief broke Velvet's voice.

"Bonsoir ma précieuse niece," he said, in a beloved, all too familiar voice. Scent filled memories instantly shrouded her, and she was wrapped in all the colors of home. Velvet forgot the tension of her surroundings and threw herself into strong arms that closed gently around her. His perfume was raspberry and vanilla.

"You're alive! How? I saw them take you away. Mother said you died in the Temple Prison...how?" Velvet gasped in a breath realizing she was on the verge of noisy tears.

Paul squeezed her body close to his chest and whispered into her hair. "I knew a white flower in England who owed me a favor, now I owe him my life."

Velvet sniffed, awkwardly wiped her nose on her arm. She leaned back and touched his smooth cheek. "I've scarcely ever been so happy to see someone in my life." Velvet looked him over, unable to help a tearful smile. Noted his deep, coal lined eyes, rouged cheeks and painted cherry-red lips. "Oncle Paul," she sighed, slipping into the old French tones, "time hasn't laid a finger on you. Mother always did say you were the most fashionable of us all."

"Armure, mon chéri, merely a suit of fine armor." Paul glanced down at the daring red dress. "I see you have worn your own."

"My choices of gown on this ship full of men, was limited," she said. Inwardly, she agreed that the dress did feel like armor. A beautiful gown that hid who she truly was under its loud, and alluring statement. The stones hid in the pocket of her stolen cloak, hanging peacefully in the cabin Napoleon's men had escorted her to not an hour past. Velvet hoped, praying as she did, to any wandering god who would listen that she would have no more need of them tonight. Tonight, she wanted to sleep, and feared she would not. She knew the unwanted vision of the last look in Henry's eyes before her spell had closed them, would terrorize her. How she wanted to run to him, dive from the rail and swim to his arms.

"There is no running now," said Paul, accurately reading the haunting in her eyes. "You are with your countrymen, and you are the last princess of the blood, so they will not let you go." A lantern flickered somewhere, a spill of soft light haloed them, highlighted the fierce set of Paul's features.

Velvet bristled at the censure she saw there. "I do not intend to run. At least, not from Napoleon. Free will brought me here."

"Fear, and sorrow brought you here. Maybe l'amour. I met him, you know? Your dark duke. I did not fight him, but I feel like I got a good measurement of the man. I did not believe he intended to hurt you. I looked in his eyes, said your name, and saw real feeling there."

Velvet shivered, and stepped back, clasping her arms across her stomach; it felt suddenly quite full of spiders. "Why were you searching for me?"

"Parce que, you are my beloved niece, and the stories attached to you are turning into fairy tales. You have the Ton on its ear." He tilted his chin. "Perhaps that is not the expression." Paul waved a white gloved hand. "No matter, you and your assassin duke are the talk of two kingdoms."

In her peripheral, Velvet could see the chattering couples edging closer, heard them quieting their talk to better hear her words. Velvet fidgeted with the soft lace edging her bodice, finding a loose string, and tugging on it. Paul's keen eyes saw it all. He gave the gawkers a regal, if slightly disdainful smile, then his arm slid firmly around her shoulder.

Velvet felt the steel in his grip on her as he guided them along the wall to a high table covered in sparkling champagne flutes all bubbling to the brim. He let her go, lifted a slender glass, and handed it to her with a cheerful smile. All at once, Velvet was ten years old again, cuddled with her family before a roaring fire, twinkling lights everywhere. Dancing colors in her mother's blue eyes. Her uncle smiling down at her, wishing her happy holidays, handing her a glass of the finest champagne. Her first. She shook her head to cast the nostalgic visions away. Her eyes, though, when they met his, were soft with a million memories. "Tell me uncle, how do you find yourself in such august company, and not elsewhere, running for your aristocratic life?"

Paul lifted his arms and gestured to the lavish room. "Like you, I exchanged some of my more annoying principles for comfort, and a head firmly attached to my shoulders." He took a step toward her. Velvet broke away from his gaze—he was right again. She had abandoned everything she loved to be here, with the enemy. She had to clasp her hands to stop herself from flinging herself from the ship's vaulted rail, and swimming back to all of them.

"I had friends in the Republic, I told secrets, and Robespierre returned a portion of my wealth, as well as some of our family's holdings. Even a title, and a seat in the new regime. I was given safe passage back to Austria. Our family mourned you, our Mother, your Grandmother, she..." Paul's voice tapered off, his mouth a grim line of remembered rage.

"What of Napoleon?" Velvet asked, casting a glance at the dominating man from beneath her lashes.

"I cast my lot with him five years ago."

Velvet's eyes flickered. "So long?"

Paul tossed his powdered nose. "What can I say? The bastard pays well and foolishly." He dropped his voice. "Mark my words, he will run out of money long before the carnage in his soul is satisfied. And you, my brilliant fool, have given yourself willingly into his tender care, all to get away from your duke?"

"He's not my duke," she said. He was hers, forever, no matter where she went or what seas parted them. She feared her face spoke her mind, throwing contradictions. Velvet swallowed a ball of fire forming in her throat, tried to blink away the burn in her eyes. "I wish it was different, but I love him. I wish I could be his forever. But this world is cruel and, in my experience, not in the habit of granting wishes. I hate being here. I had no other choice."

The ship lurched and swayed, cutting off whatever else she had meant to say. Velvet pitched forward, waving her arms to right herself, pouring champagne on her borrowed satin shoes.

Napoleon stood, and the upset room held its collective breath. He made his way straight for her, his eyes not straying from her face. He made a great show of taking her hand and pressing his lips to her wrist. The crowd tittered. Napoleon gave her a proud smile, then linked his fingers through her own, and raised their joined arms high above their heads.

"*Sons of France,*" he roared, in a vibrato that was surprising for such a tiny man. "I have found your princess, and we will conquer the continent in her name!"

His words were met with a mighty shout. Some men

stomped their feet, others clapped and cheered. Velvet knew they were enamored with their general, not her. She believed Napoleon could have said, I have severed the head of a wild goat to bring us fortune, and the crowd would have cheered just the same. They applauded the success of their tiny self-proclaimed Corsican king. Velvet glared through the crowd, beyond the melting candles and piles of half-eaten food, the shadowed portcullis showed her the darkening night. Her heart sank. Soon, the island, Henry, Nora, Devon, the beautiful ghost of Katie, would all fade to little more than a twinkling dot on the horizon.

There were times, not many lately, but a few, when Velvet wished with all her soul to be an owl once again. Now, unfortunately, was one of those times. If she was, there would be no choice. The bleeding in her soul would not allow it, Velvet knew she would fly back to him.

"There's no time, goddamn it! He won't stay. His search for her was all that kept him here." Henry's voice rose with his rage.

Nora buried her head in her hands, fearing his pacing would wear a hole in her stateroom floor. "Do stand still, Henry. Your expended energy is going to give me a fit of the vapors. Ugh! I only just got her back, so why would she leave us? I mean, I know why...but, after everything, why?"

"My fucking thoughts exactly," Henry nearly shouted.

Nora cringed at the crude word. Devon placed a pale, consoling hand on her shoulder. "Trust she had her reasons. It would have killed her soul to stay."

"I don't believe that," snapped Henry. "Whatever she was afraid of, we could have faced it together."

Nora lifted her head to stare up at Devon. "What reasons? Give me one? Your face says you know at least a few of them."

Henry pivoted on his heel to look at Devon directly, his

breathing not at all steady. "What did Velvet tell you? You two were thick as thieves when you escorted her in here."

Devon's mouth pulled down at the corners. "Velvet thinks herself to be some variant of the grim reaper. Says everyone she loves eventually dies, and she doesn't want that to happen to any of us."

"But we—" Nora started.

Devon cut her off, and his next words dropped like lead bricks. "The spell to save her brother requires the life of the one who loves most in this world. She seemed lost, out of options, afraid. She thinks if Henry knows the truth, his nobility will turn to stupidity."

Henry froze, the echo of his footsteps dying a harsh death. "She thinks I'll sacrifice myself for Louis," he breathed. The benediction of Devon's words cleared some of the red madness from his mind.

Nora pinched the bridge of her nose until her fingertips whitened, and sighed deeply, sounding pained. "I know, Louis, and we all know you don't want that. None of us do. The very thought is monstrous and makes me want to instantly hurl. Good god, I can't imagine how Velvet felt hearing such an awful thing. My heart is in my throat." Nora glanced up and found Henry's burning eyes. He looked to her like a man being flayed alive. "Would you? Sacrifice yourself to save him?"

Henry slammed his fist into the brick behind him, further damaging his busted knuckles. "Course I bloody well would. I love the chit beyond reason."

"Then maybe it's best this way. I want Louie to be human again as much as a soul can want a thing, but not at the cost of your life."

"You think my life matters at all now? Napoleon has her. He will kill thousands in her name, break cities, turn the seas red. I know him. He is a modern monster. There is nothing save war and mayhem in his heart. Strong as Velvet is, I know her soul will not survive him."

"How can you say such a thing?" Nora snapped.

"Because mine didn't."

"Henry, I can't imagine it is bad as all that. Napoleon is—" Nora's words ended in a small scream as the door flew open, banging hard on its wooden hinges. Zoe burst into the room, Rhee at his heels, both out of breath and visibly sweating. "Sorry to just bust in here, Captain." Zoe tipped his cap to Nora. "Milady, but Rhee heard from Martin who heard from Ajax, who got it from a deckhand what swabs for Little Boots. Said the general means to set sail in the hour."

Henry cursed out a violent stream of Gaelic. Rhee shouldered his way past Zoe. "Boy said he's seen her, our Velvet, in a long red gown, beautiful as the love child of an angel and a star. Thanked him for the tip we did, then clocked him right good, knocked him out cold and tied him to a beached mast."

Devon laughed outright. "What possessed the two of you to do a thing like that?"

"Well, I'll tell you." Zoe sauntered over to the table and took his time filling a mug of ale. Henry visibly bristled. Zoe lifted the mug to his lips; he took a few long gulps. Henry slammed his fist on the small table. The left leg buckled.

"If you don't finish that sentence this instant, Zoe, I vow I will lift you by the ankles and shake till it comes loose."

Zoe, unperturbed by the threat, and used a few more to finish his drink. When he was done, he returned the mug to the now tilted table. Zoe wiped his left sleeve over his mouth. "We figured not the Bacchus or even the Second song will be ready to make way in that time." He shook his head. "It will take us weeks to catch her."

"If you haven't come in here to tell me something I don't know—" Henry started.

Zoe smiled. "It's perfect, isn't it?"

Devon was also smiling. "Smart boy," he said.

Zoe looked inordinately pleased with himself.

"Seems Little Boot's crew is short a deckhand," said Devon,

turning a meaningful eye to Henry. "Can you think of any candidates?"

Henry was already storming from the room, clapping Zoe's shoulder as he brushed past.

"Henry, where—" Nora started.

"To get myself on that damn ship!"

CHAPTER 9

LITTLE, LOST CHILDREN

*V*elvet felt reborn, like the proverbial caterpillar, yet she had morphed into nothing so beautiful as a butterfly, more like a ruby viper, she thought bitterly. She focused on her uncle's face, tried to shut out all the rest. The ship's stateroom was large, with high ceilings covered in fresco, and a wide, candlelit balcony that led out to the open night. Still, it felt too close, the air tasted stale. Too many bodies. Male voices riding over each other, no music, just plots, fake laughter and lies. Velvet knew everyone was staring at her, cheering, and staring. She may as well have been naked, instead of in this damn dress; the corset was too tight; she was struggling to breathe beneath the ruched silk. Most looked at her with a mix of reverence and disdain. She was on her way to be a queen, even if in name only. The shiver that went through her at that thought didn't feel like fear; she was afraid to investigate the actual feeling, power, danger.

Napoleon dropped their hands, and spun her to face him, turning her deftly in his arms. Champagne splashed from her glass. Velvet plastered a smile to her face with the dusty taste of ashes in her mouth, and a scream building in her throat. His hands on her body made her ill, and he gave her a toothy smile.

Velvet had a vision of sticking a knife in his pudgy throat. She hated him. Hated all the men of the Republic responsible for dragging her mother through the street and slicing off her head.

"You are a triumph, my dear," Napoleon declared.

Velvet let her mind go blank in that awful way she was becoming quite good at. Her smile felt brittle, like it would crack her face at any moment.

"Merci, sir. I am pleased to be an ally of the Republic." They both knew her words were false, knew she said them only for the benefit of the listeners. The ship lurched and bucked again; the sails snapped in the balmy wind. If Velvet had a stone in her hand right now, she knew her wish would be for invisibility. Then, she would escape glittering company, find a quiet spot on the deck to bid her Island farewell. Have one last, good daydream about Henry and his hands, and she would remember what it felt like to wear wings.

Paul caught at her elbow before she stumbled and smoothly retracted her hand from Napoleon's moist grip. Velvet shivered. Her uncle's face was cold, his eyes black under his hooded brows. "Come my dear, I will escort you back to your cabin." Velvet watched him cast an imperious glance around the peopled room. Revolutionaries, murders, and peasants turned lords. The lot of them had morphed into the very monsters they once decapitated. Paul sniffed and turned away from the crush, giving his profile to Napoleon, who saw and understood the slight. "I shall retire with you," Paul declared. "I fear present company has turned my stomach."

Napoleon lifted a brow at the insolence, yet her uncle continued undaunted. "You can compel me to fight for you, perhaps one day die for you, but it is pure travesty to force me to endure this unfashionable rabble." Paul removed a snuff tin from the pocket of his waistcoat, snorted a pinch up his right nostril, then dabbed delicately at his nose. He looked down at Velvet, still perched on his arm. "Shall we, my dear?"

"Indeed," Velvet said, biting back a smile at her uncle's flare for the dramatic. In some ways the world around her had been remade the night she heard the price of her brother's life, but some things never changed.

Napoleon dropped in a slight bow. "Good evening then, we will speak on the morrow." Velvet nodded while Paul said nothing. He turned Velvet about with a firm hand on her waist and strolled away, tugging her along with him. Velvet resisted the urge to glance over her shoulder. She could feel all the eyes in the room locked on her retreating back. For someone who had spent years as an invisible creature, it was strange and horrible to be so seen. *Powerful though,* her mind echoed. *Dangerous.* She looked at her uncle. "Brave way to speak to our murderous, self-proclaimed emperor."

Paul snorted. "Pah! He cannot touch me. I am his best source of information. La revolution, killed the titled, even the rich, the truly wealthy?" He shook his head. "They survived, and Napoleon made enemies of them with his questionable, free-thinking associations. I don't think Napoleon realized that conquering the world comes at great cost. An army is an expensive thing. That's why he needs you, mon chéri, to stir up sympathies and the gold that comes with them. His motives are obvious as the excessive nose on his face. The real question is, why are you willingly helping him?"

Velvet refused to be bated. "I should ask you the same thing."

Paul laughed. "I am operating under the old adage, give the devil enough rope—"

"And watch him hang himself," Velvet finished softly. She couldn't help a sad smile. "Mother's favorite saying, she applied it often to Father."

Paul nodded. "I remember. So that rumor, at least, is false. Your memories are not gone."

"No, I reclaimed them on the island."

Paul raised a cultured brow. "I see." A host of questions flashed in his deep, icy eyes, but he said nothing. They turned a corner, then another. Their footsteps echoed a static rhythm as they walked. The corridor was narrow, with a low ceiling, and tiny, circular windows that showed little of the night beyond the hand-blown glass. The paneled walls were strung with gas lamps that spilled flame and shadow. When they came to the small door of her cabin, Paul stopped and turned to her. His face was deeply serious, all signs of the foppish lording dropped away. "What are you doing, mon coeur?"

Velvet knew exactly what he meant but chose to deflect. "I am going to lie in an extremely uncomfortable bed, where I will pray to the goddess of sleep to gift me with a dreamless repose. She will probably ignore me. She always has, I don't know why tonight would be any different."

Paul sighed at her rambling. "I have been playing devoted courtier to a monster, since I day I heard rumors of your life, praying I would find you before he did. You were free, protected by your duke, why would you willingly give yourself over? And don't flip it back on me. I know why I did what I did, money and power. I don't believe those were your motivations."

Velvet turned her head and tried to peer through the murky window. "What did you plan to do once you found me?" she finally asked, ignoring the rest.

"Take you home. You are Marie-Thérèse-Charlotte; Madame Royale; Filia Dolorosa, the Modern Antigone; Comtesse de Marnes. Born at Versailles, on a brilliant new moon. Your bloodline is from the houses of Bourbon and Habsburg-Lorraine. You were born to be a queen. I want to bring you home to our family, where we will chart a course to take back your throne."

"It isn't my throne," she said, that automatic denial that came so quickly to her lips. *Wasn't it?* She was on her way to sit in the cursed, golden chair, knowing her brother still lived, knowing it was rightfully his. Velvet shook her head. "Another glaring problem with your plan is that I have no home. I haven't belonged anywhere since the revolutionaries set fire to my dolls and slit my baby brother's throat in the nursery. *You were home with him,* her shrill mind countered. *His arms were safe and warm, the most perfect lifeline.* Velvet felt again, the sudden, desperate need to escape. Escape her uncle, and his hard, knowing eyes, escape Napoleon with his entourage of peasants and jokers dressed as lords and kings—all responsible one way or another for killing everyone she had loved. It was a sad irony; she had walked into a den of lions to save the life of a panther. Velvet felt a smile flirt with her lips at that mental image.

Paul eyed her suspiciously. Velvet shared her private observation. Paul threw back his head and laughed. "Ah, but Daniel survived the lions' den. These fools will eat you alive."

"Will they? I don't know. Owls are a predatory bird, vicious and gamey."

Paul's eyes went dark at the cryptic dribble. "So, the rumors are true?"

Velvet feigned innocence, then shrugged dismissively. "Which ones? There are so many it is difficult to decipher truth from hideous lie. Mostly it's fantasy and fables."

"The story that a Romani woman changed you into an owl, and Louie to a stag?"

Velvet glared at her delicately sandaled feet. "Oui, that one is true."

"Ah." Paul nodded. "What of the one where the British king married you to the Duke of Newcastle by proxy?"

"Unfortunately, in my case, it seems truth is the victor."

"Is Newcastle your husband?" Paul's voice was calm, but Velvet knew what he was really asking.

She nodded, unable to meet his eyes. Paul snorted. "He's a handsome devil, but I think I understand why you fled him. The bride and her betrayer. Sounds like the title of a lush French novella. The story of your life in print is inevitable. The papers are heavy with your name. Piracy, lost at sea—"

"Witchcraft?"

"Mais bien sûr. It's a label many powerful women carry, given to them by weak men."

Velvet stifled a laugh that died on her lips as her eyes flicked over Paul's shoulder. She instantly recognized the figure moving toward them. "Here comes a prime example," she said in a low whisper.

Paul raised a brow, then slowly turned to face a scowling William Pitt.

Velvet retreated into her small cabin. She shut the door firmly, threw the thick lock and dropped the chain-link latch, then leaned her forehead against the door, breathing deep, shuddering from the tips of her hair to her toes. William Pitt was the last person in the world she wished to see. With the grief and anger roiling inside of her, there was truly no telling what she would do to the villain. Velvet heard the deep voices of Pitt and her uncle receding down the hall. Velvet groaned and softly punched the door, then turned to search for the box of matches on the small table near the door and set about lightening the lantern. When the wick caught, a warm fire-glow spread through the small, damp room. It highlighted the edges of the rope bed, musty red coverlet, and metal sink. Velvet started to make her way toward it.

The ship bucked, groaning in its timbers, as it rocked hard. Velvet lost her footing, and the next jolt threw her across the room with such force she nearly splattered against the wall. Velvet caught herself, hands splayed, but smacked her forehead just the same. Hair tumbled over her face. She pushed it back, and tucked the tangled strands behind her ears, gaping, heart twisting like it would snap in two. The ship was moving. She could hear the tug and splash as the huge rudders cut through the water.

Velvet straightened, rubbed her aching wrists, and started to cry. Silent tears that slipped down her cheeks, splashed the bodice of her dress, then she sunk to her knees as the tears fell faster. A choked sob escaped her tightly pressed lips. She clapped a hand over her mouth so no more would break free. This was how it felt then, to walk away from one's heart, she silently acknowledged. It felt like acid in her veins and a fire in her chest.

The ship continued to sway; the tears kept falling. In the broken silence, Velvet heard herself call his name. She tried to imagine a world without him and came up short. Without his face, his laugh, cynical as it was, his touch, that kiss that scorched her soul. There was nothing left to do save lie down on the freezing floor and cry until the tears were gone.

Seeing her uncle, knowing he lived, was something wonderful, but it had made her miss her brothers and sisters. So, she cried for them and the life they could have had. Lying on her side, knees drawn up to her chest, Velvet rocked with the ship, holding herself tightly to keep whatever burned within from blowing apart, leaving only remnants of her smeared across this dingy cabin. She slept, finally, conjuring pictures of Henry's face, but there was no peace in her dreams, only darkness, betrayal, bloody magic, and screams.

When next Velvet woke, the ship had found a gentle rhythm, and the moon was high in the indigo sky, adorned by its crown of stars. She could see it clearly, shining through her one small window. She stood slowly, trying to go easy on her cramped, aching muscles. Her legs trembled badly but held her up. She grabbed the wall for support as her vision went momentarily black. She felt empty, spent, drained of all her light.

Moving like a drunken sleepwalker, Velvet tugged at the small clasps lining the bodice of the red dress. She ripped a few in her clumsy haste but didn't care. She would never wear it again. It fell to a glossy heap that looked too much like blood in the darkness. She kicked it away, then stood, arms clasped over her breast, shivering, and letting herself, just for a moment, pretend that everything would come out right in the end. She stared out the tiny window, and the seconds ticked by, each endless and painful. Eventually, it was the cold that made her move. She rifled through a small armoire near the window sink, her movements wooden, her fingers like tiny sticks of ice. She found nothing, save a pair of twice darned socks beside a dog-eared volume titled, A Sailor's Guide.

Sighing, Velvet moved to the bronze chest at the foot of the bed. When Velvet undid the latch, and tossed back the lid, she found it stuffed with all manner of things. She searched it slowly, methodically. Velvet shrieked when her hands touched a pair of buff breeches, and a white cambric shirt, both smelling like the sea, but blessedly clean. The garb of a cabin boy, she suspected as she pulled the shirt over her head. The hem fell to her knees, the breeches were loose, but she found a spare length of rope in the chest and used it to clinch the whole ensemble tight around her waist.

She wished for a brush with all her soul, for her hair had become its own creature. She combed her fingers through it, staring out the window, thinking inner peace was a thing more elusive than diamonds and gold. Lost in musings, Velvet lifted Minerva's cloak. The stones weighted the material. She touched them with dread, felt ill instead of vibrant when the power snaked up her arm. Cringing with disdain, Velvet stashed the stones deep in the chest, then closed the lid with a bang that made her jump.

Velvet stood, staring at the place where they rested, half fearing the power of them would creep out and attach themselves to her person, somehow. Velvet flung the cloak around her shoulders, laced it beneath her chin, then started for the door. The four walls of the cabin were too close, siphoning her air with their nearness. She needed to be free, breathe in the wild night air even if only for a few moments. Perhaps she could find a quiet nook on the main neck, where she could crouch unobserved and howl her misery at the moon. Velvet had seen a wolf do so once, after a hunter stole her cub. As an owl, looking down from her vantage of safety in the sky, she hadn't understood the activity, still, it had seemed to soothe the wretched creature, maybe it would do the same for her.

Velvet felt her humanity in every step as she moved to the

door and threw it open. Scents of night rushed in. She closed her eyes and breathed deep, then started to walk. She moved like a wraith through the dark ship. On the quarterdeck she came upon four men deep in their cups, heavily involved in a game of dice. Either they didn't notice her passing or were too involved to care. When she reached the main deck, Velvet moved toward the helm, all soaked in glistening moonlight. At the base of the stairs leading to the captain's deck, two more sailors stood, their backs to her, conversing in low tones. One was tall, dressed in a pair of cut-off breeches, and a black shirt stretched tight over his broad shoulders. He wore the garment like a second skin.

Velvet froze, unwilling to confront another soul while she was in such a state. She thought of running, told herself to do so, but her limbs refused to respond to her mental commands. Besides, there was nowhere to go. Velvet thought she might take on the Devil himself if it would keep her out of that musty, strangling cabin for a few moments more. The man turned. Moonlight touched his austere profile.

"Henry."

The sailors turned as one to face her. Velvet's heart stopped dead in her chest. Henry's eyes lifted and stared hotly into hers. She nearly expired on the spot. She saw him through a tightening tunnel, receding, while a wild thing leapt in her chest, and was forced to curl her toes into the deck to keep herself from launching into his arms. *This is truly real. He's actually here. After everything, he came for me,* she thought, realizing in that moment, she didn't actually think in her heart of hearts that he would come for her this time. She had broken her word, betrayed him again, and still he was here. The knowledge staggered her, left her reeling. They stared at each other for long moments. Henry watched her with the intensity of a predator closing in for a kill. The ghosts of past betrayals chilled the air between them. She swallowed hard, acid and fire.

Henry smiled, dark and mysterious as some foreign god. "In the flesh, my love."

CHAPTER 10

SORRY

*H*er world was crashing around her ears, her heart pounding louder than the waves. A thousand words rushed to her mind, but the knowledge of speech deserted her. A gust of wind howled through the sails; Velvet swayed with it. Whether from the forceful gale, or unmitigated shock, she couldn't be sure. Not breaking their stare; Henry nodded at the boy beside him. Rhee. Velvet felt another wash of shock, cold and jarring. Rhee took one look at her white face and threw her a rapscallion wink. He ran off then—a skip in his step—to fulfill whatever silent command Henry had given. He was gone in seconds, and they were alone.

Henry, her, a warship, moonlight, and a thousand enemies sleeping below. They stared at each other and time snared, then stretched and surged. Waves broke against the hull, and Velvet thought she heard a melancholy music in the beating red ring around the moon. There were so many things to say. Should she apologize for murdering a man, for enchanting him yet again, for running away, for not trusting enough, giving into fear over love? Henry continued examining her face, and Velvet wondered what he saw there? Could he see through her crumbling resolve to her breaking heart?

Suddenly, Velvet found her voice bolstered by a giant rush of breath. "I won't even ask how you got yourself on this ship, your grace. No doubt you rode here on a Kraken, or walked on water, but I should warn you, you will find only enemies on this ship."

"Does that include you, Marie?" he asked, low voice cutting through all her defensive shields. The intensity of his icy eyes nearly undid her. Velvet brought her freezing hands to her burning face, felt her uneven pulse jumping in her throat.

"I could not be your enemy, Henry, despite my recent actions, but my uncle is alive, and has been searching for me," she babbled, too nervous for silence.

Henry took a step toward her, then another, moving into a brilliant stream of moonlight, which highlighted the beloved curves and contours of his face. Velvet saw carefully leashed rage snapping in his eyes. She swallowed the lump of fire in her throat and stumbled back a step. His face looked hard as she had ever seen it. She held out a trembling hand to ward him off. "I'm going home, Henry, as I should have done in the beginning. In trying to do good, in trying to save what I love, I have only caused death and pain. You can say whatever you want, you know it's true. It's what you accused me of. You said I only care about myself and what I want, said I don't care who I hurt. Maybe that was true in the beginning, but not anymore. I care too much."

Her words hung in the air. Henry looked like he couldn't respond or wouldn't. It seemed if he did, he would break, pull her into his arms, lock his lips to hers, and taste her reality.

Velvet rolled her eyes at him; her hands fell to her hips. "I see you've lapsed into brooding silence, as always." He reached her in one more stride, his mouth pressed in a grim line. Velvet felt her face flare hotter. The fire in his eyes was burning her alive. "Fine! Be your morose self, stand there and judge me! I fear the fresh air is set to give me a fit of the vapors, so if you'll excuse me, your grace, I shall relieve you of my company, and retire for the evening. I wish you a good night, I'm sure."

Velvet spun, turning to go, wondering if he would let her,

hoping she could force her stubborn feet to walk away. Henry did not disappoint. He caught her arm with brutal force, his iron grip unbreakable. Her breath escaped in a shriek as he pulled her hard against him, and her backside slammed into his hips, then his mouth touched her ear. "Marie, my darling, you've never had a fit of the vapors in your life." He ran his hand slowly up her body, carefully wrapped his fingers around her throat, his thumb caressed the line of her jaw. His other hand gathered up a handful of her hair, and he twisted his fist, tilting her head so Velvet was forced to meet his eyes. She tried to look calm, unaffected, but her trembling body screamed her truth.

"Don't do something I'll have to forgive you for later," she warned.

Henry's face twisted, all hard shadow and moonlit glow. "I don't want your damn forgiveness when you should be on your knees begging mine. All I've ever asked for is that you trust me. Your response to that request, however predictable, was to cast another damn spell."

Velvet shot him a quelling glare, but her body went weak, her mind in turmoil from the accusation in his eyes. "Don't torture me, Henry, please. Depart this ship as magically as you appeared. If you've ever truly cared for me, please just let me go."

Henry's hands tightened in her hair, until the grip flirted with the line of real pain. "I can't, damn you. You are my obsession, the centrifugal focus of my world. I have told you before, I will never let you leave me. Run oft and far as you like, there is nowhere you can go where I will not find you."

Velvet closed her eyes, hearing, understanding the truth in his words. She realized all this time, she had been in love with him from afar, like an owl who accidentally loved a panther, a forbidden thing wrapped in her spells, something she wanted but could never truly have because the spells and lies that warped her life would ever keep them apart, but he was very real to her now. His heartbeat was the prose of her life.

Henry's hands gentled, instantly, became caressing, rather

than punishing. His fingers cupped her scalp, the feel of him lightly touching the contours of her throat sent wild shivers through her, making her very aware of her body. The smile he gave her then was pure temptation. "I've told you I would die to keep you."

"You don't understand," she whispered, "and I cannot explain. All you can do is let me walk away."

"Run, you mean. You are many things, Marie, but never before tonight did I think you were a coward."

"Better a coward than a murderess," she snapped, her temper rising. She lifted her arms, knocked his hands away and spun to glare up at him. Beneath the cloak, her chest rose and fell with her uneven breaths. He was spectacular, every aspect of him chiseled in brilliance. Velvet knew she was lost from the second she had seen his face tonight, or that first night, when they had been children, so many broken years, and another lifetime ago, she had been hopelessly lost. Tears filled her eyes, spilled again. "Let me go home, Henry, the thought of you, of us—it hurts. If I were a different girl, in an alternate place and time, you should know that I would stay with you forever," she said, the honest words torn from her throat. She shook in his arms, praying this was just a dream. A fantasy, torture, and relief in the same breath. He was the sum of her fears, the truth of her desire.

"If that's what you want, then I will take you home," he said, his voice so husky, she had to strain to hear the words over the wild wind.

Velvet shook her head, refusing to meet his eyes. "You are a British duke, an assassin for the mad king, and an enemy of Napoleon. Only death waits for you in France. I won't be responsible for your death. Can't you understand? It would kill me. I'm trapped, damned, no matter what I choose. The stones are evil, and I am part of them, one of them." Her voice dropped to a whisper. "I am evil, you don't know me, if you did you wouldn't love me."

Henry lowered his head. Velvet was still as glass in his arms.

"I know you, my love, like the beat of my heart. You are cunning and brave. You are a survivor."

"I've lied, I've killed," she started, her voice breaking on the words, but her hands were in his hair, pressing him closer, wanting more.

"So have I," he whispered, his breath touching her lips. "I would do it again, to save you. I would do anything."

"I don't need you to save me. I need you to stay away from me. Motivation and machination don't matter. I can't lose you. I won't even let myself consider the possibility." Her voice dropped low. "I did though. I thought about it for a moment, down in that wonderful, horrible cave, considering if I would, could, trade your life for his, but I would die if I lost you, lost either of you. There is only one path left for me in this crazy world."

"No, you're wrong. We can find another way."

"You don't know what you're talking about."

"Yes, I do. Devon told me what the spell demanded. You think I would give my life for Louis." It wasn't a question.

"Wouldn't you?" she asked, voice breaking on her breath. There was a bitter taste in her mouth, a precursor to more tears. Henry didn't answer. His lips touched hers, soft at first, void of the rage she had anticipated. Velvet struggled, fighting him, or perhaps herself. Because they were two players in a tragic romance, one of the lush tales Nora loved to read. Two lovers on a dark night, and two real people fate had driven apart so many times. Henry's arms tightened until her breasts were crushed against his chest; she could feel the heat he radiated through her cloak and thin shirt. Henry pulled back, cupped her face in his hands, pressed a kiss to the corner of her mouth. "I would do anything for you."

"That's why I have to leave. Queenie would have done anything for me. Katie would have done anything for me. Even my mother and father would have—"

Henry's mouth swooped down and cut off her angry stream of words. There was nothing gentle in his touch now. He lifted her up his body, and bit at her lower lip, slid his tongue in her gasping mouth, hot as a glowing brand. He invoked madness. Velvet wanted him, missed him even in the few hours they had been apart. She tore her mouth away. "I killed someone tonight, Henry. Remnants of his blood probably still stain my hands."

"I know," he breathed.

"Death follows me wherever I go. I don't want to hurt you anymore."

"Death follows me too, darling. Perhaps we can beat it together. Regardless, I want you too badly to have it any other way. Napoleon cannot have you; your uncle cannot have you. France cannot have you. You are mine. It is too late to deny me now, for the whole world knows you are my wife."

"I do not know it."

"You did, down in that cave. You can't lie to me; I know what we both felt. We belong together, we are inevitable. Somewhere in your soul—you know it well as I do."

Velvet chose that moment to give up, and give in, because she did know it—she might be the one who eventually killed him, but she couldn't resist him. Her mind told her to step away, put distance between them. Her heart locked her in place. So, they stood in silence, only errant wisps of night wind braved the space between them. This desire burning her bones went against everything her mind thought it knew. Perhaps the world was actually sane, and she was a madwoman.

Henry's head dipped lower, close enough that she could feel his breath warm on her lips. His eyes were nearly black with passion, darker than they had been the night he took her for the first time. Ebony curls blew across his forehead, and Velvet lifted her hand and ran her fingers through the mass, brushed the chilled curve of his ear, cupped his cheek. Henry closed his eyes, turned his head, and pressed a scalding kiss into the center of her palm.

"I broke my promise to you," she breathed, listening to the

way her voice trembled, hearing misery infused in every syllable. "I cast another spell on you, Henry, or do you not remember?"

"I remember."

"Then where is the rage and revenge?"

Henry smiled against her lips, dark and sensual. "Demolished by the power of my need. All I know is that I want you. If you hadn't left our bed, I would have had you a dozen times before morning dawned. It hurt, how easy it was for you to walk away. Had the earth been imploding around my ears, and a thousand guns pointed at my head, I could not have left you."

Velvet turned her head away from the accusation and stark pain in his eyes. "It was easy because when I left the bed, I never meant to leave you." Velvet felt heat flare in her cheeks. "I was hungry, Henry, and I didn't want to wake you. I thought I would be all right—though I am not sure what possessed me to come to that conclusion. In my life, I have scarcely left a tavern unscathed —but I wasn't. I was accosted in the kitchen by a man who thought he could."

Henry's smile gleamed like a blade. "So, you shot him with my pistol."

Velvet lifted her chin. "Naturally."

Henry chucked her under the chin. "That's my girl. No doubt the blighter deserved it."

Velvet frowned. "This isn't funny. I have killed before with purpose, but tonight I shot a man merely for taking liberties. In a more civilized climate, I should be hung for such an act."

"Then we must thank our lucky stars that we are not in civilized climes. And I take issue with your choice of words, liberties?" He shook his head, more curls cascaded over his brow, "I think you mean rape. I'm glad you shot him. Could've gone much worse for the fellow. There is a high possibility I would have pulled the bastard apart with my bare hands."

"Why are you acting like this? You've told me so many times how impulsive I am, how selfish. You—"

"I was a fool. A blind fool. I am not ashamed to say that you and your spells have driven me insane."

"You only say that right now because you have decided to be kind to me, for whatever mystifying reason. What about the next time you get angry at me? Will I still be a brave survivor, then?"

"I am angry right now, furious, actually, but it's not the only emotion I'm feeling. This time you used those damned stones to save me. You thought of me, of my life, over anyone else, even your brother. By running, you told me I was who you loved most in the world. I may want to throttle you, Marie, but I also want to kiss you breathless."

"Henry." Velvet pressed her lips to his, speaking her next words in a dizzy rush. "I wanted to jump off this cursed ship and run back to you the second my foot hit the deck. I almost wished for my wings, but magic is deceitful. It never comes to save, only to play. The price of the game is a piece of my soul each time. I can't pay anymore, for soon there will be nothing left. Then, the moment I abandoned all hope and resigned myself to whatever horror waits for me across the sea, I turn around and there you are, like some realized fantasy."

"You beautiful, darling girl, where else would I be? I just spent a horrid month—during which I aged ten years—not knowing if you were alive or dead, praying every second to a god I no longer trust, to let me see you again. Do you really think I was about to let you out of my sight? I would have set fire to this ship before I let it take you away."

"And what? What will you do, here, in the middle of the ocean, surrounded by enemies?"

Henry leaned back, stared deep in her unblinking eyes, then flashed her a rakish grin. "I've decided my men were right all along and piracy is the life for me. I will take this ship and imprison the men who once destroyed your world, then, in chains, I will lay them at your feet. Their fate will be my gift to you."

Velvet had no words. Silently, she went up on the tips of her toes and pressed her lips to his. The light stubble on his jaw rubbed her cheek. He smelled like wine, wind, and him. Want of him made her weak, and her knees felt like two pools of turbulent water. Henry kissed her back, let his hands coast down her sides, then he cupped her hips and pulled her closer. She could feel him then, hard and hot against the juncture of her thighs. She ached all over, as a desperate, wanton throb emanated from the place only he had ever touched. In that burning moment, Velvet wanted nothing more than to tear off her trousers and have him, right here on the floor, and damn whoever dared to pass by. He rocked his hips, once, twice, and Velvet's head fell back, as she heard a breathy sound of needy desperation combined and realized distantly that it was hers.

What was becoming of her? Where were her nerves of steel and regal pose? Why, oh why did a single touch from him reduce her to this? Why did she want to melt at his feet every time he put his hands on her? Was it because she loved him, or was it something more? An urgency to own him body and soul, a craving that went beyond the physical. Internally demolished, Velvet tore her mouth away. Her lips throbbed; she could count each beat of her heart in their silent pulse. "This is madness, Henry." She passed a hand over her mouth, still feeling the haunting of his kiss. "You should not be here. Not even for me. Every soul on this ship will shoot you first and ask questions later."

Henry smiled into her eyes. "It seems my life is in peril from all sides, so apparently I must live each moment to the fullest." His eyes were bright, compelling, his hard hand on the back of her neck began to drag her mouth back to his.

Velvet placed a hand on his chest to ward him off. "I hope you have a plan that does not involve you spending the night on this ship."

Henry didn't respond. For a moment he looked at her like he hadn't heard a word she said. His eyes had dropped to her body and stayed there. His hands spanned her waist, touched her legs, went to the waistband of her trousers. He made a shocked, muffled noise and, for a few seconds, he looked truly aghast, scandalized even, then he started to chuckle. "God's blood, Marie, are you wearing trousers?"

Velvet tensed. "What if I am? Nora wears them."

He stepped back to really look at her. Slowly, he reached for the edges of her cloak and pulled the falls of cloth aside. He pushed it off her shoulders. Velvet couldn't move under his intense perusal. His eyes blazed, flaming indigo. His tongue flashed out to wet his lips, then he bit at the lower one, and Velvet felt something inside her melt.

"What a rare, intoxicating creature you are," he said, his voice a husky caress. The way he stared made her dizzy. He reached out and ran a hand down the slope of her breast. Velvet felt her nipples harden to painful points, clearly visible beneath the sheer cloth of her shirt; all trace of humor left Henry's face. He untied the laces at her throat, the cloak sagged then fell in shimmering waves at their feet. Henry swallowed hard, whistling low, he spun her in a slow, full circle.

Velvet rolled her eyes, blushing. "Don't look at me like that. You've seen me naked, so surely this isn't—"

"Revealing, enticing, the most exciting thing I've ever seen? My love, I doubt Aphrodite at her finest was half as arousing."

Velvet tipped her head, peered up at him and, for a breathless moment, the world consisted of silver moonlight and the scorching fire of his eyes. There was a serious set to his jaw as he lowered his head again. From the look on his face, this time he would not stop with merely a kiss.

Velvet turned her head away. "A pack of drunk sailors lurk not ten feet away. The watch will—"

Henry shook his head. "I don't care. You're here, in my arms, not fighting me. I'll take all the moments I can get."

"Villain," Velvet accused, as she reached up and touched his cheek. "Come what may, I'm glad you came for me."

His eyes narrowed on her face. That look, his touch...

Godstars, they spun her rational mind in dizzy circles. "Don't worry my love. It is all going to come right in the end."

"How can you possibly say that?"

"Because I will it to be so."

Velvet sighed. "Fate must truly be a woman after all, if you feel you can speak an outcome and she will obey," she said, then giggled at her own wit.

Henry expelled a suspicious snort that sounded very much like a laugh. Velvet giggled again, not feeling at all herself, wondering if it was possible to be drunk on another person. She felt giddy, almost sick with relief. He was real, here, he had come for her, despite what she had done, he had not abandoned her.

Henry dipped his head to taste the corner of her smile. He threaded his fingers through her hair, tipped her head back and stared deep into her eyes. "There's something different about you tonight. What strange devilry has added to your beauty?"

"Merely deception, for all creatures know the light of a full moon plays tricks on the eyes."

His eyes flicked to her bare breasts barely covered by the thin, cambric shirt. "Eh? No trick this. Princess, even in the dark, you could drive a man to madness. Haunt him with visions of your parted thighs, all porcelain and blushed." He ran his thumbs over the tips of her breasts. "Hair like spun gold, nipples the color of a summer rose. A prize for a king."

"Or a villainous duke," she said breathlessly. Laughter still sparkled in Velvet's eyes, but Henry's were deadly serious when they met hers.

"This duke you speak of, tell me, does he have a chance of winning the fair princess's heart?"

Velvet blinked, lost in his eyes. She shook her head. "No, he cannot win it. She is already his."

Henry's eyes widened. He swallowed hard and shoved his hair off his brow with a hand that held a fine tremble. "Is she? Truly?"

Velvet closed her eyes, the vision of his face imprinted forever on her soul. "Always," she whispered. This time, when Henry cradled her face in his hands and bent his head to kiss her, Velvet was ready for him. She locked her arms around his neck and kissed him back with delicate greed. Against his lips, Velvet made an offer she shouldn't. "My cabin is just—"

"Yes," Henry rasped, biting at her lips.

Velvet disentangled herself from his arms. Turning, she bent to retrieve her cloak, unconsciously presenting him a delectable view of her derriere. Henry ran his hands over the lush curves and groaned. Velvet jumped, straightening quickly, spun around, giggling. "Follow me then, and for Christ's sakes don't let yourself be seen."

Close lipped, Henry pointed in the direction of her cabin. "Go, wench, before I rip off your clothes with my teeth and have you here on this deck—"

Velvet giggled. "Henry—"

"Twice," he avowed.

CHAPTER 11

PASSION

*V*elvet closed the cabin door, hesitated over it for a long moment, considering, in the end, she left the latch undone. Henry had been right; away from the raging inferno that was his magnificent person, old thoughts and fears came rushing back like a group of fanged monsters set to torment her. Velvet bristled, internally at war. How easy it was for him to melt her, make her forget everything, save the maddening need his touch invoked.

Listlessly, she moved to the foot of the small bed and sat down, mentally, and physically exhausted—seemed she always was these days. Velvet sighed, rubbing at her aching eyes. He could do and say anything in those moments when his lips and hands were on her, and she would submit. A hard truth for a girl whose mantra was: give me freedom or give me death.

Velvet lay down and threw an arm across her eyes, groaning. He had come for her, after everything she had said and done, he was here, saving her, again, when all she had wanted to do was save him. He said he loved her, had all but commanded her to trust him, yet in this world where only the strong survived and the wicked thrived...could she? Trust in the wrong man had ultimately ended her mother and father's life, trusting the wrong woman—in the case of Queenie—had caused Velvet to love and defend the actions of a child killer, if lord Eden's accounting of Alfonso's story was true.

Velvet pulled one of her boots off and pitched it petulantly across the room. What if it was all out of her hands? What if she already trusted him, loved him, heart, and soul beyond all reason or sanity? What if she submitted to that love, then lost him? Her body flinched away from that thought—the answer was all too easy; she would not survive it. Velvet kicked off her remaining boot and rolled onto her side. Folding both hands and cradling them under her cheek, she let her mind consider another, more appealing possibility. What if Henry was correct, and it all did go right in the end, for all of them? What if, against all odds, they found a way to save Louis without trading a life? What if Nora and Louis could be together, and Devon could pack Katie away in his broken heart and spend the remainder of his days in peace—Napoleon and his cronies would give up their assault on Europe and Charles would take a short walk off a long cliff? What if Henry and she could go somewhere, just the two of them, perhaps back to their cave, lie in each other's arms, let time run on without them and wait out forever?

In a world of magic stones, sparkling wings, and alternate dimensions, it appeared anything was possible. What if, what if, what if?

Velvet sat up suddenly and swiped a hand across her eyes. What in blazes was the matter with her? Henry was right; she was behaving like a coward, and a fool. She shook her head, deeply wishing she had this epiphany before she blindly boarded a warship of enemies. She vaulted from the bed and started to pace. She would take a page from Henry's book, and will her happy-ending, just as she had willed a pack of rough soldiers to dance, a rope to make a startling transition into a blood thirsty snake, and a host of other things she never thought to do. Sleep, love, magic, she had willed so many things into existence without even knowing how. Secretly, Velvet wondered if she even needed the stones. If Tamora was a part of her, maybe she was enough.

Velvet stubbed her toe twice in the space of seconds and stopped pacing. Her brain, heart, and left big toe were on fire. Godstars! How she wished Nora was sitting on the bed, scrunching her prim nose and spouting her perfect brand of offbeat wisdom. Velvet would ask her a million questions, and no doubt gush a little about Henry. She needed to speak with a woman who knew. Velvet sighed. Nora wasn't here, just Henry, her, and a group of bad guys better off dead.

Her eyes flew irritably toward the door. What in blazes was taking him so long? Had he been seen? Captured? Velvet's nervous, expelled breath was visible in the chilly air. It made a momentary cloud of white around her face and she knew the warship had entered deep waters. She shivered, suddenly missing her island with a sharp pang—it was hers. She was much a part of it, as the stone of Tamora was part of her. Part of a long line of ancient sages, and dead women.

The doorknob scraped, shattering the noise of her inner monologue. A pair of low voices muttering beyond broke through the thick silence. Velvet stopped breathing, and her eyes flicked to the chest at the foot of the bed and the stones hidden inside. The knob scratched again, then rattled and turned. Velvet moved quickly to stand behind the door, latched her hand over her mouth to muffle any escaped sound. She pressed her back flat against the wall, and counted, one second, two—the door flew open, swinging inward to crash against the wall where she stood. It clipped her toe, snapped back, and encountered something solid. The contact produced a low sounding thud, followed by a violent stream of curses.

"Arg! Damn. Mother of God. What the hell?" she heard Henry groan.

Velvet tried to force words through her constricted throat, but all that came out was a whispered squeak. Henry's hand, encased in a supple leather glove, braced the door, while the other went to his nose. Quietly, he closed the door, but Velvet knew he had wanted to slam the thing. He came up short when he saw her, took in her wide eyes and trembling lips.

Henry made a face. "It's not at all funny, you little vixen. I think you broke my nose."

A gaggle of giggles escaped, even though Velvet tried to bite them back. Henry tugged and shoved at his nose with the flat of both hands. There was a loud popping noise, and he cursed and groaned again. Velvet gave up trying to hold it in and dissolved into a puddle of silent laughter. She couldn't help it. The picture he made—dark hair, dark clothes, midnight cloak, and bright red nose, he looked like a grumpy grim reaper.

Henry's arm flashed out, his fingers caught the collar of her shirt, then he hauled her against him, and kissed her ferociously. Her senses instantly responded to the persuasive heat of his mouth, so erotic and tender. Just as her arms were rising to twine around his neck, he tore his mouth away, his ragged murmur was hot in her ear. "When you laugh, really laugh, there is nothing in the world as beautiful as you."

"Flatterer," Velvet accused, but her voice was soft as the fingers she twined through his hair. She tugged at the dark curls. "What took you so long?"

Henry leaned back to regard her quizzically. "Madam, did you forget that I am a stowaway and must walk only in shadows?"

"A common state of affairs for you, I think," she said tartly.

Henry smiled. "Touché, my darling."

"Can you ever give a straight answer to a simple question?"

Henry appeared pensive at her inquiry, but Velvet caught the gleam of mischief in his bright eyes. "I don't know. Remind me later to try."

Velvet smacked him hard on the chest. The blow stung her hand, and she flexed it. "Infuriating man," she gasped.

"I was talking to Rhee. He briefly spotted the Bacchus, kept an eye on it for about three minutes, but lost it in the fog. Nora makes a stellar captain, and they should catch us before sunrise.

I predict it will be a bloody dawn." His smile was all teeth. He kissed the tip of her nose, the smile reached his eyes, softened, and glowed there for a time. "Why do you ask? Did you miss me?"

"No."

"Ah, princess, you are truly the prettiest liar in all the land. If it wasn't loneliness, it must have been fear. You think my head is incredibly handsome and have no desire to see it cut from my shoulders."

Velvet rolled her eyes. "You're in a rare mood. You look more alive than you have in months. Vibrating excitement, I can almost hear your nerves thrumming. It's because you're in your element, isn't it? Espionage, trickery, battle. This is a game to which you not only know the rules but excel at its execution. Sometimes, when there's kindness in your eyes, I forget who you actually are."

Henry stepped closer, closer still, and didn't stop until their bodies touched from breastbone to hip. "Do you?" His dark brows arched high. He leaned in, his big body crowding her, arousing her. Hard fingers chilled by the night threaded through hers. He lifted their joined hands and pinioned them on either side of her head. His hips pressed tight against hers, anchored the rest of her body in place. The burning feel of him made Velvet wish her trousers were made of smoke. His lips touched her throat, his whisper sent shivers racing over her skin. "You're wrong. It's not the coming battle that's making me pant, at least not the one with Napoleon."

Velvet looked up at him through her lashes. "Do you anticipate a battle with me, my lord?"

Henry's voice dropped low. "Aye, Vixen, I have you alone, undisturbed, free to wrestle with you till dawn. 'Tis a thing so wonderful it could be a dying man's last wish."

Velvet flushed and averted her eyes and stared at the expanse of bronze skin that glowed beneath the open collar of his shirt. It looked like gold under the shadows cast by the flickering lantern light. Impulsively, she pressed her lips to the place her eyes caressed. Henry made a small, harsh sound. He released one of her hands, his fingers sunk into her hair, and he held her closer. Velvet kissed his throat and felt him tremble, then she bit him lightly and listened to his soft, ragged groan. The sound made her feel incredibly powerful and weak all over. Her freed hand went to the small pearl buttons running down the front of his shirt. She undid them quickly, despite her own shaking. He released her other hand and cupped her face in both of his, then bent to kiss her, but Velvet resisted. Their eyes met. They stared at each other for a long, burning moment, loud with their rapid breaths.

Be brave, tell him what you feel, her mind chided. She opened her mouth, but the words of devotion and love were still too frightened to pass her lips. She would show him. *Be brave, be brave,* her silly mind chanted, as if that wasn't the only thing in the world she was trying to be. She closed her eyes on a sigh and slid down his body like water. Since the night they had dimension walked, and kissed beneath a timeless tree, she had wanted to taste him, the way he had tasted her. She made short work of the buckle; the rest was a struggle. It took both hands to free him from the confines of cloth. He was so hard, burning against her. Velvet dipped her head and pressed her lips to the scalding tip, felt the hot blood pounding under the taut skin. Henry sucked a harsh breath through his clenched teeth. Velvet's lips parted, and she took him into her mouth. His hands locked on her shoulders, and groaning, he dragged her up his body and their lips crashed together.

Velvet panted. "I want to taste you."

"No, I can't take it right now. I have to have you," he rasped. His busy hands found her hips and lifted her higher. Velvet wrapped her legs around his waist. Henry made it to the bed in two long strides. "Need you. I don't want to move, don't want to think, all I want is this moment, this—" His words cut off as he tumbled them to the small, hard bed. "I want you more now than I ever have. Tell me how that's possible."

"I don't know. It's the same for me," she admitted, pushing past the terror. He hovered over her, dark and imposing, the flawless statue of a man, made flesh. Their gazes locked and burned. For the first time, Velvet thought she could read his true heart in his eyes. There was silence, but everything that needed to be said was in that look. "A single touch from you makes the rest of the world disappear." Velvet pressed a hand to his chest, just over his heart. "There is only you, Henry. I want to stop running. I want to trust you, love you. I want to fight for this, for us," she said, unable to hold the words back. Her voice dropped. "It's all I want."

Chilly air poured through gaps in the window, and it blew strands of hair around her face that got tangled in her lashes. Henry moved a curl off her nose with the tip of his finger, the sharp blue of his eyes deep and fathomless. Velvet thought she would love to get lost in their dark revelations forever. Saints! She was afraid. Afraid of being hurt by him, afraid of losing him.

"You're not going to lose me," Henry said, and Velvet realized she had said the words aloud. "I made a vow even if you did not, for better or worse, dark and light, kings and conquers." His hips pressed hers down into the mattress. Velvet rocked against him; her body was one big ache. She needed him, too. "It's you and me now."

"Forever?"

"If you'll have me."

"And...you'll want no other?"

Henry leaned back to look at her like she had lost her mind. "Never. I've had others—many others. They are all the same, one look at you and their faces blur to nothing. There is only one you, my first and last love." He started to unbutton her shirt, slowly. Velvet was panting by the time he reached the final button. He was barely touching her, and still, she was intoxicated by his nearness. Henry rolled her gently onto her stomach, and pulled the shirt from her shoulders, then his hot mouth roved down her back, pressing butterfly kisses along her arching spine. He whispered to her in that ancient language given to him in youth. Gaelic. How she loved the dark, sensual words that were more felt than understood. He bit the base of her spine and her hips lifted off the bed in unconscious plea, her nails curled into the mattress.

He was making her wait, making her want. Each touch was a scarlet scar on her soul, marking her as his forever. In that moment, Velvet decided to submit. She couldn't fight him anymore. *This free bird of prey who once soared untethered through the sky, would allow this brave, sinful, beautiful man to capture her,* Velvet thought. She pressed her hands into the mattress and tried to lift her torso off the bed and turn around, rip off her trousers and force him to take her.

With a hand on her back, Henry pushed her down. His lips touched her ear, his whisper was another type of caress. "No. I want you like this." His fingers went to the waistband of her pants, moving so slowly, like they were both trapped in the golden threads of a dream. He undid the buckle and slid them over her derrière, then pulled them off. He kept her legs spread with his knee then moved fully atop her. She felt him there, at the juncture between her thighs, hard and hot as steel burning. His knowing, wicked fingers slipped beneath her hips. "So wet," he breathed. "So hot."

Velvet shuddered. "Henry," she pleaded, her voice an unrecognizable rasp of sound. His fingers moved, sending her spiraling beyond the bounds of sanity. The ship swayed on a boisterous wave. Rock. Retreat. "You're torturing me," she accused.

His low laugh brushed the base of her nape, adding more shivers to the madness. "I'm torturing me. God's blood, you make me tremble." He pressed a finger inside of her, then another. Pleasure spiked and spiraled. Indescribable. The precipice she wanted hovered just out of reach, beckoning, waiting for her to touch it and freefall. Just when her world was beginning to go black around the edges, he withdrew his fingers and thrust into her with a force that shook the bed. His hand reached around to cover her mouth, and she screamed into his palm. He smelled like her. He moved, hard, punishing blows that pinioned her to the bed. Velvet didn't care, as she lifted her hips, wanting more, wanting everything. Sensation peaked, crested, shattered into a thousand shards of brilliance that exploded, white hot, behind her closed lids. Jagged ecstasy, luscious rapture. Some cosmic thing writhed between them as he continued to move. Every stroke of his body left more of those eternal marks on her soul. Velvet felt her legs tense as if they would break; her toes curled deep into the tangled sheets. She lifted her hips higher, grinding herself against him. Both his hands spanned her waist, and he held her close, never stopping his relentless rhythm. Pleasure rolled over her in sparkling waves.

"On your knees, my love. Yes, like that. No, don't turn around, leannan àlainn. Beautiful darling. God, you feel good." Henry's words fell, hot as his hands. His fingers found her breast, then stroked up and down the front of her body, stopping to caress that spot of golden fire shimmering between her thighs. He moved again, grinding into her, then retreating with a painstaking slowness that made her want to scream and melt all over him. In front of her, Velvet saw the lantern's jumping flame reflected in the small window. She could see their images in the glass, as they created a dramatic, fantastical picture. Like those old, religious paintings which had cluttered the halls of Versailles. A devil ravishing an angel. Their touching skin was a perfect juxtaposition of light and dark.

Staring at his face in the glass, Velvet lifted her arm, reached behind her, and twined it around his neck, her fingers clutched at the rough silk of his hair, wet and curling against his nape. Henry captured her chin, then tilted her head back so her hair poured over his arm like liquid gold. He kissed her hungrily, never stopping the intoxicating rhythm of his hips. Each thrust drove her higher, her body undulated in helpless anticipation of what it now knew was coming. He whispered wicked things in her ear and the rhythm increased, deepened, and surged. He was not delicate, his mouth and touch were hot and needy. It was everything she wanted. They clung together, their kisses endless, and he stole her breath and gave his. Hard fingers twined with hers, Velvet clutched their joined hands to her heart and wished for the moment to last forever. For a time, it seemed to.

They moved, locked together in a violent, relentless dance where the sun was in the center of her burning world. It went on and on, until she could take no more, Velvet screamed as the tension uncoiled, streaking through her with vivid release. She heard his harsh cry in her ear, felt his body stiffen, shivered when he whispered her name. When they crashed back to the bed, and he pulled her into his arms, Velvet knew she was his forever. They lay on their sides, staring at each other for a long time, both struggling to gain control over their labored breathing.

No words were needed between them. He gathered her back in his arms and pressed a kiss to the top of her head. She fell asleep with her head against his chest, already dreaming of him. Once, during the night, Velvet thought she felt him move, but before she could fully wake his arms came back around her, and conscious thought disappeared.

CHAPTER 12

IN PIECES

They lay intertwined in an afterglow so tangible, Velvet felt sure sparkles danced in the air haloing them. Both had slept on their sides, lips and noses touching, arms and legs wrapped like vines. He had fallen to sleep with his fingers threaded through hers. Their clasped hands resting beneath their chins. Unable to sleep, and wrapped in sheer wonder, Velvet studied Henry's face like there was nowhere else in the world to look. She was fascinated by how soft his mouth appeared in sleep, the way his lashes curled nearly touching his dark brows. He seemed younger, almost boyish somehow, as if the mockery and cynicism he wore like a mask had also succumbed to the allure of sleep.

How had it happened? One moment he was her enemy, the next dearer to her than breath. She recalled their childhood kiss, as he so often did. How enamored she had been with that distant, sad boy. He had been nothing like the other court dandies. It was his eyes. Even then, there had been something honest, deeper, real flashing in those clever blues. She had to admit to herself that she had loved him, even then. Loved him in the dark days after her change when her memory was all but gone. Loved him even more when it returned.

Velvet dared to reach out and brush a fingertip down his cheek, as she held her breath and touched his bottom lip. Closing her eyes, she leaned in and lightly kissed the corner of his mouth. Henry stirred but didn't wake. Velvet waited a few long seconds, then untwined her limbs carefully from his. She sighed, and sat up, tugged the twisted sheet out from under his legs, then wrapped it around her naked body. The night was cold, but not overly chilled. Velvet suspected the ship had found a patch of warmth in this watery world.

Through the small window, she could see pink streamers of approaching sunrise, threading through the murky grey mists of pre-dawn. The smooth waves were black clouds touched by rare points of light. Velvet found herself again missing all the colors of her island. Internally, she was forced to acknowledge that storming her way onto this ship had been an impulsive, stupid choice born of fear.

Listlessly, somewhere between tired and curious, Velvet knelt and searched the chest at the foot of the bed once more. After a few moments, she found an old comb, missing more than a few bristles, and a jar of tooth powder. She grabbed the treasures, smiling, feeling that if she could find tooth powder on a ship full of toothless men, everything really might come right in the end. She held the items against her chest and made her way to the small sink beneath the window, tripping on the sheet more than once. She brushed her teeth with her finger, ran the natty comb through her tangled hair, and watched the first dancing rays of sunlight lighten the eastern sky. Everything but the wind and lapping water were silent. Velvet breathed in the peace and tried to remember if she had ever felt so blissfully happy.

~

An hour later, the sun was hot in the sky. Henry slept happily on, and Velvet still knelt where she had fallen. In her trembling hands, she lightly held the piece of parchment which had been the instrument of her doom. An hour ago, she had finished her ablutions and set about straightening the cabin she and Henry had nearly demolished, with a whispered tune in her mouth and a secret smile on her lips. Her eyes strayed often to the sleeping, naked man who dominated all the space on the bed.

Velvet had looked around, trying to find charm in the musty lines of the slightly tilted chilly cabin, but her eyes just kept returning to him. She kicked a pillow out of her way, then bent, and reached for the pair of satin slippers she had worn with that atrocious red dress. Henry's discarded pants were next. She lifted them, and that's when something fell from the pocket. A piece of paper fluttered like a wet feather to land at her feet. She had reached for the letter, thinking nothing of it. She saw that it bore his ducal seal, carrying a clear indentation in crimson wax of the insignia on the ring he always wore. Velvet had held the letter for a long, indecisive moment, common sense had whispered to leave it be, stash it back in his pocket and forget she had ever seen it, but another, more self-destructive part, had urged her to open it. If she truly trusted him, Velvet knew the decision would have been a simple one, yet something needled at the back of her mind, a sinking fear, a deep and desperate dread.

Velvet had squeezed her eyes shut and cracked the seal. She blinked twice, took a sharp breath as if she was preparing to dive headfirst off a cliff, then hesitantly began to read, and instantly wished she put out her eyes with a red poker instead. The words were black ink, the handwriting was a series of hard slashes that cut through the soft fibers of the vellum. Reading the words was like drinking a glass of agony. Every single one was a taloned, iron fist that reached through skin, blood, and bone to capture and crush her heart.

She heard her own wild laugh as it escaped her trembling lips and throttled it. Rage, disbelief, misery, shame, emotions that grew with every second. Velvet remembered what it felt like to get stabbed that night of the change. The way the villain's blade had entered that soft spot just between her ribs, the memory of that pain would always linger like a specter in her mind. The bite of the blade, the tearing of her skin, it had been a touch of true horror. This was far worse. On the third time, she read the words aloud in a sparse, trembling whisper that she barely recognized as her own.

"I have the princess in my custody. I have done as you asked and gained her trust by any means necessary. The French throne is surely next. She has confessed to love me so I do not believe she will deny me. We sail for France.

    Your servant, N"

The note fluttered from her bloodless fingers. Cold wind rushed through the room, slid under her skin, and made her shiver. Velvet didn't care, she felt like she would never be warm again. What strange things words were. Just a collection of shapes turned to letters that, when spun together correctly, could produce the most powerful thing in the world. Words, even more than deeds, had the power to enrich and heal or destroy and maim. These words maimed her. If words could perform an instant kill, then she would be a bloody corpse on the ground. It had all been a ruse. All of it! Right from the very beginning. God damn it! It all made so much horrible sense. His care, his help, even when it was not wanted, his need. Every word, every look, every touch had all been part of an elaborate trap and like an oblivious rabbit, she had blindly walked into it. Had any of it been true? Anything at all?

The missive played over and over in her mind. *Done as you asked, she will not deny me, done as you asked, as you asked. She has confessed to love me. She will not deny me.*

Velvet bit down on her fist as the twisting thing in her chest caught fire. Her groan was a muted moan. In this he had not lied. She would not have denied him anything. She had run to a ship filled with enemies to save him. She would have given anything, done anything. She snatched the paper from the ground and crumpled it. The ink stained her fingers, barely dry, and she realized then that he had written it last night when she was drunk on the afterglow and thought she might vomit.

Dimly, she remembered the feel of his absence and the intoxicating pleasure of his arms when they slid back around her. Velvet's eyes fluttered to Henry. His outline was drenched in a haze of pulsating red, a mist of fury that seemed to seep from her very pores. He had played the game well. The throne of France was the prize, and she, like a blind idiot, had almost given it to him, and in doing so, gave it to an insane king who believed Britain should control the world.

Velvet stood and twisted her hands in a painful knot. If she had a knife right now, she thought she might stab it in his treacherous, lying heart, then her own. He was England's weapon, a poison that killed from the inside out, and she had been a fool. He was the dark duke of Newcastle, a heartless murderer for king and country. She should have known.

Velvet squeezed her eyes shut. They burned, but there were no tears, only various, terrifying shades of rage, all red as a sailor's dawn. Her legs swayed as she walked to the window and, with her right hand, grabbed the lip of the sink to keep from crumpling in a miserable heap, and stared at her eyes in the mirror while memories of the previous night assaulted her. She thought about the way his eyes had pierced to the heart of her soul as he lied.

I made a vow even if you did not, for better or worse, dark, and light, kings and conquers.

Velvet gripped the sink with both hands and dropped her head. The breath she held rushed out in a shattered sigh.

The French throne is next. She will not deny me.

What hurt the worst was how easily she had fallen for every calculated kiss. Velvet remembered his hot voice and the tricks he had used to chain her beneath a tree on the island, remembered the look in his eyes the night Katie died, and a spell had made him hers for a time. She remembered the unforgiving line of his lips when he told the king's men to take her, then the cold mask he wore as he stood before the church and condemned her to death, and she felt like kicking herself. She had wanted so badly for it all to be true. God damn it! She should have known.

Velvet didn't know how long she stayed in that pose, but her tears finally started to fall when the sound of Nora's triple cannons shattered the silent dawn.

CHAPTER 13

PIRATE QUEEN

*N*ora stood at the helm of the Bacchus, the wind in her wild hair and her hand on the wheel of the ship that had become as much a part of her as her soul. She stared into the ferocious dawn, unafraid. The child in her womb kicked every time her cannons boomed and shook the deck under her feet. Louis stood beside her in all his shining glory, golden antlers shifting shades when touched by the glimmering rays of the rising sun. Under his watchful eyes, Nora let go of the wheel and lifted the rifle, leaning heavy against the mast, cocked it, then peered down the sights and found Napoleon's ship through the bubbling clouds of rising smoke. Her first two cannon blasts had been warning shots. Now her long guns were finally in range. Her next shot would be a direct hit; Nora had no desire to accidentally obliterate Velvet. She was undecided in regard to Henry and Rhee. Irrepressible villains.

Footsteps sounded on the deck stairs behind her. Nora spun, gun still raised, to see Devon making his way toward her. Ajax, who was armed with a sharpened axe, walked on his right. During his time on the island, Devon had let his hair grow. Now, long strands blew around the golden stubble blanketing his jaw. The soft lines of his face had grown hard these past months. She had always been able to read him like a book, ever since they were children. Now that book was closed. There was nothing left of the witty dandy who had charmed her through life. He looked like a bloody pirate. Quickly, Nora glanced down at her own slate grey trousers and bright purple waistcoat, garishly decorated with gaudy red feathers and shiny gold chains. She sighed. With the exception of Louis and Cerberus, they were all bloody pirates now.

"The guns are in range, Captain," said Devon.

Nora met his eyes. "I know."

"The men are eager to board." Devon smiled and crossed his arms. "As am I. What are your orders?"

Nora hesitated. Louis was shouting in her mind, reading it. She knew he loathed every iota of her plan with a vengeance, but she had stopped caring two days ago. She was out of time. Ready or not, her child was coming. She desperately wanted to hold her baby, but the moment she was no longer pregnant would be the moment Louis disappeared. The thought of never seeing him again, never hearing his husky voice blast through the corridors of her mind was unbearable. Over the last six months, since the night of the masked ball when an ancient spell allowed him to hold her in his arms, Louis the seventeenth had become an integral part of her soul. Velvet's plan had failed. Nora's plan would not. She pressed her cold lips together and straightened her spine. "You will board with the men. I want you to bring me back two soldiers, bound and gagged. Kill whoever stands in your way."

Zoe stepped from Devon's shadow and raised his voice over the crashing sounds of the frothy waves breaking against the hull. "I'll find our lady and bring her to you. That's if she wants to be rescued. Our Velvet has a mind of her own."

Nora sighed. "That she does."

"I don't want this," said Louis, the voice in her mind clear, as if he had shouted in her face. The shout broke through the wall in her mind that she had tried to construct against him.

Nora shrugged, the soul of innocence, though she knew in her heart that she was guilty as sin. "What? I am rescuing your sister."

"You know it is more than that. I don't want this," he said again.

"Then it is a grand thing that it is not up to you. Napoleon's men are French soldiers. You are the rightful king. The bastards should feel nothing but honored to give their lives for you."

Louie said something harsh and profane. Nora turned away pretending she had not heard, silly really when they both knew she had.

"I will stay with you, Captain, in case the French come calling," said Ajax, hefting his ax and testing the jagged edge with the pad of his thumb.

"No, you must go. He's angry at me right now, but Louis will protect me, and Cerberus is ever my watchful shadow." Careful not to jostle her stomach, Nora switched the rifle to her left hand, and lifted her right above her head. "On my mark," she yelled. The sailors below, those who manned the cannons, repeated her cry. Nora lifted her hand higher. "Hold, hold, hold!" She brought her hand down, her gloved fingers slashing at the air. "Fire!"

The booming report of the Bacchus' cannons was instant and deafening. Nora dropped the rifle, grabbed the ship's spinning wheel, and held it steady, waiting for the rudder to bite the waves. When she felt the now familiar pull and tug of the spinning blades, she let go of the wheel, lifted her hand again and waited for three long beats of her heart. Her hand came down. "Fire!"

Another crack followed by the whistling scream of the led ball as it flew to the British warship. Its fiery tail reminded Nora of a comet she had seen in the sky as a child. Mere seconds later, the cannon ballbroke through the quarterdeck railing and careened into the mizzenmast, shattering it. A thousand oak splinters rained on the waves.

"Fire!" Nora screamed. The deck jumped beneath her feet and a gash opened in the starboard side at the waterline of

Napoleon's warship. A shout went up from her men as that ship's mainsail suddenly burst into leaping orange flames. Nora thought the sight was beautiful and terrible. She was responsible for the carnage, for the death, and it was just the beginning. At the end of this battle, no matter what blood had been spilt, two more would need to die. She shoved down the sick feeling that crawled up her throat at that thought. Five years ago, she hadn't wanted to kill a fly. Debutant diamond to bloody pirate. It was a transition she had never in her wildest dreams intended to make.

Shouting for her men to reload, Nora caught the spinning wheel and turned it sharply. Over her head, the mainsail snapped, the ropes groaned, stretching, and tugging on their metal links, but the Bacchus obeyed. It swung its bulk to the left and Nora again gave the ship its lead letting the burners below do their work.

Devon unsheathed his sword. "Make ready to board!"

Nora was awestruck by the moment as the Bacchus dipped on a crashing wave and Napoleon's ship pulled up alongside them, dark and dangerous as a sea monster. Her men yelled and waved their weapons. The French soldiers on their burning deck, responded in kind, screaming their own battle cries. For a few tense moments, the two ships sailed parallel, making piles of froth in the ever-narrowing space between them. Nora held her breath and steered the Bacchus closer.

The French brought their guns into a fighting stance. The early morning sun sparkled on the sharpened bayonets. Nora's pirates began to howl as they lowered the first plank. Ropes flew over her head as men swung across the space between the racing ships and disappeared into swathes of cannon smoke. She knew they had landed safely when the sing-song sound of clashing swords rang out, crisp and clear.

Nora sighed and rested her hand on her kicking child, rubbing the spot where his little foot bruised her skin. "Zoe, take the wheel. Keep her steady."

Zoe touched the soft brim of his hat. "Yes, Captain."

Nora drew her sword. Louis still stood close behind her; she could feel him, sense his every move. He may hate her plan, but he would not let her face her coming fate alone. Nora wanted to glance over her shoulder, look at his eyes, and assure herself of his reality, but she wouldn't. Seeing the pain in his eyes might put her off course, so she kept her eyes trained ahead. She could see Alfonso and Abigail standing close, Alfonso held out his hand to help Abagail up onto the plank, but she slapped it away and he laughed. Martin and Ajax were already across, shouting at the top of their lungs while cutting down the French soldiers standing in their path. Ajax was smiling as he hacked through men. Nora couldn't blame him, as there would be treasure aplenty to pillage. They were welcome to it, for she had no need of shiny things, only two souls delivered to her on their knees, bound, gagged, and ready to die.

"I will never forgive you if you do this. These are my countrymen. There is honor in a battle death, but what you plan is murder."

Nora's whole body went cold. She squeezed her eyes shut and shook her head. "It's all murder." Nora sighed. "I am not seeking your forgiveness, Louis. I will settle for your transformation. Most of these men, French or not, would kill you given half the chance. Some were directly responsible for stealing your father's throne practically right out from under him."

"My lady, I come from a long line of murderers, kings who killed in the name of justice, personal right, or pride. I will not be like them. Kill for me and you will lose me, anyway. I cannot love a cold-blooded killer; my life is not even in jeopardy."

"Nay, my lord, only your humanity!"

"I will walk away from you, forever."

Nora opened her eyes and looked out at the fire-lit waves. "So be it," she whispered. "At least you will be a man."

Louis snorted and stomped his front hooves. *"So, just another animal then, stupid and twice as vicious as the one I am now."*

Nora threw up her hands. "Louis, please."

"Nora, please," he echoed. *"I don't want anyone to die for me. I*

don't want to be king. I never did. Besides, I believe I would make a terrible one."

"Or the best that ever lived," she snapped back, then fell quiet for a time. The silence stretched, on and on, until she could bear it no more and turned to face him. She saw a fine tremble in her hand when she reached out to stroke his silky nose. "Don't fight me, Louis. Not here, in the ninth hour. I am doing this for us."

"No. Do this, my love, and you will break us."

"I have no choice," she breathed.

"So be it," he said, echoing her words and tone, then he turned and walked away from her. Descending the stairs that lead to the main deck, his bearing ancient, and regal.

Nora stared at his retreating back and willed him to pause and look at her once more. He didn't. He simply left her standing in the wind, salt and sea splashing her face. He took all the light with him; his absence turned her world dark and cold. She swallowed hard. The knot in her throat turned her stomach, and she tasted tears on her lips. He would forgive her because she would die if he did not. As the bastard daughter of an insane king, Nora had learned the hard way that precious things were easily lost. Even if Louis hated her, stars forbid, she could not, would not, lose him. Louis didn't want blood on her lily-white hands, not for him. Yet, what he didn't know was that she would bathe in the damn stuff if it meant she could have just one more night with him.

Lost in the misery of her thoughts, Nora jumped when something cracked. Smoke bloomed like a hothouse rose between the two warring vessels. She had come armed with the element of surprise, but the French soldiers were no untrained bunch, peasants perhaps, but most of them had been with Napoleon at the coup of Brumaire. The fighting was fiercer than Nora had anticipated. This would be no easy route.

A shout went up from the main galley as the Second Song was spotted flirting with the blazing orange horizon line, wide black sails flapping in the breeze. Coming to join the fray. Ten minutes, no more, and Nora could see Henry's first mate, Ritchie, at the helm. He stood tall, a bright red kerchief tied around his silver kissed hair and a toothy grin on his chapped lips. Fifty of Henry's best fighters stood at his back, each man wore a black mask that covered all but their eyes.

Nora swallowed a gulp of fear, remembering the night they had come for her and Velvet. A night that seemed to have taken place a thousand years ago. When she noted the twin swords each of the warriors carried—curved and designed for bloodletting alone—the colorful memories of that night were enhanced. Many French men, boys, brothers, fathers, sons, would die tonight. The pain she felt in that moment was sharp and bleak. The feel of it made her breath catch. Would he truly walk away from her, after all they had been through? Could he? Endless questions plagued Nora's mind like a barrage of flaming enemy arrows while the battle raged on, and time passed.

Nora watched Henry's men, under Ritchie's command, board Napoleon's much-abused ship. They moved like wraiths, or the ghosts of brave men lost at sea. They wasted no time coming to the aid of her men, and more French soldiers fell to their slashing blades. *Blood offerings for Davy Jones*, Nora thought, and more chills wracked her bones.

It seemed an eternity before Napoleon's men readied their cannons—British men of war, she had heard them called. Their report was terrifying, as the ball whistled its warning song, then, somewhere below, a piece of her haul shattered.

"Return fire!" Nora screamed. Her men obeyed, and more blood stained the decks. The sun crawled to the top of its perch, and still there was no victor. Cannon smoke sucked the blue from the sky, bodies littered the choppy waves and the macabre décor spoke of heavy losses on both sides. Suddenly, Nora's smoke-soaked eyes found Velvet in the crush. She wore a garish, fantastical red dress that made her look like a queen. Her unbound hair cloaked her in a wild mass of shimmering silver. Her mouth was set in a grim line as she held a sword in one hand, and a loaded pistol in the other. Beside Nora, Cerberus began to whine, then howl upon seeing his mistress.

"Go to her, boy," Nora whispered. Cerberus obeyed with a speed that would have hurt her feelings had he been running to any other but Velvet. She watched as the giant beast made his way across the rickety plank in three wide bounds. He skidded to a stop beside Velvet, who stroked his face and kissed his freezing nose. Hand clinging to Cerberus's scruff, Velvet scanned the warring crowd, her people fighting her friends. Nora cast her eyes about, and found Henry was nowhere in sight. Nora sighed. That did not mean he was not near.

Velvet grabbed a hold of the slender rope twining the mainmast, then wrapped what was left of it around her arm and held tight. Cerberus faced off a group of bloody men. He bared his teeth at them in a feral snarl. The French soldiers paused, red cheeked and plumb shocked. Nora laughed aloud, then quieted the outburst behind her gloved hand. The stunned men looked from the monstrous canine to their lost princesses, who was at this very moment climbing the mizzenmast rigging with the blade of her slender sword clutched between her teeth. The smoking ropes swayed under her feet, but she held fast and climbed higher. Velvet reached with her right hand and grabbed the thick netting above her head. Long chunks of fat, braided twine wrapped by shredded bits of the main sail.

Nora gasped as the warship swayed, tossed by the rising waves. She realized almost immediately that there was no need for concern, Velvet only locked her knees and held tighter, then she lifted her chin in that stubborn way she was wont to do. A darkened memory of the first night she had met the princesses flashed through Nora's mind. Even then, drenched in blood and confusion, Velvet had been a force to be reckoned with, but now, eyes flashing, hotly reflecting the silver of her sword, hair flying about her beautiful face, golden and wild as a summer storm, she looked like a daughter of conquerors and kings. A rare creature born to lead and rule.

The sky above their heads suddenly darkened and Nora mused that Poseidon must be in a mood, giddy from the blood they had poured into his waters, for the sun hid its face behind a single black cloud set to burst, and the waves rose higher. Velvet cast her eyes to the turbulent sky, and Nora watched her take a long deep breath, then she drew back her shoulders and shouted, loud enough to carry.

"Sons of France, my brothers," Velvet cried. Beside her, Cerberus began to howl a fit to wake the watery dead. The fighting stilled as the men at her feet grew silent, nearly as one they looked up at the girl burning like a flame in their midst. "Soldiers of the Republic, hear me. I am Marie-Thérèse, Duchess of Angoulême, daughter to Louis the sixteenth, the last king of France. My blood is old and pure as yours. I am the direct descendent of Charlemagne, king of the Franks, before we were a nation. We are countrymen, neighbors, family, and I wish no more to taste death today. You fight for a tyrant. Napoleon cares nothing for us. We are pawns to his plans. We must beware of those who name themselves kings to make us their slaves. You are free men, with the right to choose who you will fight and die for. You have the right to rebel, and we all have the right to fight for the France we love."

"You are dead!" one man exclaimed.

"A mirage," swore another, crossing himself.

Velvet smiled. "I assure you, sir; I am quite alive. I am not captured. I am not tamed. I am a queen and if Napoleon wants the throne of France, he must take it over my dead body. I ask you, my brothers, to help me reclaim what was stolen. Help me now. Fight for me. Help me make a France that suits us all."

Nora stood transfixed. Whether it was a trick of the approaching storm or the flames licking across the warship's deck, Velvet seemed to be...

"Gore! She's glowing," one of the soldiers cried, taking the words right out of Nora's mouth.

"Blimey," said Rhee, who had not yet witnessed this particular phenomenon.

"You look like your mother," another man said. An aged warrior who stepped forward and shaded his eyes. "She was kind, your mother was. Those stories about her, they were nothing but lies." He wiped his bloody hands on his stained trousers. "God has cursed us for killing her," he finished, then bowed low and crossed himself.

"She is an angel," another shouted.

"A witch."

"A beauty."

"A true queen."

Nora watched each minutia of the men's expressions. Those she could see through the fog all shocked her. Had the Madonna herself materialized in her midst, Nora doubted the men would have looked at her any differently. Worshipful. Like they would gladly fall on their swords for her.

"It was a sin to kill her," another said.

"A sin," more agreed.

"Then you will help me?" Velvet asked, pausing to search the eyes of the men closest, with a heartfelt plea in her own. "You will side with me? Fight with me? For her?"

As her words fell away, the world around them hushed. Nora felt that even waves stilled, listening, waiting. The whispers began, slow as the chills that rushed across her skin. "La dame, la Reine, las belle femme," they said, then the men began to say her name, over and over, until it was a shout.

Nora shook her head, smiling. The girl was unpredictable and deadly, and Nora had never been prouder. The men reached out their hands to touch the silky hem of that horrible dress, one kissed her satin shoe. Velvet started to descend, a perilous quest to be sure. Nora found herself gripping the rail. Movement on the quarter deck caused a rumble to run through the crowd. Velvet paused, her satin toes clinging to a swaying rope. She turned her head toward the commotion. Whatever she saw turned her blood to ice. Nora could not see who it was, but Velvet's face went white as fresh fallen snow and the smile on her lips died a broken death.

After a few moments, the sea of men parted enough for Nora to see the source of the commotion. It was Henry, who stood near the set of stairs that lead to the captain's cabin, wind, and water at his back. His hair clung to the sharp lines of his jaw in disorderly strands. Nora saw that he had a black line of soot on his left cheek, and a streak of blood on his shirt. He looked dangerous, from the fearsome stare he leveled at Velvet, to the tips of his toes. Dangerous and furious. He had eyes only for Velvet, and she for him. They stared at each other with such heat, which, had she a fan in hand, Nora knew she would have used it with vigor.

Nora leaned over the rail, hating to miss any detail of the strange exchange between the lovers. She saw that Henry had a length of chain wrapped around his left wrist and hand. Nora followed the chain to its end and caught her breath. Napoleon and William Pitt stood shackled together, identical expressions of wounded shock on their pale faces. Nora laughed aloud and clapped her hands. Instead of the smile she expected, a snarl curled Velvet's lip.

"Ah, my lord duke," called Velvet, dropping into a dramatic, somewhat mocking bow. "You have done as you promised and brought me my attackers in chains. Tell me, lord, who will shackle you?"

CHAPTER 14

I FELT YOUR BETRAYAL, THEN I FELT NOTHING ELSE

*H*enry stood transfixed. He couldn't move, couldn't take his eyes off of her. Gorgeous, powerful as the coming storm and just as angry. He had woken not an hour ago, smiling, drenched in bliss. He could smell her on the sheets, on his skin, roses, and starlight. Eyes still closed, Henry had reached for her and encountered only empty space. His eyes flicked open, and instantly he threw up his arm to shade his face from the single beam of sun shining through the small window like a searchlight. He blinked and dropped his arm. The chilly cabin was empty. Henry had sat up quickly, heart pounding. A cannon boomed in the distance; it shook the ship and brought him fully awake.

Nora. Henry smiled; the smile died when his eyes fell to the crumpled missive lying in the center of the floor. He knew immediately what it was. He had written it only last night as he watched her sleep. It was what old Georgie wanted to hear, but she would never understand.

He tossed off the sheet, then stood up and strode naked across the room. The trousers and shirt she had worn were folded and had been placed neatly on the only chair in the room. The red dress and satin shoes were gone. Another blast of steel and thunder rocked the room, but horror stiffened his limbs. She would never understand, and any chance he had of her trusting him had been murdered by a slip of paper. Henry lifted the lantern and threw it against the wall with all his strength. The air had grown suddenly thick, and it seemed a struggle to breathe, then the cabin had become a prison he had to break from or die. He had to find her, had to try to explain before she did something he knew they would both come to regret.

He stumbled into his clothes, cursing his own stupidity all the while, cursing her for believing the worst as he knew she did. He knew that in her heart and mind, she had not given him a chance. Those quickly written, thoughtless words confirmed the guilt she had always believed was his. Placing the note in his pocket, he thought, God! If that wasn't the stupidest thing he had ever done in his life, Henry didn't know what was. Pure hubris really, to believe she would trust him enough not to open the damn thing. He had believed her, believed she had finally started to trust him, love him.

Motivated by adrenaline spiked terror alone, he had thrown the small door of the cabin open, and nearly bowled over a shrieking William Pitt, busily trying to scurry his way to safety.

In a rage, Henry had drawn back his fist and punched the man directly in his bright red nose. Pitt crumpled like a piece of paper. Capturing Napoleon had posed a greater difficulty, as the man was surrounded by a retinue of guards who fought like berserkers. If adrenaline hadn't been pumping like blood in his veins, Henry thought he would have lost his life or at least a limb this night. After dispatching the men, he had hauled the emperor and his traitorous fool topside, meaning to drag them through the battle and toss them both at her feet as he had promised. Then he had seen her, high up and tangled in rigging, and the world had simply stopped spinning. Her eyes were wide and turbulent, dark blue as the rumbling sky. They were hot and drenched with passion as she spoke to the men, then cold as glacier ice when they finally locked with his.

More cold terror rushed over his limbs and speared through his heart, causing him physical pain. Outwardly, he somehow managed to remain calm while inside he was yelling. She had loved him. He had seen it in her face last night, felt it in her kiss. If he blinked his eyes, he could see it all, the way her body had shivered and bucked when he pressed himself inside of her, the way they had watched each other through that dusky mirror, eyes locked as they moved together in the dark. She had finally given him the thing he wanted most in the world, and he had broken it with his stupidity and a few poorly timed words. He looked at her now and saw no love in her eyes. No understanding. No forgiveness—there would be no quarter given, no mercy. He stared at her with a bleak sense of futility. He had lost her. This one final time, he had lost her. He knew it was true. His chest burned and squeezed with the pain of it. Unmoving, heart hammering against his ribcage, Henry watched Velvet jump down from her perch, lithe and nimble despite the clinging red dress. He remembered how she used to trip over her feet on flat ground and mused on how far she had come from the wounded girl who once blindly attacked him on a dark and terrible London night, then promptly stole his soul.

Men gasped and panted after her as she moved, and Henry wanted to bare his teeth and kill them all. *Mine! She's mine,* he wanted to shout. The deep lines of pain bracketing her eyes and mouth kept him silent. There was a terrible thing hollering in his gut, telling him she would never be his again. He lifted the chain to which the men were bound, noting indifferently that his hand was shaking. She met his eyes across the crowd, and what he saw in her gaze made his soul roar with fear and pain.

～

One moment the night was empty and cold, in the next it was infused by a ripple of warmth. He was there, staring at her, watching, waiting, desperation and fear sullying the piercing blue of his eyes. For a fleeting instant, Velvet was possessed by the urge to run to him, fall in his strong arms and beg him to save her from the pain that he himself inflicted. Just the sight of him hurt, prickles of awareness turned to agony rushed over her skin. She wouldn't show him another feeling, for she had given him an ocean of emotion, and she refused to bleed another drop. Squaring her shoulders with a determination she did not feel, Velvet walked through the men. No one said a word, even Devon, who appeared to have much to say, locked his lips and blessedly kept his peace.

Velvet's feet stopped less than three paces from Henry. She folded her arms across her chest as the temptation to touch him was too high.

"My lady," he said, inclining his head. "You have a habit of leaving me, and I don't enjoy it."

"Good," she spat. When he opened his mouth, she held up her hand. "While I would like to go on about how much pleasure your fury brings me, I fear now is not the time to exchange pleasantries. Truly though, tell me, I must know, what was the plan when you discovered you could not kill me in cold blood? What did the king command you to do? Seduce me? Put a child in me? Goddess of earth and sky, I am so stupid. At least your actions since the first begin to make sense. You couldn't find it in yourself to murder me, so the move was to steal my heart and break me?"

For a moment, Henry held silent as the muscle in his jaw ticked. It seemed he did not wish to give credence to her accusations by arguing his innocence. Finally, his face like a mask of stone, save that telltale tick in his jaw, he said, "Yes, it was always the plan."

Pain, more pain, so sharp, so intense, so much all at one time, Velvet thought she would die of it. She swayed a little as if from a blow, then she reached out and grabbed the rail to her left for support.

Henry took her hand, his touch a brush of fire, eviscerating her. "It might have started as the plan, me following orders, doing as the king commanded. I held you and everything changed, you know it did."

Velvet jerked her hand away. "Don't touch me," she cried, anger and pain in her voice. "Don't ever think to touch me again."

Henry paid her outburst no heed and closed the distance between them. "Marie—"

Velvet smacked him hard across the face and, in the preceding silence, the sound was like a thunderclap. "That's Velvet to you, my lord, and you shall address me as such, or Reina, if you prefer."

"Marie, those words I wrote to the king, they are part of the game—"

"Really? Which game would that be? Do you mean you didn't set out to make me trust you—love you?"

"Yes, I did, but that knife cut both ways. I fell in love with you. In a world of lies, that is the only truth I know."

Velvet laughed. It was a vicious sound. "You play the part so well. You may drop the act, my lord. I am wise to it all."

"You are a fool," Henry said, his husky voice sending a yearning, miserable ache from her head to the tips of her toes.

"Yes, you have made me such."

Pain flashed through his eyes; his mouth tightened into a stiff line. Velvet thought he had the look of a wild animal preparing to howl into some dark night. She wanted to lift her chin and smile at his hurt, show him she was unaffected by what he had done, but she couldn't quite manage it. Instead, horribly, tears overflowed her eyes and poured down her cheeks like poisoned rain. Velvet suspected the tears would one day dry up, but the pain? That she feared would be felt until the end of days. She was exposed, raw as an open wound, and all she wanted to do was hide it from him so he would never know how badly he had hurt her. It was impossible.

Emotions roiled inside of her while a cacophony of inward screams terrorized her brain. Just looking at him, with all his hard lines and bronze perfection, made her weak in the heart and knees, made her loathe him, loathe herself all that much more. He loomed over her, proud and unrepentant, and she wanted answers from him more than she wanted breath. "Forget all the rest. Why would you give my throne to that horrid king? He wanted to kill me; he would have—"

"I wanted you to be safe. Those words I wrote were calculated. I need the king to think the plan is progressing for a while longer. I would never give him your throne, I—"

"I don't believe you," she snapped.

Henry's hand flew to his heart. "No? Truly? Gad, I fear I shall expire from the shock," he said, extreme mockery lacing his devout tone. "Marie, I could tell you the sky was blue right now and you wouldn't believe me."

He folded his arms across his chest, accidentally tugging on the chain, causing William Pitt to let out a choked squeal. Devon reached down and clocked the man squarely on the head, then smiled as if he was inordinately pleased with his timely actions. Pitt screeched again, outraged. Velvet hardly bothered to throw the sniveling man a snarl before her eyes flew back to Henry. Their gazes locked and her world spun like a dizzy top. Godstars, she loved him, even after knowing it had all been a horrible lie.

Henry stepped closer, unaware or uncaring of all the eyes watching them. His own looked hooded; his thoughts unreadable. "Not all of it was a lie," he whispered, seeming to pluck the words right out of her mind. "It started as duty, it changed the moment you attacked me in that shop. You came at me, a wild, wounded hellion, then I put my hands on you and it all changed."

"More pretty lines. It's finished, I do not need them anymore, though, it may content you in the coming days to know that you were right, I would have betrayed the crown for you, I would have done anything, because you made me feel guilty, like I was the betrayer for not giving you my blind trust. You made me feel damaged, as if the fault was mine, when all the while it was you," she stabbed him in the chest with her fingers, punctuating each word with a poke, "lying to me, toying with my heart and all the while setting me up for the final fall. You are a master of deception, my lord, and should take comfort in the fact that you did your work well. No one could have played the part better than you, and I am deeply ashamed to admit that you had me convinced, body, mind, and soul."

The look in his eyes was like a shot to the gut, and she realized that both of them burned on this pyre of his design. It melted her anger like sugar over an open flame.

"Marie," he rasped, unlocking his arms and reaching for her. Velvet moved toward his touch instinctively—she was the moon, and he was the sun—forever was she caught in his orbit. His finger coasted down her cheek, just the breath of a touch. The emotion that raged in her was a blinding, inarticulate thing. She was burning on the inside, crying, dying. She froze in the act of flowing into his arms and flinched away from his touch. The lurch in her stomach was like an old unwelcome familiar. The pain in Henry's eyes was a knife cutting through the shredded remains of her heart.

She took a step back. This man had consumed her entire being from the very first. Perhaps that was why it hurt so bad, because she loved him so much. If so, then love was truly the greatest curse of all. It made you weak. Velvet decided then and there that she would never be weak again. Only the strong survived, and it was her fervent hope that she would survive him. Velvet cleared her throat of a few burning tears. "You have betrayed me for the last time, my lord. Would that we had never met. If I were a true queen, like my grandmother, I would have your head. You are a traitor and, in the end, they all share a similar fate."

"I am a soldier and merely followed orders. Nothing in the world could have prepared me for you," he said, his eyes deep and earnest. "I never planned to fall in love with

you—"

"Fall in love? Sir, you do not even know the meaning of the word. You do not get—"

"To need you badly as I do," he growled, cutting harshly across her words. "You consume my dreams, my thoughts, wake or asleep, you are what I see, what I crave. All that I am belongs to you." He reached out and tucked a curl behind her ear. Struck speechless, Velvet let him run his knuckles over the slope of her cheekbone. His fingers left a wash of fire in their wake. She let him because she couldn't help it. He cupped her cheek in his palm. His hand was cold, but the touch was white lighting. Velvet closed her eyes; she couldn't look at him a single second longer.

As it is with all wonderful moments, this one must come to an end. When it did, she would need to walk away, scrape her bleeding heart off the ground and find a way to start again. The thought was daunting. Velvet blinked, her eyes opened slowly, immediately focusing in on a small piece of white protruding from the side pocket of his trousers. She grabbed it without thinking, the feel of it brought her back to reality with a slap sharper than the one she had given him.

"Gentlemen," she said, stepping out of Henry's aura to a place of safety, near Devon and his swords. "This man is a British duke, and a spy. He is an enemy of the Republic," she continued, hating him, hating herself. She dragged in a choppy breath, shot with tears, and raised her voice so it would carry. "France needs no more enemies. I implore you to detain him, gentlemen." Velvet felt more than saw Henry stiffen.

"The first man to touch me will be the first to die," Henry promised in a low, acidic tone.

The men held back, eyeing the duke with equal parts wary respect, and open fear. His eyes were wild and blood shot, his clothes blood spattered and torn. He looked like a highlander from medieval times.

Devon placed a hand on her arm. Velvet met his eyes, which were full of a knowing sadness, and a host of untold secrets. "I'll take him," Devon said.

Henry lowered his freshly drawn sword. "Eh tu Brute?"

Devon shrugged, smiling. "Will you fight me, Newcastle, or will you surrender peacefully? I have no desire to clap you in irons."

"Turncoat. I see you have chosen a side. Nice to see that our twenty years of friendship count for nothing."

"Not at all. I'm here as your friend, offering to stop you from doing something stupid, as you so often are wont to do. Come, let us lock ourselves in the captain's quarters, since you have the man in question at the end of your metal leash. I wager there is a good scotch in there, and our best course of action would be to find and drink it posthaste."

Henry grunted, passed the chain he held to Ajax who had materialized like smoke on his right. Ajax took the chain with a smile that crinkled the skin bracing the thick scar on his upper lip. Henry's gaze moved back to her; it was impossible to drop her eyes. "This isn't over, Marie—"

"That's where you are wrong. Whatever this hopeless thing is between us, it is most definitely over." She dropped in a slow curtsey, never taking her eyes off of him. "Goodbye. I shall do my best to ensure we never meet again."

"You cannot do this," said Napoleon, speaking for the first time.

"I believe I can. The land is mine. Your palaces are mine. Versailles, Château de Saint-Cloud, Luxembourg Palace, which I believe you are currently residing in, and many others. I own eighty percent of the country you have called your own these past ten years. Land you gained by killing my parents and aiding those who slaughtered my family. Feel fortunate that I do not kill you here and now, make you walk the plank, then leave you as fish food. I am Marie Therese, princess of France. I believe I can do anything I desire."

Devon turned to Ajax, and Zoe. "Do escort our lordly guests to the brig, for I fear my time will be consumed by drowning my sorrows with the duke and seeing what we can do about the holes Nora blew in this ship."

Velvet felt her eyes go wide at hearing Nora's name. She spun, searching out the Bacchus through the fog. She found Nora instantly, dressed like a pirate and standing on the deck of her ship. Tears stained her cheeks, which were white and wind splotched. Even from where she stood, Velvet could see the shock of the girl's adorable freckles, the exact color of her storm lit, auburn hair. Their eyes met and Nora held out her arms. Suddenly, Velvet was running. Running away from Henry, away from all the sickening pain and straight into the arms of her friend. Crossing the plank was terrifying as the waves were wild and trashing, black tar, and foam. Velvet kept her eyes on Nora's freckles and didn't look down. She was across in seconds, then they were running to each other.

Velvet suspected she was going to start crying again when Nora's arms folded around her, and she was engulfed in a fragrant hug.

Velvet gently resisted. "No, I'll hurt you and the baby," she gasped.

Nora stroked Velvet's hair from her forehead. "The two of us will be just fine. It is you I'm worried about." Nora leaned back to inspect Velvet before shaking her head and tisking loudly. "Oh, dear, you look like the living embodiment of death."

Velvet rolled her eyes and impossibly started to laugh. "That is too profound a proclamation for such a stormy Tuesday."

"When last I saw you both, Henry was mooning over you like a lovestruck moon-calf, and you were looking at him like he hung the sun. Now, after the exchange I just witnessed, I believe you would relish the idea of seeing him skewered to the deck."

"Oh, Nora, it is all such a terrible mess."

"What has he done? He adores you. I'm sure there is a way to get through it."

"There is no way. He wrote a letter to King George." Velvet shook her head. "I had this idiotic idea that honor demanded honesty, but it was all a wretched lie." Velvet tore the letter from her bodice and shoved it in Nora's hand. "Here, read it for yourself."

Frowning, Nora took the letter and opened it slowly. She read it with a deep furrow in her brow. Then sighed deeply when she finished. "Stupid man. I must admit this is some damning evidence that does paint him in a rather dastardly light." She met Velvet's eyes. "I want to say he could not have done this, but—"

"It's what he does," Velvet concluded.

"Yes, sadly, espionage is breath to that man." Nora threw her arms around Velvet again and hugged her so tightly it almost hurt. "I'm so sorry, darling. You must feel like crawling a hundred feet beneath the ground."

"And dying there," Velvet finished.

"Oh!" Nora stroked Velvet's hair and wiped and a tear on her cheek. "My poor girl," she crooned, with such kindness that Velvet began to sob.

"I love him, Nora. I love him still. And it was all an act, an elaborate play for my throne, Louis's throne."

"Oh, I hate to think what will happen when Louis learns of this."

"He practically forced me to love him, but I have, loved hi...hi..."

"And there's the rub." Nora sighed. "Now, now, don't blubber, or you'll cry all your beauty away."

"I never want to see him again. I fear what I will do. The spell to transform Louis demands I spend Henry's life. I almost feel like making the exchange."

"Never say that my dear," gasped Nora. "You may think our dark duke of swords is a villain to the core, but I have known him most my life, and I know his true heart. It may have started as a mission, but it isn't like that now. He cares for you, hell, you've driven him mad. He senses your presence from a mile away, and when the two of you are in a room together...honestly, the way he looks at you when he thinks no one is looking could set fire to stone."

"Lies!" Velvet cried. "All of it was nothing but lies. The way he spoke to me, the words he used, the voice—" Velvet shook her head, swallowing lump after lump in her throat. "I didn't want to love him...I—"

Nora snorted. "I need no details. I can only imagine. No one does heartbreaking drama like the duke. Just ask the women littering his past. He missed his calling on the London stage, the man would have been a sensation."

Velvet hiccupped and wiped at her watery face. "I always wondered what it was that drew Henry and I together from the first. I thought it was fate," said Velvet, shuddering. Just speaking the words aloud made a sickening blush rush up her cheeks. "I loved him the moment I saw him, even without having my memories, some part of my soul remembered. I thought it was cosmic, inevitable, magical. I was wrong. It made me an easy mark."

Nora opened her mouth, most likely to make some loud-voiced protest. Velvet held up her hand, unable to hear another word without bursting into more noisy tears. "I know you love him, Nora, but defend him no more, I beg you. If we continue to speak of this horrid affair, I fear I will throw myself in the sea. It is done. I mean to be a queen now. I will go to the home of my ancestors, find my peace at Versailles and I will think no more of him. France has mages, apothecaries, witches, and dark arts aplenty; we will find a way to change Louis, and Henry will become a distant memory. All will be as it should."

Nora rolled her eyes violently. "If you say so, dear, if you say so."

CHAPTER 15

OLD FEARS, NEW BEGINNINGS.

*D*iamonds of sunlight danced on the vibrant foliage blanketing the south Parterre of the sprawling Versailles gardens. It ran over the espaliered hedges and carefully manicured trees. Summer blooming daffodils and narcissus twisted and climbed their way through the bushes that clung to the semi-precious stones lining the pathway, glittering and polished to perfection. André Le Nôtre had planted all this beauty over a hundred years ago under the watchful eye of her great grandfather. Velvet sat near the center of the eastern hedge maze, arms wrapping her legs, and diaphanous gown, chin resting on her drawn-up knees. Nora paced in front of her, occasionally harassed by clenching pains that made her shake.

"Breathe in deeply, then out," Velvet directed. "I watched my mother do this five times. It's all about the breathing." While Nora wrestled with her ragged breaths, Velvet tugged at the confines of her bodice, trying to keep her movements subtle, not wanting her small discomfort to take precedence over Nora's agony. Yet, truth be told, it had been years since Velvet had worn a bone-in corset, a strange piece of torture inflicted on women, for what crime Velvet did not know, but she decided the punishment was monstrous.

Nora saw her struggle despite Velvet's efforts, and she smiled knowingly. "Be still, my dear, or you'll topple that diamond crown right off your head."

"It was my mother's," Velvet whispered, reaching up a hand to brush her fingertips over the heavy piece.

Nora sighed, tight-lipped as if enduring an exquisitely painful torture. "It suits you," she said.

Choking back a groan, Velvet sat straighter, arching her spine, sighing when she was rewarded with a single second of relief. "I know this is a stupid thing to say to you, at this exact moment in time, but you told me the pain would become manageable."

Nora laughed. "The pain of the corset? Or the pain of having our favorite duke locked in your dungeons."

"Both." Velvet snapped, then sighed. "The corset. Henry is where he belongs, and it is no more than he deserves."

"How long do you intend to keep him down there?"

"His cell was designed for the late prince of Prussia. It has more luxury between its walls than most palaces—he will survive."

Nora rolled her eyes. "If you allow yourself to think about it rationally, you will realize you can't imprison a man for hurting your feelings."

Velvet felt her lips lift in a half smile. "Can't or shouldn't?"

Nora made a face, then shook her head derisively.

"He did more than hurt my feelings."

Nora pursed her lips. "Undoubtably, but Charles has stayed at the bequest of my father. He's offering a king's ransom for our duke's release."

Velvet grimaced. "Figures. Old George must be stumbling in the dark without the use of his right hand," she said stringently, dropping her eyes to avoid Nora's searing gaze.

"I want him gone," Nora huffed.

"The duke, or Charles?"

Nora smiled. "Both. Charles most of all. I don't want him here when I have this baby."

"Do you think he will try to claim the child?" Velvet asked.

Nora arched her fine brows, a scowl pulling at the slender bridge of her nose. "I wouldn't put it past him to try. Though, it would be the fastest way to have his throat cut by yours truly." Nora placed a gentle hand on her taut stomach. "For better or worse, this child is mine."

"You will have someone who loves you, no matter what, forever," Velvet said, sounding melancholy even to her own ears.

Nora cast her a sympathetic glance. "Is that what you had with Henry?"

"What I thought I had."

"And if he wasn't lying? If he truly did fall in love with you, what then?"

Velvet flinched. She could not withhold the sting of agony which came with that thought. "How could I ever be sure it was me he truly wanted?"

"Faith," Nora said succinctly.

Velvet raised her eyes and regarded her friend. "You mock me," she said, feigning a lightness she was suddenly far from feeling.

"No, I mock love itself with all its nefarious ways—the cruel tricks it plays on the unexpecting." Nora pointed to her stomach, which appeared to be bursting the seams of her beautiful gown. "Just look at what love has done to me. Now I must labor in agony to bring yet another bastard into the world. Some would say I'm cursed."

"Many know that I am," whispered Velvet. Her gaze wandered over the gardens, built with such care. She thought of the fortune Louis XIV, the Sun King, spent creating them, indulging in pure opulence while his people starved and died. "I don't know what to do about any of it," Velvet whispered, saying what she hardly had the courage to admit to herself. She leaned forward to rest her head against Cerberus's face. His fur was still damp from his morning prowl. He basked now in the few weak threads of sunlight fighting their way through heavy rain clouds. Velvet sunk her fingers in his scruff and scratched behind his ears. Cerberus licked her cheek with a tongue the size of a large trout and mewled happily.

"What have you done with Napoleon?" asked Nora, pressing her hand to the small of her back and making a sound somewhere between a groan and a mewl.

"He is my honored guest...I haven't fully decided what to do with him yet. I can't very well kill the man; he's made himself something of a god."

Nora's body stiffened, and she let out a small squeal. Velvet was instantly contrite. "I'm so sorry. Listen to me, babbling about my own nonsense. Can I get you anything?"

"No, but you are a darling for asking. This child wants to kick his way out of me, and I am half inclined to let him."

"How much longer, do you think?"

"A fortnight, if your pious court doctor is to be believed. I feel as if it will be tonight. He battles inside of me." Nora suddenly took Velvet's hand, her eyes wide and earnest. "You will stay with me, won't you? When the time comes, you will—"

"Nothing in the world would make me leave you. I'm afraid you won't be able to get rid of me." Velvet dropped her voice. "Are you afraid?"

"I would be a fool not to be, and I am many things, but not that." Nora closed her eyes. "Fear of labor is not why I dread the passing of every minute, every hour, every day. I fear—"

"To lose Louis," Velvet finished, her heart crushing painfully when she spoke his name.

"Yes," Nora breathed.

Velvet buried her face in Cerberus's neck. He smelled of wet dog, sunshine, and salt. "I haven't seen him in so long, not since the island, that night—" Velvet words broke off, much had transpired that night. Instantly she could see Henry's eyes, clear as if he stood in front of her. She could hear his harsh breaths in her ear, feel his hands setting fire to her skin. She didn't want to lose him. She wanted to revel in his flames, even if they were merely contrived. Velvet cleared her throat of unshed tears. "The magic on the island was so strong, I grew accustomed to it. I had wings," she admitted.

"Yes," Nora said with a derisive snort. "We've been here less than twenty-four hours and the story already circulates your court like smallpox. The lost princess returned, the girl who can fly." Nora laughed, a weak, wheezing sound. "An angel and a god. In another life, I believe you and Napoleon could have been powerful allies."

"He is not my enemy. I cannot condone it, but I understand why he killed my parents, why they all did."

"What do you mean to do with him?" Nora asked.

Velvet turned her head and met Nora's searching gaze. "I don't know. What would you do?"

"Let him do what he does best—invade and conquer. You are more than capable of holding the French throne in his absence. Every queen needs a general."

"And what will you do with the two French soldiers in your custody? You mean to exchange their lives for Louis, don't you?"

A shameful blush crept up Nora's neck, but she straightened her spine and squared her shoulders. "They are merely insurance, just in case all else fails as up until this point, all else has."

"I understand, though I don't wish them dead. Battle is one thing, cold blood is another," said Velvet. "Trust me, I speak from experience."

"I know. Louis said much the same to me. I can't lose him though, I won't."

"The thought is pure horror, but perhaps there is no other way. The curse demands too much."

"What will you do if I kill them, and turn Louis human?"

"I will give him the throne with a smile on my face, then, perhaps I will run away, back to the island where I can spend the reminder of my days flying in silence. Return to the nature I love, with the exception of lord Eden, and your illustrious self, I've had my fill of humanity."

"I will come with you, of course," Nora said, sitting down and fluffing the wide pink skirts of her hooped gown. She straightened the white lace roses that adorned the ruched silk like drops of diamond rain. The full skirt flared as she knelt, then squirmed, clearly trying to find a comfortable position. She made a sour face and stood again, clenching her teeth to hold in a whimper.

Velvet stood and held out her arm. "Come, let me take you to your chambers. I think you need to lie down." Nora linked her arm through Velvet's, and a few steps saw them free of the maze. Two footmen in full livery materialized at Velvet's side. Nora cocked her head and raised a questioning brow.

Velvet shrugged in answer to the unspoken question. "My shadows, since the moment we arrived in Versailles."

Nora scrunched her nose. "Somber fellows, aren't they?"

Velvet smiled. "Quite. I doubt either of them can fight, or hold a sword, yet somehow, I feel safer with them. In this place, before that wretched day when it all fell apart, I was always safe here." Velvet let her eyes rove the grounds as they made their slow way back to the palace. In all her wild imaginings, she had never dreamed she would actually return to this place. "There are so many memories here," she observed softly, unintentionally speaking her thoughts. A kind of dull amazement had taken hold of her. The grounds had remained primarily untouched. Blood had run through the streets of Paris but seemed not to have reached the golden gates of Versailles. In her gown of blue silk, golden trim reflecting the waning sun, and blushed rose petals fluttering under her feet, it felt like no time had passed at all. Like the decade had all been nothing but a dark dream. She half expected to round the orangery, and see her mother holding Louis on her lap, and smiling her sparkling smile. They turned the corner, and her mother was not there. The truth was cold.

"Where do you suppose Louis has taken himself off to?" Nora

asked, lifting up a hand to shade her eyes and look out over the flower strewn, sprawling grounds.

"Wandering somewhere around these eight million acres, lost in memory as I. This place is the setting of many frightening dreams."

"I'd wager, it has some good dreams too." Nora said, giving Velvet's hand a squeeze.

Velvet closed her eyes, felt the tickle of her lashes as they rested like butterfly wings against her cheek. "Yes, good ones too. Unfortunately, those are the ones that hurt the most."

Twilight came with silence. Fireflies played in the wind, shining under the blanket of starlight, swirling around each other in a mating ritual old as time. Velvet watched the brilliant creatures at play from the window of her mother's room. Lightly, she ran her fingers over the wall, bracing the window frame. Marie Antoinette had loved the Orient, and adored Chinese silk, which covered the walls and draped the giant canopy bed in a thousand shades of rose gold. The plush rug beneath her feet offered the same rich color, covered in peacocks and, as a child, she had named each one. Thick, satin drapes framed the floor-length windows; the cloth shimmered like the contents of a champagne flute.

The irregular panels on the walls hinted at secret doors, and Velvet knew exactly where each of them led. The story of these walls had oft been relayed to her as a child. In seventeen eighty-one, after her mother had finally given birth to an heir, the definitive décor to the polished wood paneling had been added. Beautiful motifs carved by the talented Rousseau brothers, who her mother had so admired. In these delicate motifs, the king, her father, was symbolized by the egale of Jupiter, her mother, the queen, by the peacock of Juno done in bronze and scarlet.

Garlands of roses, bows and arrows had been carved to symbolize the royal couple's love.

Velvet knew the fascinating murals were a lie. There had been no love. Her parents had married too young, her mother too wild, her father too vain. Velvet turned away from the window and walked toward the bed. Despite the royal blood they carried, her family had always been cursed in love.

A knock sounded at the door. Velvet jumped, startled. A maid entered without waiting for her response and dropped into a quick curtsey. "Bonne soirée, madame," she said, in a high, soft voice that matched her pointed, pixy face and restless dark hair. She rushed forward, caught Velvet's arm, and drew her toward the adjoining Starlight room, done in shades of pink and ocean blue. "I laced you into that dress, so now it falls to me to get you out of it."

Velvet smiled weakly and held out her arms. "Do your worst, and thank you, these clothes are a prison."

"True, they are designed this way, to keep us meek and submissive."

"And forever unable to breathe," Velvet observed on a gasp.

"Yes." The maid laughed, a high laugh that rang like a bell. "Yes, that is the way."

"What is your name? I'm sorry that I did not ask when we arrived."

"You were crying over a man, n'est-ce pas?"

"You are bold," Velvet said.

"Je suis Français, madame," she said, by way of explanation. "I always know when a woman is sad. Besides, the court whispers about the British duke in your dungeons." She tilted her head and regarded Velvet seriously. "It is not often a queen asks the name of a peasant."

"I am not a queen, not really, so there is no difference between us. Well, perhaps a few. For example, you know how to undo the laces of a corset, while I do not—I—oh!" Velvet gasped when the last lace slid from its eyelet, and Velvet was finally free. She closed her eyes and rubbed her hands over her aching ribs.

"My name is Fleur, and I was born here, in Versailles. I saw you often when I was a girl. Once, at chapel, I saw you take your communion, your golden hair reflected the light from the stained-glass windows. Vous es tres belle, madame. You had flowers on your dress, yellow as sunlight, I thought you were an angel."

"I am no angel," Velvet observed.

"Quoi qu'il en soit," Fleur said, then repeated the sentiment in English. "Be that as it may, I'm happy to see that you are unharmed. I feared for your life, many of us did, madame." Fleur dropped her voice to a whisper. "If ever you find yourself in need, you should know that you have friends here at court, wealthy, powerful friends."

"Thank you, Fleur. I will keep it in mind."

Fleur smiled, and tugged on Velvet's hand, then continued leading her across the room to the ornate vanity, with its plush, gilded chair, where she had seen her mother sit a thousand times. "I used to sit on the floor, just there," Velvet said, pointing to a spot on the thick, blush-colored rug. "I would read poetry to my mother, for she loved Voltaire and Jean-Jacques Roussea."

Fleur tugged the pins from Velvet's hair, and it tumbled around her shoulders, jumping, and curling in every direction. Velvet stared at her reflection, noting the changes since last she looked. She was sad and pleased to note that there was nothing left of the girl she had once been. She was terribly pale, all hard lines and sharp angles. The face she had seen in the looking glass at the Blind Pig was nowhere to be found in this mirror. Against her chalky skin, the blue of her eyes was startling, and her lips looked bright red.

"Vous êtes magnifique, madame," Fleur said.

"Do you think so? I hardly recognize myself."

"Une affaire de Coeur. It gives color to the cheeks, or it takes it away." Fleur shook her head. "Sleep will do wonders for your constitution. Your own men are posted outside of your door, a pirate, and a British lord. You will not be harmed tonight. You must sleep." Fleur lifted a brush from the vanity, then ran it through Velvet's hair. When she was done, she went to fetch a nightgown from the armoire in the adjoining suite. Fleur returned with a skip in her step and placed the garment in Velvet's outstretched hands. Velvet lifted the soft silk and buried her face in it, then breathed deep. Her eyes filled with tears. Ten years and it still smelled like her mother, vanilla, and night blooming jasmine.

Velvet hardly noticed Fleur leading her to the bed, dousing the lantern and tucking her beneath the cool silk sheets. Velvet curled on her side, drawing her knees to her chest like a wounded creature. She didn't want to sleep for fear of what she would dream, but exhaustion tugged at the threads of her consciousness, and she could feel herself falling. Dreams came swiftly, where she ran in darkness, chasing the sound of her mother's voice. The nights had never been kind to Marie Antoinette's daughter.

CHAPTER 16

THE MISERY OF YOU

*V*elvet's dreams changed, as all dreams must. Colors seeped through darkness, and the sound of rippling water replaced the silence. She opened her eyes and found herself lying on the rocky shelf, back in their cave, with her legs twisted in the sheets of the dead lovers. *It's only fitting I would dream of this place,* Velvet thought. *Why wouldn't I? It's the place where I gave Henry my innocence, and my heart.* The thought was sad somehow, in this magical beauty, sadness seemed wrong.

The water in the surrounding pools looked cool and green, aqua ripples topped by diamond froth. The waterfalls were crystal chandeliers raining diamonds. Velvet stretched her hands behind her head and closed her eyes. She knew she was only dreaming of this place; knew that she had somehow willed her mind to travel here, and she wanted to stay. A dream within a dream, she realized, and laughed, delighted.

A sunlight streaming from nowhere wrapped her in startling warmth, taking the eternal chill of misery from her bones, unraveling her in slow degrees. She stretched again, languorously, deciding to keep her eyes closed. This was a dream she had no desire to wake from. It was just too wonderful. In all her life, she couldn't remember a time when she felt so warm and peaceful.

The warmth extended from the roots of her hair to her toes. Touching points of brilliant pleasure on her body that made her arch and shiver. Heat on her neck, her jaw and collarbone, shoulders, and the tips of her breast. It touched her stomach, dipped into her navel, then went lower, lower. Velvet squirmed and gasped. Something brushed between her thighs, more fire that made her arch. The fire, she realized distantly, was created by a pair of hands, hard and battle scarred. They were hands she recognized, hands she loved.

Velvet's eyes flew open as she came instantly awake. She looked down at her body in shock. Her nightgown was bunched up around her waist, and a man's dark head rested between her drawn -p knees. Velvet opened her mouth to scream, but Henry clapped a hand over her lips and lifted his head.

"Good evening, my love, how nice to see you." His eyes dropped between her legs. "To see so much of you." He bent and licked a spot high on her upper thigh that made her moan. "Even when you're cruel, I love the taste of you." His eyes met hers, so intense she could drown in them. His pupils appeared to fill the blue of his eyes with indigo ink. They expanded further as his nostrils flared, his voice was a low rasp. "I've missed you."

Velvet's whole body felt stiff with shock. "Never has heaven turned so quickly to hell," she railed, and kicked at him, trying not to feel her body, trying to ignore all the trembling nerves he had set aflame. She grit her teeth, kicked again, and struck something solid. Henry grunted; the sound was immensely satisfying. "Little hellcat," he snarled.

Velvet made a fist and swung it at his face, but he caught her hand before it made contact, and locked it above her head. Velvet despised the way he so easily overpowered her. He climbed on top of her, captured her thrashing legs between his own, and squeezed till it hurt. He grabbed her other hand then, and it went the way of the first. She was stretched beneath him like a prisoner on a rack, and he was hard as a rock, pressing against her, bearing her down into the soft mattress.

"How did you escape?" she asked, infusing as much hauteur and command as she could muster in her current position. It was woefully insufficient.

Henry only laughed. "You really think that a two-hundred-year-old steel door with a faulty lock can keep me from you? That hurts my vanity love. Indeed, it does."

Velvet stared at him defiantly, refusing to be bated. His sensual, mocking smile did not distract her from the anger warring with the passion in his eyes.

"There were guards posted at my door, Lord Eden, along with one of Nora's men. What have you done with them?"

"Nothing at all. I suspect they are both peacefully sleeping on the floor, doing their part as always."

"Then how—"

"You are not the only one who grew up in this place. I know all the secret door locations, as does most of your court."

"Used for your numerous liaisons, no doubt."

"No doubt," he said.

Velvet had a bitter taste in her mouth, and she wanted to buck him off, but did not dare. She knew from past experience that all her struggles would do is drive their panting bodies closer together—that she could not bear. She would give in to him, again, and then she would hate herself. Hate him.

"Get off me," she spat vehemently. To her surprise, he did. He let her go and sat back on his heels, rested his arms on his knees, and regarded her like a hungry hawk. Well, she was no prey. She was queen, and she would remind him of that. Dumb and innocent were her shields no longer, he had seen to that. "What are you doing here? I meant what I said on Napoleon's ship. I want nothing to do with you anymore."

"Ah, darling, how quickly you believe the worst of me." He touched a place above his heart. "Another terrible blow." His smile was sharp as the blade of a dagger.

Velvet scrambled backward. She tugged her nightgown down over her naked hips, then hugged her knees to her chest. The space between their bodies seemed insurmountable, and simultaneously too close. "Every word of that letter you wrote is branded in my mind." She swallowed hard. "I always thought it strange how quickly you wanted me, and how hard you chased me. The way you made so much of a childhood kiss, which I am sure you hardly remember. It was all done under command of your mad king. You made me depend on you, give myself to you. You refused to let me go, even when I begged for my freedom. You tracked me onto the Bacchus before Katie died. I did not mean to cast the spell on you. You were there of your own accord. Yet you bound me to you with the guilt of that night. You hounded me until I gave you what you wanted, gave what I had saved for the man I will one day love. My innocence and my trust were wasted on you and your lies. You wanted whatever power and acclaim I would bring you, you never wanted me."

"Little fool," he snarled, his expression darkening. "I wanted you the moment I saw you. Do you really doubt my desire? I promise, there is no man alive who can fake a hard cock."

Velvet flinched at the crude language but refused to be cowed by his anger. Refused to be felled by the misery that trembled her bones. The force of his presence was over whelming, he twisted her heart and mind in knots only he could untwine. She lifted her chin, tried to show bravery, but she could feel her lower lip trembling. "So, you enjoyed your deception. What of it? You had your cake and ate it too, as it were. By the way, the pocket of your trousers was a stupid place to leave such damning evidence— strange choice, especially for you. It's almost like you wanted to be caught. My guess is that you are tired of all the lies, tired of me."

"I have never lied to you," he said in a muted roar.

"I have gained her trust as you commanded. She will not deny me," she said, bitterly reciting his words.

"I wrote those words because I do not want the king on our backs. He is on the brink of war with France, and he will not hesitate to sacrifice you if it gets him the throne he so covets."

"Will you?" she asked softly, hating herself for the way he affected her, despising the weak tremors in her voice. "Will you hesitate to sacrifice me?"

Pain twisted Henry's face, pain that wrenched at her heart. "How can you even ask that? You must know I would die for you."

"I don't know anything!" she cried. "My world has been turned inside out. The ship of my life crashed with you at the helm."

"Marie—" his voice broke over her name.

"No." Velvet shook her head, then buried her face in her hands. It was all rushing back, every touch given, and kiss felt in that cave, on the ship, every moment in his arms a scorching memory she couldn't run from. "I don't want to see you anymore, knowing that I will never look at you the same way again. How can I ever believe you? How? Everyone in my life has always had their own ulterior motives. I thought you were different; it gulls deeply to realize I was wrong. One always thinks they are so cunning and wise until they trip on the knife lying in wait for their heart. Luckily, there is a way to see myself clear of this mess. For better or worse, it appears fate has made me queen. It is now in my power to petition the Pope for an annulment."

"To the devil with that!" he roared. "The marriage was consummated, and you well know it."

"I will offer him a new chapel built somewhere of his choosing. Perhaps an abbey will be sufficient motivation," she said, speaking over his denial as if it had not been voiced. She sighed. "It should be enough. I don't believe he will deny me," she finished, using his words, and twisting the knife.

"No!"

Velvet's eyes flew open. Just one word, full of such heartbreak it made her eyes water. She pushed it away, buried it under doubt. "You are a terrific actor, my lord, but if you have any honor left in you at all, you will leave now, and swear to never again darken my door."

"You are mine," he said in a thick voice. "Whatever my feelings were at the start of this plan's inception, rest assured, they are not my feelings now. I want you, not just in my bed, I want you in my life, as my duchess, my companion through life. I will not lose you over this."

"You cannot lose me, Henry. Because of you, I have already lost myself."

Henry's mouth tightened. It was the only warning she had before he lunged forward and pulled her against him in a single, fluid movement. There was strength in his touch, but no pain. It invoked madness and need. His head dipped, a foreshadowing of his intent, then his mouth met hers. His hot breath blended with her own. At the first touch of his lips, all the emotions boiling just beneath her surface charged to the forefront. Passion, desperation, a craving that was unlike anything she had ever known. She wanted him more than she wanted a home of her own, or Louis, even more than she wanted to see her mother's smiling face again. Velvet tried to stiffen her limbs, but they were soft and pliant, rebelliously wrapping themselves around his hard body. Muscles tensed and flexed beneath his golden skin. The feel of him under her fingertips was better than soaring down a mountain side, wings splayed and catching the wind.

His kiss was gentle at first, such a soft touch, it would have been easy to mistake it for tenderness. He licked and bit at her lips until she parted them, then his tongue swept inside her mouth, hot, caressing. Velvet dug her hands into his biceps, pressed herself closer, closer. He threaded his fingers through her hair and cradled her head in his warm hands, then kissed her breathless. The moment was timeless. The room spun, the air heated, and she was caught up with him in the center of the storm.

They fell apart, panting, staring at each other. Even in her pain and rage, she loved his face, the way his lips moved, the way his eyes yearned. The heat in them was divine, if she lived to be a thousand, Velvet knew no other man would ever look at her this way. With a look, he saw through her barriers, skin, and bone, then touched her soul, carved his name into her very being.

He took hold of her upper arms, drew them both up to their knees, and leaned in close. "Hate me if you want," he breathed, softly kissing her between each word. "Despise me even, convince yourself that I had only evil intentions, but never doubt that I want you. Crave you. Desire is too pale a word. You are the blood in my veins, even when your kiss is full of need and loathing. If you truly want no part of me, then I will go. But know this, if time and fate force me to find comfort in another, it is your face I'll see, your name that I'll call."

The thought of Henry in another woman's arms made bile rise in her throat. She turned her head so he would not see the bitter emotion surely twisting her face.

"Look at me, Marie," he commanded. She did, their gazes locked, held. "You are beautiful," he whispered. "You are the light of my life; without you, everything is darkness. Beautiful, strong and brave, don't ever think I don't want you."

Velvet's throat tightened. She felt beautiful with him, only him. The way he touched her, looked at her, made her feel like the rarest thing on earth. He stroked a finger down the slim column of her neck, and they both felt her pulse skitter wildly. He did it again, then ran a thumb over her bottom lip. Her breathy gasp hung in the air between them. Her mouth opened slightly, leaned closer, and their lips brushed, lingered.

"God's blood!" Henry pulled away and raked a hand through his hair. "I must leave you now, or you will find yourself on your back with me inside you this instant. I'll worry about the consequences tomorrow." He sat on his heels again, his huge shoulders hunched, his hands balled into fists. "Since it is clear your mind no longer wants me, and you refuse to listen to explanation or reason, and I do not relish the thought of rotting in your dungeon, I will go."

"I will always want you," she whispered, closing her eyes, because it was too painful to watch him leave. He went out the front door, the sound of it slamming was loud and echoed for a time. When she heard his footsteps receding down the hall, she buried her head in her hands, and allowed her tears to fall. She knew she was indulging in self-pity, yet she couldn't help it. She had lost him, for real this time, and blast it all, but it hurt.

CHAPTER 17

IT IS ONE THING TO BE QUEEN, RULING IS ANOTHER MATTER ENTIRELY

The days that passed at court were as long as she remembered. Endless, poignant, wonderful days full of people. The people were her joy. Despite popular rumor, they had loved her mother, French and Romani alike, and they loved Velvet in turn. Truly. Velvet remembered all of them from her childhood. Each of their names and occupations was easy to recall, as if she recited an old, beloved rhyme. Her days at Versailles were now filled with their smiles, gifts, and complaints, and that was all good and well, but her nights...her nights were torment. Every night since the night Henry had slammed his way out of her life, she had been plagued by dreams of him. The things she had said to him replayed in her mind like a slow-killing poison. Such cruel words could never be fully taken back.

Devon stood behind her, one hand resting on the hilt of his sword, two more blades crisscrossed his back. His presence brought her safety, if not comfort. Everything reminded her of the Duke, especially his best friend. Velvet placed her hands on the double doors guarding the entrance to Napoleon's suite of rooms. Taking a deep breath that trembled as it went down, Velvet pushed the doors wide. Napoleon was waiting for her, standing tall as he was able, paunch extended, hands folded somewhat primly behind his back. His peasant face was hard, with a three-day growth of beard that sported streaks of startling silver. His close-set eyes were a muddy grey, but wide and alert. Velvet nodded at his two guards, and they faded from the room, closing the door quietly behind them.

Napoleon clicked his heels and bowed. "Welcome, my queen. I must say, I expected you days ago. Yet do not fret. I have not been idle. This was your father's reading room, and there are real treasures in here, so I have been well entertained, which I believe is what you intended, so I thank you."

"I'm glad, ennui is truly an affliction that attacks blue blood alone and am pleased to see it has not affected you."

If Napoleon noticed the slight insult, he gave no show of it. He simply stared at her like a predator too long without a kill. Behind him, Velvet could see his morning meal wilting in the midday sun. Brie spilling onto China plates, lemon cakes topped by browning slices of melon, scattered eggshells and a half-eaten crust of brown bread. Behind the mahogany desk where sat the unappetizing affair were long French windows, curtains thrown back, yet the wide shutters were closed against the boisterous wind. The room was stuffy as a tomb and smelled like a sailor's old boot.

Napoleon clicked his heels and clapped his hands, bringing Velvet's attention back to him. "So, what's it to be? Will you have Lord Eden take my head?"

"Why would I do that? Because you helped my mother lose hers?"

Napoleon pressed his lips tight and rocked back on his heels, each swinging movement highlighted his paunch. Velvet could see his shrewd mind ticking, and she lifted her hand and waved away whatever answer he could contrive.

"No matter how badly I would love to have your head delivered to me on a rose-gold platter, I must sadly disabuse such violent fantasies. Killing you is not in the interest of France. I respect you. I always have. You alone have the ability to bring a greatness to France that even my grandfather could not achieve —for however brief a time. Men like you always have a way of coming to a gruesome end, kill to be killed and all that. I think you know this, sir. Build your empire, conquer the world if it suits your fancy, all I ask is that you leave Versailles to me." Velvet lifted her chin and squared her shoulders, silently praying to the sun god for courage. "I will help you to care for the people of France. I will even help whisper in the right ears and fill your coffers, but I am no man's puppet, not even an emperor."

Napoleon smiled. "A female tirade, but a worthy one, perhaps." He took a single step toward her.

Devon's hand tightened on the hilt of his sword. "That's close enough," he said.

"Thank you, Lord Eden. He won't hurt me. The time of killing princesses is over," Velvet said softly, staring into Napoleon's eyes. "I believe the emperor and I understand each other perfectly."

"The French army is mine," Napoleon said in a tone that brooked no negotiation.

Velvet smiled, remembering the ship and the way the men had listened to her words, the way they had looked at her—like she alone could save them, solely because of the blood in her veins. "Is it though? I have my doubts. I wonder what the sons of France would do if I asked them to fight for me?" Velvet met Napoleon's sharp gaze, unflinching, then lifted a challenging brow. "I believe we both know they would choose me, but I am happy to put it to the test if you're in a gaming mood."

Napoleon sighed. "Do not try my patience, child. The army is mine and shall remain so."

"No," Velvet snapped, her voice cracking like a whip. "They are my men, my army. You, however, will remain their commander." Velvet spun to leave, then paused to glance over her shoulder. "And I am not a child. I am, for the moment, queen of France, and if the church of England is to be believed, a vengeful and powerful witch. I have survived things that can only be imagined if experienced. If you betray me and mine, by the power of god or the devil, I will kill you. I swear you will not like the taste of my wrath."

"Just ask the Duke of Newcastle," Devon said solemnly.

Velvet spun toward him. His eyes were staring over their heads, seemingly fixed to an unknown spot on the distant wall. His voice was colorless, but Velvet was not fooled. She could see the corners of his mouth twitching.

Inwardly, she fumed, while Devon pretended not to see the hot blush that climbed up her neck. "This *child*," he continued, "has bested him many times, a thing I believe you, yourself sir, were unable to do," he finished the sentence with a click of his heels, stoic as if he spoke of the weather.

Velvet felt that Devon was teasing her and chose to ignore it. She turned back to Napoleon. "If you accept my terms, you are free to go. You may continue to borrow my army, fortunately I have my own."

Napoleon chuckled. "Free slaves, pirates and turncoats," he said, casting the last disparagement directly at Devon.

"Brave and loyal warriors all," Velvet said.

Napoleon held up his hands. "I do not fault you for keeping such company, as one can often find jewels among thieves."

"Furthermore, I have not turned my coat, sir," Devon said. "As you can see, it is quite red. I serve Marie-Thérèse of France, and I serve England, or rather, the England that should be."

Napoleon snorted and turned away from them both. He walked to the desk and lifted a stack of papers, then deposited them in a gilded chair. It was clear the menial task was merely employment for his hands while his mind raced. He let the silence stretch. Finally, he cleared his throat, then spat out a wad of mucous in a tin cup. "Very well, I accept your terms."

His begrudging tone warned Velvet that he probably had an arsenal of tricks up his sleeves—those, however, were problems for another day. She wanted him gone, wanted him to take the loud men and camp whores with him—she wanted silence. Craved a few days of peace before Nora had her child and Louis was lost to all of them forever. She took a deep, weary breath and dropped into a pretty curtsey. "Very well. I bid you good day and god speed."

Napoleon grunted. He was shuffling through stacks of charts and maps; it was clear he had already dismissed them both from his mind. Velvet whirled and stalked from the room without another backwards glance, for today, she had no more time for plots and machinations.

Sunlight shone through the Hall of Mirrors, spearing through the hundreds of diamonds dangling from the chandeliers so that the floor and walls were engulfed in a thousand prisms of rainbow light. She could see her childhood self in the mirrors running alongside Louis; could see the hem of her lacy white dress getting tangled with the ribbons on her satin slippers. If she closed her eyes, she could almost hear the way their laughter had bounced, and echoed off the high, golden ceilings. Her stomach twisted with a sudden jolt of fear, her mouth filled with the acid taste of it, for she would never hear Louis's laugh again. The thought was so horrible, Velvet almost sunk to her knees, right there in the center of her great grandfather's masterpiece.

Devon caught her elbow when she swayed. "Steady, now." His grip was powerful, and Velvet leaned on him for a moment while she found her balance. She smiled despite her dark thoughts. "Some of your old strength has returned. That's good, I hated seeing you so—" She shrugged, not finding an appropriate word.

"Indeed, life as a turncoat and scallywag has agreed with me." He paused, then said, "Velvet, if I may be so bold?"

Velvet made a face. "When are you not?"

"Fair point." Devon rubbed his beard growth with his free hand. "I fear I must speak in Newcastle's defense—"

Velvet groaned. "I beg you not to."

"I must. I have known him my whole life, saw him with his first woman, and I have seen him with many since."

"Yes, we both know he's bedded down with half of the haut

ton. You should know your words are doing nothing to endear him to me," she snapped.

"I know how he is and know all the games he is a master at playing," Devon said, speaking over her.

"Sweet lord, is there a point you are trying to make? I warn you, I will burst into tears, and it will be on your head."

Devon grimaced. "It was different with you, Velvet. For one thing, he laughs with you. I hadn't seen him laugh since his mother and sister died. He had a reason for what he told the king, and though I cannot say what it was, I do not believe it was betrayal." Devon met her eyes directly. "He would die for you. Those thirty days he searched for you, I have never seen a man so broken, the thought of losing you was unbearable to him. By your own admission, I know you love him, and I would swear on a stack of bibles that he loves you to distraction and beyond."

Velvet had to swallow a mouthful of tears. "If that is true, then why is he gone?"

Devon arched his golden brow. "Because you threw him in a dungeon, then told him to leave?"

Velvet locked her teeth, and her heart turned over as she thought of what she had said to him. "I was a miserable bitch."

Devon threw back his head and laughed. Sunlight sparkled in his golden hair, and Velvet wondered what he would look like with wings. "With good reason, but honestly, I don't think whatever you did changed anything for him at all. I believe he loves you more than anything on earth. There is something rare between you, and I would not be so quick to throw it away. Believe me that I speak from experience. To my great misfortune, I will live out the rest of my life as the king of regret, mourning the girl I lost. I will never find another.

Velvet swallowed hard, felt the bitter wash of guilt flush her cheeks.

"It wasn't your fault," Devon said.

"That's kind of you to say, but we both know better. Do you

still hold the stone, do you...see her?" Does she hate me? Velvet wanted to ask; she couldn't make the words come.

"I do, though not as often. That does not mean she is not constantly in my thoughts. I am always daydreaming about the adorable chit, ever wanting to be nowhere else except with her. The stone was killing me. I used to think if I really wanted to die and be with her, all I would have to do is close my eyes and the stone would take care of the rest. Sometimes I almost did." Devon's eyes went soft, and his voice dropped to a tone of near reverence. "I've never loved anyone but Katie, and I never will. The worst travesty is that she is dead while I am still alive, half alive at least." Devon shrugged. "Come, I must escort you to your apartments, and from there I will take my leave. Our lady N, has tasked me with finding Charles, and 'keeping an eye on his miserable face'." Devon smiled. "Her words."

"Fleur tells me he spends much of his time at the gaming tables or fainted beneath them."

"I would expect nothing more of him. He is a shrewd fellow, though I would not make the mistake of underestimating him. Even when drunk as a virgin, he listens to whispers and hatches plans. I don't think he much cares what happens to France. I believe it's the stones he's after."

"He will not find them. Anything can be hidden at Versailles. It is said that this is the palace of lost treasures. My mother used to write secret poems, penned to all the men she could not have. She would hide them in the walls, the floors, even inside a fountain, though I can't tell you which one."

Devon touched her cheek. His hand was ice. "After all these months of endless danger, it's good to see you home. You belong here."

"Do I? During the day, I feel like I might, but at night, the dreams come, and I'm lost. From the Pairs gutters to the Mediterranean sea, every place I have ever called home has taken a piece from me."

"We all lose pieces of ourselves in the game of life, but the goal is to try and hang on to the important ones," Devon said. A long look of understanding passed between them.

Hand in hand they left the Hall of Mirrors and moved on to a slender corridor, braced by the castle wall on the right, and open sky on the left. The roof was a mess of thatched beams that sat one atop the other. She had climbed on those rafters as a child looking for birds' nests. Now, thick cobwebs hung where she used to place her feet. A breeze rustled through the wide courtyard and brushed her face. The sun shone directly on them, and still the day felt dark, the very air haunted with all the ghosts of those she had lost. They walked under a low arch and the narrow hall flared into the sprawling courtyard. Devon let go of her hand as they moved across the cobblestones to the entrance of her apartments.

Devon touched her arm when they saw Ajax moving toward them from the east. Velvet smiled. His ax was on his back, for once he had showered, and some brave barber had taken a pair of scissors to his hair and beard. He had somehow managed to stuff his gigantic bulk in a smart, violet waistcoat, a starched, high-collar shirt, and a wide silver sash that was the color of his eyes.

"I will leave you here in Ajax's capable hands. Rhee, it seems, has taken a bit of a shine to Fleur, so he is helping to light the lanterns in your bathing chamber. The women of the court say all you do is bathe. They swear you are half mermaid."

"It's better than other things I've been called," Velvet said, then sighed when she saw the flash of worry in his eyes. "Not recently, you don't need to fear. I'll be fine. It's as you said, I belong here. I don't think the residents of Versailles have it in them to kill another royal. We are all but exterminated. Really, I'm all right. You've been a good friend to me from the very first, Lord Eden...I...I thank you."

Devon brought his right hand to his heart. "Serving you has been my greatest honor, princess." He smiled a devilish smile that reminded her of the man he had been before he watched the love of his life die, then touched a poisonous amethyst stone. "Or, should I say, my queen?"

"No, you should not say that. Ever. It sounds very strange," she said, then impulsively, she went up on her tiptoes and kissed his cheek. "Go and play nice with Charles, and later, when you sleep, I hope you dream of her."

Devon smiled into her eyes, then chucked her under the chin. "I always do."

Rain came at dusk. Velvet watched it fall while she picked at the contents of the tray Fleur had sent to her rooms. She had not yet mustered up the courage to dine in the great hall with all the eyes of the court fixated on her every move. Velvet ate what she could of the smoked salmon drenched in salt and butter wine. She picked at the raspberry soufflés, and le gâteau au fromage, then sat still as Fleur brushed out her hair. Finally she managed to bustle the girl out of the room, swearing she could accomplish the simple task of climbing into bed unaided.

For a long time after she left, Velvet sat beneath the North window, her body curled up in a pink, brocade chair and watched the silver moon on its nightly trek across the sky. Sleep was far away, and try as she might, no other thought in her mind would stick, save ones of him. Henry. Horrible fears assaulted her from all sides. What if he had told her the truth? What if they really had touched something beautiful, and her fear and pride burned it all down? Godstars! She had read the words with her own eyes, traitorous, horrible, heartbreaking words. She was only doubting her resolve because she wanted so badly for her heart to be wrong. If Velvet slept at all that night, she slept in the chair.

The next day dawned bright. Velvet, exhausted from her sleepless night, went cheerily about the business of her day, determined to stop feeling sorry for herself, to stop crying over broken things she couldn't fix. She was given six new ladies, who showed up on her bedroom doorstep chattering and carrying on as if they had never been anywhere else. They were the daughters of the few remaining, powerful lords; men whose gold Napoleon was in desperate need of.

Nora had taken it upon herself to organize the giggling herd who finally quieted. Nora, however, prattled endlessly, no doubt to distract herself from what was coming. The babe was bearing down low now and brought her constant pain. Velvet could see in the scrunching of her nose and tight lips, the deep breaths she would take when she thought no one was looking. Properly disguising her pain like true British ladies are wont to do. Velvet was in awe of her. At supper, Nora somehow managed to convince Velvet to throw a ball in her own honor, a ludicrous idea if ever there was. Velvet had no idea why she had said yes. Never in her life had she attended a formal ball. What's more, no part of her felt like dancing. None at all. She felt like crying constantly. "It's the way she looks at me with those big eyes," Velvet muttered mournfully, disrobing as she climbed the golden stairs to her bathing chambers. "Like the sun would fall straight out of the sky if I refused her."

Velvet pushed the door open, stepped into the grand, marble room, then paused. Through thick reels of white steam, she could make out the curved line of Nora's stomach. She sat near the steaming bathtub, holding a stack of towels in her lap. "Damn," Velvet muttered.

"Were you by any chance talking about me?" Nora asked sweetly. She stood groaning, then set the towels on the vacated chair.

"I didn't know you were here," Velvet said.

Nora laughed and squinted. "Velvet, dear, are you blushing?"

"Not for the things I said. I would have said the same to your face, but I'm not enamored with the fact that you caught me talking to myself."

"You talk to yourself all the time."

"I do?"

"Umm hum, constantly. Like a drunken cockatoo. I saw one once, sitting on his perch, spouting all sorts of gibberish. Actually, I—oh!" Nora gasped, grabbed her stomach with both hands and curled her body protectively over it. She made a growling sound behind her clenched teeth. "Sorry, this child desperately wishes to be born."

"You have nothing to say sorry for. You're incredibly strong. I would be terrified."

Nora met Velvet's eyes. Her pale cheeks were splotchy red, her lips bone white. "I am."

"Are you going to kill the two French soldiers you took prisoner?"

Nora knocked the towels off the chair and sat back down. "I see you've dispensed with pleasantries, or preliminaries."

"You look like my mother the night before she gave birth to Louis. You can't hold that baby in much longer."

Nora leaned back in the chair and closed her eyes. "Would you kill them to save him?" Nora pressed her fingers to her temple. "Henry and Devon are right. Killing during a battle and killing in cold blood are two entirely separate things. Tell me what you think I should do. This baby has scrambled my brain like an egg."

"I wouldn't kill them. I would like to, but it's not what Louis wants and the cost to our souls would be dear."

"It's all too horrible!"

"Yes, it really is." Velvet let out a long, pent-up breath. She had been afraid to ask Nora, and even more afraid of her answer. "Besides, I'm not sure if it would work."

Nora opened her eyes and sat up. "But the spell? One, if that life is willingly given, two if it is forcibly taken—"

"I think that the transformation stone's requirements are different. The spell I saw on the wall combined the things Minerva told me—"

Nora cut in. "Minerva?"

"She's a story for another time, but she told me that to take back the thing you love, you must sacrifice what you love the most. For me, that meant Henry in exchange for Louis and, as you know, I couldn't do it. I have been thinking about it though, quite a lot, ever since Devon told me Alfonso's tale. Queenie wanted to put Louis on the throne with her standing right behind him, helping him to ensure a safe kingdom where her people could live and thrive, a country where they would never be outcasts or slaves again. She wanted it so badly that she killed two children in cold blood."

Nora's shrewd eyes sparked. "You don't think the two children were random," she said. It wasn't a question.

"No. I don't. Queenie never did anything without a reason. She must have loved those children. Queenie has a daughter, still living far as I know, but there were rumors. People whispered that she had birthed two other children. Some said they were children born of rape. Others say she loved their father deeply and after he was killed, the children were too much of a reminder of what she had lost. I was an owl and not much concerned with the affairs of humans, but campfire gossip was a guilty pleasure of mine. No one believes those stories, whatever the case—"

"You think the two children are the brother and sister Alfonso lost to her knife?"

"It has crossed my mind," Velvet admitted from where she sat on the floor near Nora's feet and rested her head against her knees. "So, you will release the men you captured? That's good, Their families will thank you."

"Hopefully, their families will never find out that I did something so monstrous." Nora sighed and pushed her foot into Velvet's lap. "Rub my feet, if you please, they are killing me. You needn't look at me like that. I am not evading your question, I just want a foot rub."

"Fine."

"I released the men, really, they were no more than boys, two days ago. Not on account of a soft heart, you understand. The stress of it all was weakening my constitution and ruining my appetite. I—what are you smiling about?"

"I was just thinking about what a strange fate intertwines our lives. How many dots had to connect to bring us to this point? If you didn't have an affair with Charles, your shadow would never have darkened the streets of Cheapside. If I had not been randomly attacked by bandits while running for my life, if they had not thought me dead and dumped on the street in that exact spot, you and I never would have met. If you hadn't fallen pregnant, you would never have seen Louis on your street, or that day in the forest, never heard his voice. We wouldn't know what he wants, and I probably would have killed to get him back...killed and failed. Like a million golden spiderwebs linking in all the right places transporting us to this moment, this choice."

Nora sniffed and wiped at a tear rolling down her cheek. "Now we will lose him."

Velvet closed her eyes. "Yes, now we will lose him." She blinked her burning eyes and looked at Nora. There was no one around, no one to put on a brave face for, and both realized it, so they held each other's hands for a while and let themselves cry.

CHAPTER 18

BRIGHT LIGHTS, A MAZE OF STARS

*T*he surrounding night was black as pitch, but Versailles was lit up like a star, shining bright enough to rival the three rings encircling the new moon. The huge courtyard was packed with golden tents strung with flickering candles. All around were bunches of lilies, red, white, and blue roses, forget-me-nots, and clusters of chrysanthemums huddled together like dozens of sleeping butterflies. Everywhere, people laughed and danced. Women spun in beautiful gowns, surrounded by yards of flowing fabric, light as a dragonfly wing.

Beyond the courtyard, the vast gardens had been lit with ten thousand torches, the jumping light reflected and sparkled in the numerous champagne flutes.

Nora argued that too many people had met their bloody end in the grand ballrooms of Versailles for her to host a respectable affair. Less than twelve hours from the event she had decided the courtyard would better suit her plans, then she had moved like a drunken whirlwind. Velvet was left speechless by the way the girl had sprung into unbridled action. Velvet had sat back and watched in awe as Nora transformed the castle in a mere matter of hours. Velvet hadn't minded the change of scenery, because this way she was free to invite the town's folk, so she had, and they had come in droves.

Camille, the baker's wife who Velvet had known since infancy, took Velvet's hands and kissed her cheeks. "Bless you, lady," she whispered.

Velvet placed a few gold coins in her hand. "For you and your family."

Celine and her brood of four curtsied. One of the boys tugged on Velvet's hair, nearly dislodging the golden circlet holding her mess of curls in place. Madame Chloe, Versailles's finest dress-maker, had hair like amber and fire-bright eyes. She kissed Velvet's cheeks with three noisy smacks that echoed, then she brushed her well-manicured nail down Velvet's shimmering, silver sleeve. "You make my finest creation even more beautiful, for you are the rarest jewel, madame, like a drop of moonlight, n'est-ce pas? Against all that golden Hofburg hair the effect is quite startling, you look like your mother."

"Merci, Chloe. This gown is the most beautiful thing I've ever worn. You are a true artist," Velvet said, her mind suddenly full of the way her mother used to sparkle, right here on this storied ground.

"The people love you, lady," Abigail said. Velvet cast her a side glance and smiled. The pirate lady cut an astonishing figure in a peach, satin dress that clung like skin, a daring side-bustle of deep purple and scarlet hung to the ground. In one hand she held a crystal decanter of wine, in the other, a sheathed sword.

"Truly touching devotion," Devon said, his smile gently teas-ing. "You are rather splendiferous in that dress. I'm afraid to look directly at you."

"They look at you like you're the virgin mother, so I don't think anyone here plans to hurt you," Ajax said.

"True," Devon agreed. "I'm not sure what purpose we serve."

"Merely ornamental," Nora snapped. "It's a wonder any of them dare approach her at all, with you three standing behind her, armed and looming like hungry dragons."

"I beg your pardon. I do not loom," Devon said haughtily.

"Velvet. Ah! There, look. It's the Comte de Bruxelles. My...he is handsome, and he's walking this way. I believe he desires a dance."

"I won't," Velvet said, not bothering to raise her voice, but added a fair amount of steel to her tone.

"Oh, sure you will," Nora said. "It will be fun, no one needs a spot of fun more than you, my dear."

Velvet cast her eyes to the ground as the Comte stopped in front of her and took a knee. Not bashful, only wary. "Bonsoir princesse, I was most honored to receive your invitation. Thank you for thinking of me."

Velvet had not known of his existence much less thought of him, and she cast Nora a look. Nora shrugged and lifted her chin, the very epitome of smug. The Comte stood and captured her hand, then held it lightly between his spotless white gloves. He bent and pressed a kiss to her knuckles. Even through her silver gloves, she felt the heat of his breath. "My Lord Comte, thank you for attending."

"How could I not? I am now one of the fortunate few, as all of France wants a chance to set their eyes on our lost princess." The Comte clicked his heels. "The gossips say a waltz is next, perhaps you would honor me with a dance?"

Velvet glanced up and studied him through the veil of her lashes. Chocolate swirls of hair, emerald, green eyes, and soft lips. Nora was right, as usual; the man was very handsome, and there was something generous in his eyes, maybe kind. He was red cheeked and innocent, different from Henry as day was from night. No. She would not think of her duke now; she would not let his darkness intrude on this place of sparkles and light. "You are quite young to be a Comte, my lord?"

"True, but my father was beheaded, and alas, the title fell to me."

"Well, we have that in common at least." Velvet sighed, relenting a little. "Though, I hope that is not all. I would love to dance," she said, realizing she actually meant it. "It's been a while since I waltzed, and never at a ball. I mourn for your toes."

The Comte's smile was brilliant. "I promise I will not let you miss a single step."

Velvet smiled and placed her hand on his proffered arm. A shadow fell over them both, briefly blocking out the distant, flickering torch light.

"Saints preserve us, this isn't going to end well." Velvet heard Nora mutter, then she knew, knew before she glanced up, knew it was him. *No, not here, not with flowers and laughter everywhere, not when my guard is down. He will touch me now, and I will fall to pieces at his feet,* she thought miserably. Then he spoke, and Velvet felt the words like an arrow through the heart.

"This dance is mine."

Velvet refused to look up. If she looked up, it would be real. In her heart, she knew she was a ninny, but she held to her delusions; avoidance was better than the alternative, soul rending, bone crushing sorrow. She loved him, and he had betrayed her, yet she loved him still, loved him always.

The Comte laughed. "Not to worry, mon bon garçon, you may have the next one."

Velvet gasped as her gloved fingers were rudely snatched from the Comte's arm. "All her dances are mine, and I would kindly ask you to take your hands off my wife, before you find yourself without them."

Velvet knew she should do something, but she couldn't move; there was a high-pitched ringing in her ears, and her hands had gone ice cold. Somewhere behind her, Velvet heard Abigail's throaty laugh. "My, my, it seems the night god has come to claim his prize."

From the corner of her eye, Velvet saw Nora drop some coins in Devon's waiting hand and, shaking her head, she shrugged. "Told you he couldn't stay away," Velvet heard Devon say.

Velvet had no chance to berate them for profiting on her misery, when an arm snaked around her waist, and she was pulled against a hard body she knew well. Her breath came out in a shaky gush. *Godstars, I've missed you Henry, I've missed you so much,* her mind howled. Her body wanted to shake and melt and come apart. She wanted to link her arms around his neck and kiss him as the world burned down around them and the past lost its power, faded to shadows and dust. It seemed strange that he had been the one to deceive her, when for so long in her world of broken promises and lies, he had been her only truth. If he meant to have her tonight, Velvet knew in her heart she would not be able to resist. Goddess! Why did good sense turn to mush in his presence?

The first haunting strains of the Viennese waltz tasted air, and Henry tugged her closer, then whirled them into the spinning crowd. Velvet finally met his eyes. Blue flames, vibrant and pulsing desperation, passion, madness, need. Emotions she knew were mirrored in her own eyes. They said no words, none were needed. His arms were her home. She could wish it was otherwise, but wishes were for nymphs and fairies—she was neither, therefore had none.

The feel of her in his arms cooled his rage, for he had tasted hell fire when she put her hand on the arm of that pretty boy. When her fingers had crushed the delicate silk of his evening coat, he had seen only red. Henry knew his feelings were irrational, but how dare she walk willingly into another man's arms after spurning him. Seven days, seven days away from her. Seven days of madness, seven nights of torture, so grueling that Zoe had thought him possessed by a sea demon and had taken to leaving small stick dolls outside of his cabin door. Henry had been in the process of returning to England, but dreams of her had forced him to turn his ship around. What a fool he was to think she might have missed him, needed him, even a fraction of the way he needed her. He would kill a thousand men to have her smile at him just once, the way she had smiled at that drooling boy.

Henry moved them skillfully through the crowd, having successfully navigated his way through the crush of many a ball. He could feel her breathing, her perfect breasts rising and falling against his chest, could smell the maddening, intoxicating scent that was hers alone, roses, rain, and starlight.

God's blood he was shaking. Together they swirled through the waltz, his moves perfunctory, performed by habit alone. He danced her to the edge of the crowd, through the first flower garden, and on into the spiral maze. If she noted his intent, she said nothing. She moved flawlessly, dancing on the tips of her toes, light as a feather in his arms. He dragged her around one leafy corner then another, until they were well sheltered from any prying eyes. Then there was nothing but her. He couldn't push her up against the hedge wall fast enough, couldn't kiss her deep enough. Her lips were soft as silk, and she tasted like raspberry. She moaned in his mouth. He could feel his body trembling with the need to have her here on this mossy ground, worship her with his mouth, somehow make her irrevocably his for always. Yet, he was ever afraid because the tighter he tried to hold her, the more she slipped like water through his fingers.

He ran his hands down her torso, cupped her beautiful breasts in his palms. Her dress appeared to be made of silver starlight, as it clung to her every curve, cloaking her in exotic mystery. The shimmering material slid and hugged as he tugged the dress down over her soft, white shoulders. She stared directly at his face when he bared her breasts to the cool night wind, and his starving eyes.

She breathed a tremulous sigh. "You shouldn't handle me so, Henry, no good can come of it."

Her words were the stuff of madness. He shook his head. "Stubborn darling, leave me then, right now. Turn around and walk away...if you can."

"You don't play fair," she whispered. "My lord, you use tricks, toy with my senses and sanity. I cannot think when you touch me like this. My mind tells me I should rage at you, but I—"

Henry cut off her words with his lips. It was beyond reason, he had to taste her. He lifted her closer, tilted her head and ravaged her lips. The kiss was savage, and he couldn't control it any more than he could control the rise and set of the moon. Tentatively, she returned his kiss, then she grew bold, bolder still until their breaths merged, and became a desperate symphony. He drew back, then licked and bit at her lips until they were wet and flushed, rose and scarlet.

"God! I missed you. I haven't been able to eat or sleep—"

"Nor I," she breathed. "I've missed you too, Henry."

"I can't stand a single day more without you. I am so sorry; you were right about everything. It was all a ploy, plotted by a mad king and his right-hand man—yours truly. The initial idea was mine, but I only suggested it because I wanted you, so damn badly. When the king held me in his dungeons, I envisioned only you. My days, my dreams, my every waking thought was possessed by you. I played and replayed each moment of us in my mind, and when I could take it no more, I told the king I would do what it took to bring you and France under his control. There were glances, touches—the way you spoke to me, I believed I could make you love me." He cupped her face in his hands when she would have turned her head away. "I lied to the king, to myself, but I swear, I've never lied to you. I was angry when you cast that love spell on the Bacchus because I wanted reality with you, not some passion contrived by a twisted magic. My anger was telling. It told me how badly I truly wanted you. I married you by proxy to save your life, but mostly so I could call you mine. What you felt between us was never a lie. The way I feel for you has been the realist thing in my life."

She blinked rapidly for a second and he saw tears suddenly spike her lashes. "And mine," she breathed.

Henry closed his eyes on a deep sigh and dropped his head to rest his brow against hers. The intoxicating smell of her filled his senses. He could feel his body hardening further, aching to a nearly unbearable degree. "I'm sorry," he said softly, moving closer, pressing his hips against hers.

Velvet folded her fingers across her naked breasts. "For what?" she demanded, and Henry knew she wanted her pound of flesh. He would give it to her, willingly. He would give her anything. "For all of it. For wanting you past sense or reason, for breaking all my rules of right and honor just to have you." He captured her hands and drew them to his chest. His eyes fell to the barred tips of her breasts.

Velvet stared up at him, torchlight threaded through the golden strands in her hair, making each of them glow. She shimmered in his arms; he was breathless just looking at her. He wanted to fall to his knees and worship her. He bent to kiss her again, but her spine straightened taut, and she stepped back. "You think you can just walk into this place and command me? I am not the girl you once deceived. I am queen of France. I am not your property, so you cannot claim me. I will not be—"

"By damn woman! You are mine, my wife, and I will have you tonight by love or by force, both will be my pleasure, I assure you."

She stumbled another step back, eyes flaring and sparking with warning signs of an approaching storm. He wanted to throw back his head and howl at the sky. Her jaw dropped, but she recovered her shock at his outburst with a low shriek. "You rutting bastard. Say what you want. You will not have me tonight. You have hurt and humiliated me. I wish to wound you with the edge of a blade, not lie with you."

"I see. So it is torture you have planned for me. Do you have no mercy?"

"None for you, my lord."

"Do you know that I could take you in my arms right now, and in moments you'd be begging for me?"

Velvet said nothing. There was no need, for they both knew his words were true. Almost gently, she wrestled her hands from his. The flurry of action made her breasts bounce, and her silver gown slipped a little lower.

He cleared his throat, still his voice rasped over each word. "Marie, I have rarely cast my coin for a lady's bed, nor wielded my will past a woman's power to defy me, but on occasion, there comes a point where a man is tempted beyond his will to resist."

"What the devil do you mean?"

"That rape does have its rewards, even if they be one sided."

Velvet smiled at that. "Villain," she muttered, stuffing her breasts back into the confines of her exquisite gown. They fought with her seeming intent on escape.

Henry closed his eyes so he would not simply attack her. "Take me to your bed, Marie. Fight with me tomorrow. For the love of my sanity, let me have you tonight."

"What will you do with me, my lord? Once you have me, will you find more pieces of me to break?"

"No. In all of this, even in the depths of my worst confusions, I never wanted to hurt you, never. I swear it."

"Just own me."

"Yes." He touched her face, adoring the petal softness of her skin. "Yes, Marie, that's all I want. Do not make me beg, love. What is one more night?"

Velvet snorted; it was a sound he had come to realize was among the most adorable, endearing things in the world. "Nothing," she snapped, lifting her eyes to his face. "Not a damn thing, just the price of my soul." She sighed, fidgeted, and pinched her cheeks. It looked like she was doing everything in her power to hold back a burst of tears. "Henry, I honestly don't think I can take this anymore. Just leave, before you do greater damage. Not to mention, you are ruining my first ball. Nora will not forgive you. Leave, or I will use the stones to break this connection between us once and for all."

Henry felt his entire body tense as if readying for battle. "I would like to see you try," he rasped, his snarl sounding menacing even to his own ears.

Velvet didn't flinch but cocked her head to the side and regarded him thoughtfully. The moment between them stretched and shimmered. "Just one more night, then you will leave?" she asked finally.

Henry's whole soul seemed to fight against speaking the answer that came to his lips. He nodded. "If that is your wish."

"My wish is to dance, at least one real dance. I've always dreamed of dancing at a ball. Give me one dance and I'll take you to my bed."

This time, Henry did fall to his knees. He wrapped his arms around her slender waist and pressed his lips to her stomach. "I'll give you ten."

CHAPTER 19

BRIGHT LIGHTS, A MAZE OF STARS

They danced three dances. It was scandalous and wonderful. Henry was perfect. Truly flawless in the way he mercilessly kissed and teased her. Velvet blushed and laughed until her cheeks ached. She knew that not all was settled between, but Henry was right. Tonight, the world was saturated in the charged magic that always sizzled in the space between their bodies. Who knew what twists and turns destiny held in her devious hands? Tonight belonged to them, belonged to her, and she would not squander it. Lies, revenge, blood, death, and war would always be with her, true brilliance was rare, she would treasure it.

Henry pressed glass after glass of chilled champagne in her hands. Velvet knew his game but decided she would play and drank down huge gulps of the sweet, bubbly liquid until her vision grew hazy, and the flames of the surrounding torches cast swaying beams of brilliance. All past rages between them dwindled away with the incendiary ticking of time. He never stopped staring at her, his gaze hot as his hands that, never once in all the hours of her first glimmering ball, lost contact with some part of her skin. She told herself that it was the endless barrage of spirits that had muddled her mind and dulled her anger, but she knew it was a lie. It was him, only him, always him.

"I hate the way you do this to me," Velvet breathed as he guided her off the dance floor after they had completed their third and final dance. Henry turned till her back met a stout pillar situated at the south side of the courtyard, hidden in the dappled shadows of an old maple. Beams of moonlight splintered through the branches and puddled around their feet.

"Do to you?" he rasped. "It's dangerous to say such words to me. The things I want to do to you, dream of doing to you, are vast and varied. I think I could make you come just by describing just a few of them. I think I want to try, right here, surrounded by all your lordly guests. I will put my lips to your ear and whisper my intentions until you melt, then, I'll put my hand up your beautiful skirt and make you scream, show each painted peacock at court that you are mine."

Velvet said nothing, as she didn't doubt a single one of his words. She knew she wouldn't be able to stand it if he did and said such things. She was already melting, panting, wanting. She wanted to scream the denial to his despotic statement, the one she had voiced a thousand times, but speech abandoned her.

Henry raised a brow, easily reading her. "Have you nothing to say?"

"Why bother? I fear now that you will state your claim until one of us draws our last breath."

"My love, you will be mine much longer than that."

Velvet rolled her eyes. "I know that you think so, and all my protestations to the contrary have brought me nothing."

Henry crowded her, forcing her hips harder into the unyielding pillar at her back. He kissed the corner of her mouth, ran his tongue lightly down the shell of her ear. Velvet's shiver of pleasure reached her core, and she gasped for air and breathed him in. He smelled like mint and champagne. Velvet laid her hands against his chest, feeling the crashing beat of his heart. "You are too close, my lord. People will talk."

"That's the point, darling," he said, again wearing that wicked smile. A dark curl fell perfectly over his brow, dangled in his eye, and he flicked his head to fling it away. Velvet had to clench her hands into fists against his chest to keep from running her fingers through his hair. "I have even admitted that I was yours, yet it was to no avail. Instead of treasuring me, you chose to chain, trap, and betray me."

Henry stiffened. Anger flashed in his vivid eyes. "May I remind you that when given a choice between your brother and my humble self, you chose to run, chose to betray me with my worst enemy. A man who gave me over to be tortured for weeks without remorse."

"I did not betray you! I made a choice. I chose to save—"

"My life, of course," he snapped, cutting her off harshly. "God damn it, Marie. Did you ever stop to consider that for me there is no life without you?"

"Henry," she breathed, stunned by his words. She dropped her head so he wouldn't see the tears that suddenly rushed to her eyes. There was no life without him either, not for her, Velvet knew that now, perhaps she had always known. The last week had been a misery, the nights without him an endless torment from which she could not retreat.

"Pushing me away is a knife that cuts both ways," he whispered, placing his hands over hers, then bringing her knuckles to her lips. The action drew her close, dragged her nipples across his chest. The sensation was dizzying, and she moaned behind her sealed lips and felt him shudder. "You know me, Marie. You know I am a man of my word; I swear I've never lied to you," he breathed in a barely audible rasp. "I meant what I said. The act became real the moment I touched you." His hands roamed her body, cupped her hips, lifted her so her legs parted slightly, and he was cradled between her thighs. "I don't know how to prove myself to you if you won't believe my words, so throw me in your dungeons if you must since I've found it's simply impossible to leave you."

Velvet gazed at his face, noted the perfect way his lips moved when he spoke, and wondered if he meant what he said. Then she wondered if it mattered at all. The heat between them was spiraling out of control. She took a deep, steadying breath, yet it did nothing. Her heart lurched. "You gave me the dance I asked for, didn't you?"

Henry inclined his head, his eyes twinkling. "I have my queen, and more."

"Then, how can you be in the dungeons when you will be in my bed? I must keep my word, after all, and you will keep yours. One more bargain struck between us."

"You play games," he accused darkly, his mood changing like weather on an autumn day. "I swear this is more devised torture to punish me for wanting you. Am I ever to be grilled on this rack? Ever wanting, craving, never—"

"Ma Belle niece," said a high voice at Henry's back. Velvet glanced up, startled. She relaxed when she saw the face of the speaker.

"Good evening, Uncle. Are you enjoying the festivities?" Velvet kept her question casual as she discreetly tried to disengage herself from Henry's arms. Henry resisted emphatically; his huge hands clamped down on her hips.

"I am, ma Belle, I'm here to see if you are," said Paul, nearly going up on his toes in an effort to see past Henry's bulk, no doubt to assess her level of duress.

"She is fine," Henry snapped. "She is with her husband, who is doing his utmost to see to her safety."

Paul unsheathed his sword and strode forward. Velvet violently rolled her eyes. She spun from Henry's arms, and he sighed but let her go and she positioned herself between the two men. "He is telling the truth, Uncle. I am fine. It's a lovely evening, and my...my—" Velvet swallowed hard, she simply could not say the word.

Henry threw back his head and laughed. The sound was real, surprising, and gorgeous. It made her feel warm all over. It was infuriating, really it was. Velvet shot him a venomous look. "His grace," she said finally, "has chosen to keep me company. I felt the need for some fresh air."

Henry cleared his throat and pulled a face. "It's an outside ball," he said reasonably.

Velvet smiled and slapped his arm. "You are supposed to be on my side," she whispered, and he laughed again. Paul stared at them both for a moment, and from the look in his eyes, Velvet suspected he noted the way Henry's body unconsciously pulled toward hers, and hers toward his, the way they seemed trapped in each other's orbit, meshed, combined.

While Paul watched, Henry reached for her hand and twined his fingers through hers. The action offering comfort and stating possession. Velvet took the comfort and ignored the rest.

Paul smiled, and Velvet guessed they appeared genuine in their affection. Velvet was sure of it when Paul sheathed his sword. "I will leave you then. I suppose if he is truly your husband, there is no cause for gossip. I will spread the word. Our princess has wed England's sword. The scandal mongers on both sides of the Atlantic will swoon."

"Good night, my lord," Henry said curtly.

Paul bowed, turned to depart, then paused. "You should know your brother is making much of some mismatched magic stones he swears are in your possession, my lovely niece. He's saying these stones can topple mountains, break empires, destroy, change fate and other such maudlin things. He says you, my dear, have used them many times, swears he has seen these stones with his own eyes."

"My brother is a braggart and a cad."

Paul seemed to muse on this for a moment. "True, but not, I think, a liar." Paul looked into her eyes and offered her another bow.

Velvet closed her eyes in relief as he finally walked away. "They will call me a witch, the church has denounced me as such and already questions the validity of my claim to the French throne," she whispered. "All the people I love, the ones who are just getting to know me again after all these years. I can only imagine the way they will all stare up at me when the Pope inevitably condemns me, and I once again lay my neck on the executioner's block."

Henry leaned in and pressed a light kiss to her brow. His lips were warm, filled with the promise of safety. "That will never happen again."

"You can't promise anything, Henry. I used powerful magic. I spent too many lives. I failed to save my brother, then, after which I stole his throne. The one thing I swore I would never do. I promised my mother that I would save him, and I failed, failed, and failed again. It is bitter knowledge." Her voice dropped to a whisper. "I have tried to love you and I...I have failed at that too."

"We tried with Louis. If you want...if you ask me nicely, I will willingly give my life for his. English or French, I don't think it much matters. I was born to die for a king. Perhaps it would be nice to have the choice of which one."

"I won't cast the spell to change him. I refuse to sacrifice you even after all you have done. I can't. Much as I wish it was, otherwise, I fear my soul would not survive the loss of you."

Henry moved closer, 'til the toe of his boot flirted with the shimmering hem of her dress. His voice was so husky and alluring, it made her eyes close, and her breath catch. "Does that mean you've forgiven me?"

"No," she breathed, "that's not what it means. It means I can't spend one more night without you. These last seven days it felt like half of myself was missing."

Henry took her face between his warm hands and, in that way he was wont to do, he tilted her head, and forced her to meet his gaze. "Truly?" he whispered, and his honey voice made her tremble. He ran a thumb over her lower lip. Velvet was too captivated by him to say a single word. His eyes dropped to her lips, ran down her throat to trace the arched line of her neck, followed the bare skin to the mounds of her breast. His breathing grew heavy. Velvet thought her own sounded like a breathy chorus of uneven screams.

Finally, Velvet nodded. "Truly."

Henry's smile was slow and sensual, and it broadened as his head descended toward her. His lips brushed hers, his hands fell to her skirt. Her back hit the pillar again, the marble was equal parts smooth and rough against the bare skin of her neck and shoulders. Henry leaned into her, bit her neck, and she felt the dress's shimmery cloth move over her legs in a relentless, upward slide. His fingers touched her thighs, then moved between them, gently brushed over the center seam of her silk drawers. The material was wet and clinging. Velvet gasped into his mouth as he gently slid it to the side.

"Henry, not here," she panted, shocked there was strength in her to resist. Henry's answer was a hoarse growl against her throat. He tugged the silky lingerie further to the side and pressed a finger inside of her. "Ah, angel, I could come just by touching you. Did you know that?"

Velvet shook her head as it fell back, and she heard her own shattered gasp. She blinked as his fingers moved and sensation spiked. Stars cartwheeled overhead and shot across the sky. With his free hand, Henry took her own, and brought it to his lips, pressed a hot kiss in the center of her palm. Velvet looked at him the second his eyes lifted. Their gazes crashed. Burned. "I'm sorry, Marie, truly."

Velvet wanted to rail at him, tell him that his 'sorry' was nowhere near good enough, but the gesture, the honesty in his eyes as he said those words, disarmed her. Velvet's anger melted away, flowing out of her with such force its absence left her weak. "Villain," she breathed.

"Vixen," he groaned, his fingers moving, working magic, making her eyes roll back in her head. "Say you want me, need me...say it, Marie, I want to—"

"I need you," she gasped, and tugged at the hand between her thighs, but it was to pull him closer rather than push him away. "I'm yours."

"All mine? No more running?"

Velvet shook her head, unable to speak. Her body was flush with fever, her heart beating out a rhythm they both could hear. "God's blood, I'm going to pull you down to the floor and take you right here. I never imagined I could need someone like this. You are a fire in my blood, woman."

Velvet stared at him, loving the roughness in his voice. He kissed her lips, softly, biting kisses while he moved his fingers in a rhythm that was driving her mad. She couldn't move, couldn't think. There was nothing to do but submit to his wicked fingers and lose herself in the infinity of his eyes. "I think—I think I would let you. I want you. Now. Always. You've ruined me completely; I fear I'll die wanting you."

"My lord," called Devon as he rounded the edge of the crowd to their secret place of shadows and passion.

Velvet felt Henry's taut muscles tense further. "What is it?" he growled, not taking his lips from hers. "If one more person tries to pull me away from her tonight, I swear to Lucifer, Devon—the sky better be falling."

"Worse," Devon said. "Much worse, I'm afraid. Nora is having her baby."

CHAPTER 20

Life, death and all the stages in-between.
I cried because I would miss you, I lied so you would not know, I
raged so I could save you, I died because I love you.

The babe refused to come. The labor had gone on for twelve long hours, and Nora, perfect daughter to the King of England, pirate and proper lady divine, was much worse for the wear. Her face and hair were drenched in sweat, despite Velvet's best efforts to wipe it away. The white silk nightgown she wore clung wetly to her swollen body. Beneath it, Nora's pale skin was blotchy as Velvet had ever seen it.

Velvet could tell Nora was trying constantly to be brave, but her bright blue eyes were wide and drenched in fear. Nora hardly screamed anymore when the pains came. Instead, she made soft, mewling sounds in her throat and bit at her bottom lip until it bled. Velvet, for the most part, had hovered at the fringes of the room, letting the silver-haired midwives do their work. Between the frequent bouts of agony, she would wash Nora's face and arms with a cold cloth, and let the poor girl squeeze her hand until Velvet felt sure the bones in her fingers had snapped a hundred times over.

Nora was on her knees now, breathing through a particularly bad batch of pains when a knock sounded at the door. Velvet set down her wet cloth and bowl of chilled water. "I'll go," she said softly, and slipped from Nora's bedside and went to the door. When she saw who it was, Velvet stepped into the hall and closed the door quietly behind her.

"Lord Eden," Velvet acknowledged, scrubbing her sore hands over her tired face. Her body swayed, and she leaned back against the wall, bracing her head on the polished wood paneling.

"How is she?" Devon asked. Through her fingers, Velvet could see his face—a pale mass of worry.

"There is no change," Velvet said, dropping her hands and wringing them. "Actually, that's not true. She's weaker than she was when last you asked." Sighing, Velvet glanced down the golden hall to the spot where Henry's incessant pacing would soon wear a hole in the lush rug. Velvet wiped again at her tired eyes with the heels of her hands, then ran her trembling fingers through her tousled hair and found them instantly tangled in a horrendous mess of knots. She sighed and dropped her hands. "It hurts me to see her struggle so, but the babe refuses to come. The midwife says it is doubtful Nora will live to see the morning. I refuse to believe it. She's a fighter."

"That can't happen. It won't," said Henry, materializing behind Devon in the time it took her to blink. Velvet dared a glance at him, then grimaced. He was badly mussed, cravat and jacket gone, collar undone, and he smelled like sweat and whisky. Velvet dropped her eyes and studied the satin toe of her shoe. "It might be..." Velvet paused for breath, "It might be that she doesn't wish to have the child. Louis is in the room with her now and has been for hours. She whispers answers to his questions when she thinks no one's looking. The moment she has the baby, that tangible connection between them will be forever severed. She doesn't want that. Nora has an indomitable, steel will, as well we all know. I think by that will alone she is not allowing the baby to be born."

"That's physically impossible," Henry said softly.

Velvet shrugged. "It is only a theory. Now, will that be all gentlemen? I don't want to leave her for longer than necessary."

Henry placed a restraining hand on her arm. "Marie, you've been on your feet for hours. You need to rest."

Velvet gently disentangled herself from his grasp. "No. I will rest after the child is born."

"Wait," Devon called the moment she turned to leave. "Just wait. That can't be it. There must be something we can do." Velvet swallowed hard when Devon's voice broke over the last word. He sounded miserable as she felt, and the thought of losing Nora was a pain that struck right to the center of her soul.

Velvet closed her eyes. Stupid, useless tears were close again battering at the walls of her defenses. She brought her fingers to her temples and tried to rub away the throbbing ache. "She keeps asking for Katie," she said finally, the admission so broken and hollow Velvet almost choked on it. "At times I can't decipher if Nora can actually see Katie, or if she just wishes for it to be so."

Henry's eyes darkened to the color of huddled pine trees in an evening storm. Concern and fear were at war for prominence on his pale face. "I feel helpless," he said in a whisper, low enough for her ears alone.

Velvet lifted her chin in a nod. "I know. There is nothing we can do right now but try to keep her comfortable, wait and pray to whatever deity you think might be available for listening. You should sit, as your hair is standing up on end." Velvet raised her hand to absently smooth the wild curls. "You should put your hands in your pocket, for you are in true danger of tearing it all out by the roots."

"It's like sitting outside my mother's door, listening to her screams and quiet sobs, grateful because both were proof of life. I can't lose Nora. My mother would never forgive me, and I wouldn't put it past her to haunt me for the failure."

"I will do everything in my power to keep her with us." Velvet met his broken gaze and spoke with feeling. "Anything, Henry."

He closed his eyes and Velvet saw his lips were white as grave lice. She went up on her tiptoes and placed the lightest kiss on his cool cheek before she retreated down the hall, Nora's heart-wrenching screams punctuating her every step.

Back in the birthing room, the nightmare returned in force. Sweating, crying, panting, screaming, intolerable minutes that ticked by like years.

Five more hours passed, then ten. Twenty-seven hours, even the seasoned midwives were beginning to sway on their practiced feet. Velvet sat beside Nora on the bed, where she had been for the past three hours, stroking her hair, wetting her brow with a cool cloth, and wishing with all her heart that she wasn't so bloody useless. Nora, for her part, slipped in and out of consciousness with each tired blink of her eyes. The shimmering shadow to Nora's right told Velvet that Louis had chosen to remain through this madness. Velvet was glad of him, his presence alone seemed to ease When he spoke to her. Nora's eyes would sparkle, and she would smile through her pain. Velvet knew Louis was speaking to Nora in that secret, silent language that was all their own.

"She will die for want of you," Velvet whispered, knowing her brother marked her words. The shimmer shifted, then Nora's leg twitched, and the taut muscles in her stomach visibly cramped. Nora started to scream again.

"It's a lie, Louis," Nora wailed. "This has nothing to do with you a'tall," she gasped, while her sweaty body tensed and trembled. Muttering a stream of curses, Nora rose up on her knees. Her hair poured over her shoulders like a waterfall spilling copper curls on the twisted bedsheets. "No!" she suddenly shrieked. "If you walk out that door, Louis, I swear I will take my last breath." There was silence proceeding her outburst for a few moments, then Nora's head dropped, and she began to cry, pitiful, wrenching sobs that shook her shoulders. "Please, Louis, I want a life with you. I want to laugh and dance with you. I want... I want..."

Velvet tried to stroke Nora's hair back from her face and whisper soothing things. Nora knocked her hand away. "No," Nora gasped, "there is no life for me without him. He is my only home, and if I lose him today, I'll be forever lost."

It was too much, and Velvet found it impossible to hold back her own tears. She crawled more fully onto the bed and pulled Nora into her arms. "It has to be over, I can't hear him, but I know Louis would never want you to die for him." Velvet wiped fiercely at her tears, trying to breathe over the knot in her throat. "It's o... over," she repeated, choking on a sob. "Over. We have to say goodbye. It's time to save...save yourself and the baby." Velvet swallowed hard, no more words would come, just tears.

Nora's body slumped forward, then she rested both hands in front of her on the bed and shook her head. "No, please no. I've lost everything, please..."

Velvet felt like something was blowing apart inside of her, and her hand clutched her stomach to hold it in. "Nora..." she gasped, speaking through a mouthful of tears. "We have to tell him we love him and let...let him go."

Nora wailed a wordless denial and pounded her fists into the mattress. Neither said a word for a time, during which Velvet had a moment to note that tears made a rather dreadful, unearthly sound. Finally, Nora dragged in a ragged breath, sat back on her heels, then pushed handfuls of damp hair from her tear-stained face. "Alright," she said, her voice small and deflated. "You're right. You both are. I don't want to lose my baby."

"Or your own life," Velvet cut in.

Nora shrugged. "Wouldn't really care right now. Death would be a blessed relief."

Velvet smiled. "It won't feel like that when you're holding her. It will be worth everything."

Nora lifted her head and met Velvet's eyes; her face was the very picture of misery. "I don't think I can let him go."

"I understand," Velvet admitted honestly. "I've loved Louis from the moment he took his first breath. If I could trade my life for his, I would do it in an instant. Without question. One thousand times over." Velvet turned her head to stare at the shifting, glimmering cloud standing ever sentinel at Nora's back. "I would, Louis. There will never be a day where I don't think about you, wonder where you are, and pray to all the goddesses that you are well. I would change places with you if I could. It was evil of Queenie to transform me first." Velvet's hands dropped to her lap, and tears splashed her open palms. "I would die for you, Louis," she said again. "But I can't, I want to...I just...I can't—"

"I can," Devon said, his low, sure voice coming from the foot of the bed. Velvet and Nora both swung their heads toward the sound. Devon and Henry stood shoulder to shoulder, faces pale, eyes bloodshot and red-rimmed.

"You can't be here—" one of the midwives began, but Henry held up his hand and the woman fell silent.

"Devon," Nora nearly shrieked, "Lord, you look awful."

"Said the swollen pot to the shapely kettle," Devon retorted. Velvet saw a real smile light his eyes, the first in twenty-seven hours she suspected.

"Get out, the pair of you," Nora railed. "Can't you see I'm rather in the middle of something?"

Devon made a horrified face. "Are you really only in the middle of it? Gad, my dear, it's been a little over twenty-seven hours. I pity you, deed I do."

Velvet rubbed her eyes, wondering if they would ever stop aching. "Nora, Lord Eden, this really isn't the time or place for one of your famous brawls."

Devon strolled forward. "I have no intention of brawling. I came here to offer my life, debonair gentleman that I am. It seems you ladies need one, do you not?"

CHAPTER 21

ALL THE THINGS WHICH MATTER, THAT WE DO NOT SAY

*D*evon stared down at Nora's flushed, pretty face and shook his head in unmitigated wonder. Twenty-seven hours. Inconceivable. The woman was an amazon. If Hannibal had this lady on his side during the battle of Zama, Carthage may not have fallen to Rome. He didn't know how much longer Nora could take the agony. He had seen grown men felled by a tenth of the pain she felt with every passing moment.

Devon took his eyes from Nora and glanced around the room. No one had spoken in a full minute. He laughed. "I must say I find myself rather flummoxed, since 'tis a rare man who could make the lot of you speechless. It isn't such a preposterous suggestion, you know? The life of a girl I love," Devon gestured at Nora. "A mother and her child, in exchange for the tarnished soul of a soldier who, by all rights, should've taken an enemy blade to the heart years ago. What do I need with old life, anyway? For my part, I am well done with it."

"Devon," Henry started, but Devon spoke over his protest.

"From the moment that cursed pirate dragged his blade across Katie's throat, reality for me ceased to matter. The beating of my heart became merely incidental. I want her. I want Katie. I've wanted her my whole life."

"I know," Henry said.

Devon raised a brow.

Henry's smile was sharp and brief. "I've always known."

Devon shrugged. "This world, as experienced from my perspective, can't give her to me." Devon reached into the right breast pocket of his redcoat and withdrew the amethyst. Slowly, he folded his fingers around the burning stone. Katie materialized instantly, as she always did. His heart hesitated, then pondered its next beat. Her eyes focused. She saw him. Her grave features softened, the smile that lifted her lips was for him alone.

Devon reached for her as she reached for him. She ghosted closer, her feet hovering above the ground, and she moved like steam beneath water. Devon took her hand and gently clasped her icy fingers between his own.

"I want to be with you," he told her, not caring that the other occupants of the room stared at him like he had suddenly sprouted two heads. When he spoke, the amethyst began to glow, the violet light traced a well-traveled path up his arm.

"Be with who?" Henry asked, spinning in a tight circle, eyes scanning all the dark corners of the room. Devon knew his friend couldn't see the girl he touched, but Devon also knew he could sense her from the hairs rising on Henry's arms.

Devon felt that the smile which touched his lips just then was nothing if not beatific. "Katie, of course. By the by, Nora, darling, Katie says you're doing a bang-up job m'dear."

"Liar," moaned Nora. "I am an utter failure at this child-bearing nonsense and well I know it. Now, all of Versailles knows it too."

"Don't be ridiculous," Velvet said, kneeling down beside Nora, looking exactly as a princess should. Devon watched her lean in to kiss the top of Nora's head. The princess didn't care that Nora's hair was a damp mess, and he loved her for it. It brought him peace that he was leaving his friends in the best of hands, each other's. Their disagreements, battles, earthquakes, and traumas had only knitted them all closer together, somehow binding them with ties that went deeper than blood.

"You are doing a spectacular job of playing host to this stubborn child of yours," said Velvet, speaking words to fill the silence. Henry stood near the pair of women flexing hands that hung uselessly at his sides, looking the very definition of lost. Devon understood the feeling, but for once could not relate, for the first time, probably ever, he knew exactly what he was doing. This was going to be the strangest, most painful, wonderful day of his life. Devon was sure.

Velvet drew in a long, audible gasp as another wrenching pain came to twist Nora's limbs. Nora moaned and drew into herself, her arms and legs curling to protect her tense stomach. "Devon, Henry," Nora wailed. "You must leave. I can't do this with the two of you hovering about. I don't want either of you to see me like thi..." Nora's breath broke. She gritted her teeth with enough force to make Devon cringe and shudder as another contraction came. "Dare not think it, m'dear," Devon told her over a cough. "I swear, 'tis a vision I shall take to the grave."

Nora awarded what Devon had thought was a rather timely display of his wit, with a vicious scowl. "Don't even jest about such things."

"I don't think he's jesting," said Henry, then turned so he faced Devon to the exclusion of the others. Katie moved closer and laid her head on Devon's shoulder. He stroked her hair. Henry said something irate, and Devon understood the tone but didn't hear the words because he was staring down at Katie's adorable face. Today her eyes were an unearthly fusion of brown and storm grey. That tiny detail suddenly seemed more prominent and important to him than anything else.

"I want to be with her," Devon heard himself say. Those six simple words appeared to answer whatever question Henry had shouted and forestalled another. His words did not have the desired effect, so he said them again. "I want to be with her from the second I wake, 'till the moment my eyes close in sleep. In my dreams, she is always there, singing, laughing, haunting me. I could stay alive—if that's indeed the correct word for the shadow I've been these past eight months—but every breath I took would ache for want of her. I wasn't brave enough to have her in life, perhaps I can redeem myself in this final act of death."

"Madness," Henry breathed.

"With a wealth of sanity at its core. Nora wants Louis, quite desperately, I think. If the prince has any sense at all, he wants her too, perhaps with his whole heart. They have a real chance to be together in this reality. Katie and I don't have that luxury."

Henry started to speak, but Devon shook his head and continued. "What would you do, I wonder, if our stories were reversed, and it was Velvet's transparent hand you held, Velvet, who was waiting for you beyond the mortal veil?"

Henry folded his arms across his chest and shuddered. "I would do everything in my power to be with her."

"Even die?"

"Yes," Henry said. Devon smiled; he had caught Velvet's eyes glowing before she dropped her head, then turned his attention back to Henry. Neither man spoke for a long time. Finally, Henry ran a hand through his hair. "I'll miss you," he said.

"And I shall be none the wiser—it's the beauty of the thing. Though I may check how you fare from time to time. Don't wish to frighten you, old chap. Alfonso is another matter. That man deserves a good haunting. It will be my absolute pleasure to personally see to it. Speaking of the bastard, give him this stone after I'm gone. The man wants to see some dead children, and it is payment for a debt. Louis understands. Some other time he can tell you how he attended a masked ball as a human still trapped in an enchantment."

"Damn it, man! Even if I understand your motivation, do you honestly think we are going to be able to just stand here and watch you die? In all your crazy ideas this one is—"

"It is madness, Henry," Nora gasped, her weak body tensing over another teeth grinding pain.

Devon sighed and sat down on the bed beside Nora. He took her sweaty hand and kissed it. "For once, I'm being serious. My life has not been my own. It's my greatest wish to control my death."

Velvet made a sound of distress and found Devon's eyes. "The stone poisoned you. Katie is a ghost. No good ideas are spawned by fraternizing with the dead. Perhaps she calls you to your doom."

"Then I shall go to it with a smile on my face," Devon avowed. "I would rather die for the idea of her, then live in a world absent her voice, her laugh. I will not let this stone go. Eventually it will kill me. I can feel it sapping my life force. Best to trade in this life of mine, and die for something grand."

"You're asking us to trade one life for another," Nora said.

"I want to give you what you want, but I don't think it's in my power to stand by and watch you die," Henry was saying, talking over Nora in emphatic tones.

"I'm not even sure how it would work," Velvet said, her eyes flicking rapidly between Devon's face and the slight, visible shimmer of Louis's aura.

"I believe I am. I've had some time to think on it while I was gallivanting around after the pair of you. Velvet, you told me Queenie used the stone of Tamora to transform you and your brother the first time. During the second changing you remember seeing the emerald. Initially I was confused, but of course after the dancing, the snake, and the love spell, I realized the emeralds give you what you ask for, if you have the strength of mind to imagine that thing. Your Queenie was holding the stone of Tamora in one hand, then offering something to the emerald, which was, of course, clasped in the other."

"I wonder what she offered?" whispered Nora, panting through yet another pain, and Devon pitied her, indeed he did.

"I believe she offered her life," said Devon, giving voice to all his theories. If there was any time to say his piece, it was now, here in what he intrinsically knew were the final moments of his life. He took a breath and continued, speaking through the burning pain the violet light rushing up his arm constantly inflicted.

"The emerald gives the user their heart's desire. Queenie was a woman in the eve of her life, a woman who killed her own children, a woman who would have done anything to reach her goal, a veritable Agamemnon, if you will. I think she meant to trade her own life for yours, but something backfired, and the spell took more blood than was offered."

"Makes sense. I learned in the cave that I can't trade my life for Louis. Perhaps Queenie never visited the cave, never met Minerva," Velvet admitted weakly, and shuddered. Devon wanted to ask who the hell Minerva was, but there was no time. Just one of life's many mysteries he wasn't fated to solve. "The stones want blood," Velvet continued, wiping surreptitiously at the single tear rolling down her cheek. "They want it, crave it, and I believe they will take it by any means necessary." She lifted her head suddenly, jerking her neck, her eyes locked with his, and Devon felt a chill sliding down his spine at the dark flavor of her gaze. "Any means necessary. That's why I hate this idea, and I don't have to read his thoughts to know Louis hates it too."

"I won't use the emerald. I will give my life to the amethyst, and hope the stone of Tamora accepts the trade."

"What makes you think it will be any different?" Velvet asked.

"Because Queenie had demands. She needed something from the magic. I offer only sacrifice. I think it will be enough.

"I have cause. Louie told me a few weeks ago that you informed him of this miserable plan months ago. You told him you wanted to die, wanted to be with Katie. You said helping him was only a happy accident."

"Or a divine fate," Devon said.

Nora paused to glare flaming daggers at him. "You've lost all semblance of sanity. You aren't being reasonable, Devon."

Devon had to bite back a number of heated responses, as the look on Nora's face told him she wasn't playfully bantering anymore. He enjoyed riling her, always had, but now was not the time. Fighting with a woman in labor had to be in bad taste, and Devon was made of better stuff, at least he liked to think that he was.

"I've hidden the stones," Velvet declared. "I won't give them to you no matter what you say or do, so this conversation and all resulting rabbit trails are moot. I refuse to assist you in this madness. I want my brother back more than anything. Every single thing I have done in the past eight months was to that end, but it's over. Louis will live a good life. I will miss him with all my being. If we use the stones, you will die, Devon, or your baby will die, Nora, and I will lose more than I care to. Permanently."

"M'dear, that's the idea. I must say, Velvet, you disappoint me, and it hurts not to have you on my side," Devon said, and watched the princess drop her brilliant eyes. It sounded for a moment like the girl had forgotten how to breathe. She looked guilty and miserable, so he pressed his advantage. "You once told me that you would do anything to save your brother. Anything."

"What did I know?" Velvet cried. "I found my limit!" She came to her feet in a rush, pinning Devon with a sharp glare. "I won't lose another friend. I won't trade your life, not even for my baby brother, and that's the end of it."

Devon stood and began to pace. The hesitation of his friends acted like acid on the salt of his resolve. Now that he had spoken his intentions, truly, after all these months, his nerves had responded to his declaration by trembling. Romeo and Juliet were heroes in their own right, but Devon would bet his last sovereign that both had feared the poison. Death was a terrifying concept even to the most savage, determined mind. Devon had never truly feared it, stupidly had not registered, or believed in its power to take him. Now that he stood before the grim reaper, his neck barred for the scythe, he could taste the fear in his mouth like dirty rain. He stopped pacing and turned to stare at Katie's face so he would remember all the reasons that had come together to formulate this choice. She floated listlessly beside him, her mouth turned down at the pretty corners, her big eyes wide and sad. Her tears turned to grave dust as they fell.

"What if I can't get to you?" Devon breathed, reaching out his hand when he could bear their slight distance no longer.

"I fear that too," Katie whispered.

"What is she saying?" Nora cried, struggling to raise her head. Devon was not too proud to admit that the pallor of Nora's face terrified him.

"She is saying that she can hardly wait for me to take my last breath," Devon lied with a cheerful smile.

Velvet gasped, but Nora snorted and shook her head. "Fraud. Katie hates this vile idea even more than I do."

Devon smiled down at Katie, and saw his reflection in her eyes. Katie twined her fingers through his, then placed her right hand on his heart. Her eyes were soft now, watching him with love. "Perhaps not as much," Devon said, wanting nothing more than to lean in and kiss Katie's mouth, run his lips down the slender curve of her bloody, ruined neck. He reached out and touched her cheek, stroked her twisted, tangled corpse hair. "We are wasting precious time. My decision was made months ago, since that fateful day on the Bacchus when I held his stone and saw my murdered darling, then promptly fainted like a dowdy matron with a debilitating case of the vapors."

Velvet laughed, then clapped her hand over her mouth. Her eyes said she was shocked and horrified that she had made such a sound.

"Make the hangman laugh before he slings the noose," Devon told her and winked, then turned to Henry. Though Devon knew the man in front of him, his oldest and dearest friend, stood in direct opposition to his plan, Henry was the only man in this sprawling palace that he trusted implicitly. He was too honorable to stop a man from sacrificing himself for love, when Henry knew he would do the same, make the identical choice in a fraction of a heartbeat. "Your Grace, kindly fetch the remainder of our princess's stones as I believe a riveting trade of souls is in the offing. The prince of France in exchange for a moonstruck swain in love."

"I won't," said Henry, folding his arms across his chest.

Devon had to laugh. The dark Duke of daggers sounded like a rebellious child. "You will, because as much as you hate it, you know it is the right thing to do."

Henry didn't bother to hide a jolting groan that sounded heartfelt. Devon's chuckles continued. "Good to know how you feel about me, old chap."

"You can't simply fetch the stones," Velvet argued in that imperial tone of royalty which she now owned to perfection, so different from the terrified girl he had met almost a year ago. "I've hidden them."

Henry grunted. "Not well, for I found them days ago in the nook behind the chapel pulpit, the very place your mother used to hide love notes to her courtiers."

Velvet scowled, looking deeply put out. "Oh, I didn't know that."

"Yes, well, I decided to have a search for them the day before my failed attempt at sailing home. The thought of Charles finding them was one of the things giving me my sleepless nights. That hiding spot is nearly as famous as your mother herself. It was only a matter of time before he got his hands on them."

Velvet violently rolled her eyes. She stood and walked away from Nora to place her hand on Henry's arm. "Don't do this, Henry, I don't want this."

Devon observed the tenderness with which Henry touched the girl's flushed cheek. "Nor I, but I believe the choice is Devon's alone," he said, which made Devon smile.

"Right you are old chap!" Devon exclaimed. "Now sod off and

fetch the stones, as I have some dying to do," he finished blandly, and Nora promptly burst into noisy tears, each sob punctuated by weak little screams. The sound broke Devon's heart, indeed, it did. A dastardly turn of events really, but his own eyes started to water, as he tilted his head down to stare at Katie's face so he would not lose his resolve.

CHAPTER 22

AND THEN WE DIE IN THE BRILLIANT SHADOWS
OF WHAT PASSES FOR DAY AND NIGHT.

*I*t was a solution. Not one she would have wished for, not one she could even have imagined, but life and death had their own plans. Velvet felt soul sick and mentally wounded. Her gaze traveled the room almost listlessly, simultaneously seeing everything and nothing at all. They were inwardly bleeding, all of them. When her eyes moved to Devon, they stayed. It was beautiful, the way his body seemed to unintentionally curl around the living ghost in his arms. So stunning the light in his smile, the way it left his mouth and touched his eyes. Velvet wondered if Katie was smiling, too. Was this really what Katie wanted? If so, then Velvet feared her past actions had willed a good man to death.

Velvet felt like she had struck a deal somewhere along the way, a deal with fate, a deal whose terms were a mystery to her. A deal that said take all others, take my very soul, but save my life. A stupid deal if ever there was. What was life if you had to watch everyone you love die? Slowly, painfully, endlessly, death by hundreds of tiny cuts, bleeding slowly yet dying truly.

In her mind lived a persistent thought. If there is nothing coming that is not already here, then she was wrong, and had been wrong all along. She wasn't cursed, her bloodline wasn't cursed, the truth landed much closer to home—the curse had always been her. Destiny played the cruelest games, and if felt like no matter what cards she held, she was fated to lose. If strength was in numbers, then they were growing weaker.

Looking back to Nora and the ever-present shimmer behind her head, some part of Velvet didn't wish to argue anymore, some part of her wanted to shove the stones in Devon's hands and be done with it. The other part of her wanted to press a cold blade to Henry's throat and dare him to defy her by leaving this nightmarish room. She glanced away from Nora to find Henry staring at her in that way that rose her hackles rise. It was like he knew the contents of her mind, and could read each one of her thoughts.

He mouthed some words at her, which she easily read off his lips. "Don't hate me," he silently said.

Velvet closed her eyes so she would not see the steel in his. This was actually going to happen. Devon was going to die, and she was finally going to see her brother's face again. The knowledge was devoid of any semblance of joy. A hot tear rolled down her cheek. All she could do was stand here and cry, helpless as a cork in a storm.

"Don't cry for me, dear," said Devon. He came over to stand at her side and placed a consoling hand on her shoulder.

Nora started to moan again. The midwives rushed over. Nora slapped their hands away. "Velvet, no! Are you honestly acquiescing to this madness?" she wailed, her rasping voice now pitifully weak, the barest thread of shattered sound. She froze seconds before her face fell, then waved her trembling hands through the air. "I don't care, Louis! I don't care if it's what Devon wants. You've been against this idea from the first. You railed at me for offering the lives of two rogues, but this! This is acceptable to you? I don't understand. Whatever is between us will always be tainted by this."

Whatever Louis said in response was lost on Velvet, but she

knew it was harsh by the way Nora's tears fell faster, by the way her tired shoulders drooped further.

"What's he saying?" Velvet wanted to know. Her question was too late. Nora was in the grip of fresh agony and had finished the speaking of any word that was not a curse. Velvet tossed a rage-filled glare in Louis's direction, and hoped he saw it.

Henry turned to leave. Velvet jumped up and chased after him. She caught his sleeve as he opened the door. He paused, then turned. His eyes traveled slowly over her face, dropped to her lips.

Velvet let her head fall. His eyes were fire, as ever they burned. "This can't be the only way," she whispered. "Louis isn't going to die, just go invisible. We can keep trying, keep searching for ways to save him."

"I thought you gave up," Henry said, running a hand through his impossibly mussed hair. Velvet said nothing, her lips pressed together so tight it hurt.

"Trust me, I like this less than you do," Henry said, when the silence stretched to a scream.

Velvet lifted her head and met his eyes. Unflinching. "Then help me stop it," she demanded.

"I can't. I want to, but I can't. This is his choice. I won't stand against it. I can't," he said again, then shook his head like it was all just too much. Velvet understood and sympathized.

"He's my friend, my brother," Henry continued. "I won't remove his right to choose in such a fundamental way."

Velvet felt like more tears were coming, and she took a deep breath to ward them off. "So much death," she breathed, "so much blood all over my hands."

Henry touched her chin, lifted her face until their eyes again clashed, then he caught Velvet's fingers and brought them to his lips. His kiss was hot as an open flame. "On our hands, my dangerous love," he said, in a deep voice that resonated in Velvet's ears long after he turned and left the room.

Velvet walked back to Nora, her mind a cacophony of confusion. Sighing, she sat on the edge of the bed, and stroked Nora's hair away from her face. Nora was too weak now to do more than twitch and moan when the pains came.

"Twenty-eight hours," Velvet heard one of the midwives exclaim.

"We'll need to cut out the babe if there's any hope of saving it," the other midwife replied.

Velvet scowled at the pair of them. "No," she cried, then turned and shook Nora. "Nora, and her child will live, both of them, do you hear me?" she hollered, and shook Nora again, with a barely leashed violence. "No more of this, Nora!"

Nora's eyes rolled back in their sockets, and her chest heaved like she wanted to cry, to protest, but simply couldn't find the strength. Velvet shook her again. "Wake up and have the baby this instant. You need to sit up. You need to push. Stop fighting it, or your baby is going to die, do you hear me?"

Nora nodded. Her eyelids fluttered. "Help me," she whispered.

"I will," Velvet said, gently taking hold of Nora's shoulders and lifting her into a sitting position. "Look at me. Look at me!" she repeated as Nora's eyes seemed to roll back in her head. "You will have the baby this instant. You are my best friend in all this wretched world, and I command you to have this child, and demand you live through the experience. I don't care about stones or spells, or ancient, bloody curses. Louis can just go to perdition."

"Changing him human is all you wanted since I first met you," gasped Nora, fingers clinging to the bedsheets like they were a lifeline. Each breath she took was a clear strain.

"Priorities change. I was alone in the world for so many years, now...I have you, Devon, even Henry."

"Not for much longer, darling," Devon said, a smile in his voice.

Velvet struggled to hold in a gasp that had the potential to morph into a sob. "I'm going to ignore you, Devon, or find myself in grave danger of bawling my eyes out. I can't attend a successful delivery while blinded by tears."

Velvet scanned the lavish room until her eyes settled on the two exhausted midwives. Little help would come from that quarter, of that, she was sure.

"Come, Nora, let's finish this," said Velvet. Nora took one last longing look at the golden light hovering near the door like the ghost of a felled angel. Velvet cleared her throat. "Goodbye, Louis. I'll miss your voice every single day for the rest of my life."

If Louis responded, Velvet didn't hear it. Nora started to cry, slow tears that slid down her pale cheeks like oil. Her eyelids tumbled closed, then she scrunched up her nose, and tilted her chin in the smallest sign of assent, as if to say, I'm ready, but I don't want to be. "Let's get this over with," Nora whispered. Velvet was pleased to hear a thread of steel stitched through the shaky words. Nora gripped her hand, squeezed until her knuckles turned white as bleached Spanish lace.

Velvet nodded. Her heart raced like a stallion crossing the finish line as Nora's body went tense all over. Velvet could feel the pulse in her friend's wrist, a weak, tremulous flutter against her palm.

"On three Nora, alright? We can do this darling," Velvet panted. "When I say three, I want you to push with all your hard-headed strength. You are the most determined woman I've ever or will ever know. You're the girl who was fighting for her life one day, and a pirate queen the next. If anyone can do this, it's you."

Nora's lips drew into a taut, white line of agony and grit.

"One...two...three!" Velvet's countdown sounded like a battle command; one Nora obeyed with fervor. To Velvet, it felt like every muscle in the girl's body was tense and trembling. "Push!" Velvet hollered. Nora did. Her scream was a long, angry wail that twisted Velvet's gut. Velvet had to swallow the desire to run. To cry out like a mad woman and pound her fists on the fancy, papered walls.

"Breathe," Velvet commanded. Pleaded. "Breathe, Nora. In and out, in and out. That's it! Now...push!"

Nora's back arched like a drawn bow, her trembling legs were spread, her tiny body strained and stretched to the max. It was a strange horror, like watching a butterfly morph to a fire breathing monster. "Push!" Velvet said again.

Nora complied with a traumatized scream that seemed to go on and on forever. Finally, when Velvet truly feared the whites of Nora's eyes would burst blood, she saw the top of the baby's head.

"I see him, or her, maybe her..." Velvet babbled. Overcome.

"Is she hideous?" asked Nora, trying to look down at the crowning child.

"I don't know yet, but if she's anything like her mother, she'll be the most beautiful thing in the world. Now, push, Nora, once more."

"No! I can't, don't make me," Nora mewled. "You do it for me, please."

"Oh goddess, if I could, I would. Look at me Nora, look in my eyes," Velvet commanded. Nora complied with a dizzy stare. "Come on. You can do this. I know you can."

"Fine then, if only to have you leave me alone, damn you," Nora snapped.

Velvet reached out her hands, waiting. One more push, one more heart-rending scream—which Velvet strongly suspected may have come from her—one more minute of terror and pain, then there was a woosh followed by a shattered sigh, and a gooey, slippery, squirming little baby girl was in her arms, screwing up her tiny face and squeaking out the most wonderful, wailing sound.

"Nora! Oh, ma déesse! You have the most beautiful, adorable baby girl," Velvet could hardly speak. When the midwife patted her on the back and told her to cut the cord, she could barely see the blade because of all the tears. With trembling fingers and blurring vision, Velvet pushed perfect golden ringlets that were stuck in the goop on the child's forehead. The baby didn't cry after that first lusty wail, but popped a pink thumb between her rosebud lips, then stared up at Velvet through a tilted pair of thoughtful, crystal blue eyes.

Nora fell back against the pillows with a huff that sounded more pleased than exhausted. "Is she perfect, Velvet? Tell me she's perfect."

"She's the most beautiful thing I've ever seen. She has your eyes and a full head of curly hair. It's the color of pure gold at sunset. I think...I think I love her," Velvet finished emphatically as she sliced through the cord, then tied it off in a clean knot. Velvet held the little girl close to her chest, not caring about the sticky birthing mess being smeared all over her fine clothes. She wrapped the child in a soft, turquoise cloth, handwoven with silver stitches wrapping the edges. She tucked the fold of remaining cloth under the girl's chin, as she had seen her mother do for her younger siblings dozens of times. When it was done, Velvet placed the baby in Nora's weak, yet waiting arms. Nora made a stream of soft cooing sounds and kissed her daughter directly between her beautiful eyes.

Devon patted Nora on the shoulder in a consolatory fashion. "Well done, old mum, for a moment there I saw the reaper knocking at your door, but no worry, he's circled back to mine."

Nora shook her head. "No Devon, we'll find another way," she said, staring down at her daughter, tears and love spilling from her eyes.

"He's gone from your mind, isn't he?" Devon asked.

Nora said nothing, kissed her baby again, but the happy, cooing sounds stopped, and some of the light drained from her eyes.

Devon stepped closer to her, then sat on the edge of the bed. "Nora, can you still see him?" he pressed.

Nora's lips thinned. Velvet sensed her escalating tension and ire. After a long moment in which none of them scarcely dared to breathe, Nora shook her head. "No...I don't...I don't see or hear him. He's gone," she said in a voice devoid of life. Her eyes moved slowly up to stare at the light by the door, and she clutched her daughter tight, tighter still until the girl began to fuss.

Velvet reached out to take the child from Nora who now bore a strong resemblance to a wax doll. Like one of the little beauties that artist from Holland had created of her mother, for the life of her she couldn't remember the man's name. She had watched him work for hours, days even, and remembered well how she had thought herself enamored with him. A free spirit with stormy grey eyes. Velvet wondered if the Revolution had swallowed him as it had so many others, wondered what had become of the little wax figures of Marie Antoinette. There wasn't much left of the woman who had once laughed with such abandonment and joy. Strange really, but if one looked at it in the right light, Louis, and herself, even their royal mother and father were just like anyone else in France. The surviving casualties of a bloody war.

Barraged by memories and musings she didn't want, Velvet held the child close, and rocked her gently. "Nora, that look in your eyes is killing me. We will find another way. I swear," Velvet said, standing as the child started to wail in earnest.

"Pair of lungs on this one," Devon said.

Velvet smiled, staring down at the baby's bright red cheeks, like she was hiding summer apples under her porcelain skin. "She's hungry."

"Leave it to you, m'dear to give birth to the loveliest child I've ever seen," Devon said.

Nora gave him a weak smile.

Devon cleared something that sounded suspiciously thick in his throat. The violet light wrapping his arm pulsed, steady as a healthy heartbeat. "Katie—" Devon's voice broke, he coughed, then hauled in a deep breath. "Katie says she wishes she could hold her. She says not being able to tell you in person how good you did, how brave you were, is the worst thing that's happened to her since she died. She...she says, she loves you so much, Nora. Says that you will always be her lady." When Devon finished speaking, he was visibly holding back tears. "Also, uh, she wants to know what you plan to name the little doll?"

Nora's sigh moved her whole body. For a time, she didn't answer as the midwives fussed around her, changing the birthing sheets, then helping her into a fresh, soft nightgown. Finally, they left Nora alone, and Velvet moved to sit at the end of the bed, still holding the babe close. Nora lay her head back, where it sunk into the fluffy, goose-down pillows, her eyes tumbled closed, and two tears slipped from beneath her bright red lashes curling against her pale cheeks. "That she would even have to ask. I'm going to name her Katie, of course. Kathrine, Marie."

Velvet's throat burned as she swallowed tears. She held Katie Marie closer as the little girl started to cry. "Hush," she breathed. "Hush now, little love."

"Marie is for your mother, Velvet, but you knew that," Nora said, a wry smile on her chalky lips.

Velvet didn't mind then that baby Katie was crying, she was crying too, it seemed tears not misery were the ones who loved the company. Happiness was in this room as well as sorrow; it lived in the smile filling Devon's eyes, and the fresh promise of new life infusing the air. Velvet lifted her face to scan the room for Louis's glow and found nothing, only the muted pallet of a stormy dawn.

CHAPTER 23

FIGHT TO DIE

*H*enry stomped through the golden halls leading from the private bedchamber of the queen, small bag in hand stuffed with stones that had no business existing. Power, Machiavellian, and lethal marched up his arm, raising the hairs and tensing every strained muscle.

The whole mission to fetch these cursed things took much longer than he expected. There had arisen a complication in the form of his goddamn brother. Charles had found him rushing through the queen's chapel on the way to Velvet's suite of rooms. From the desperate, wild, noxious glare lurking in his brother's eyes, Henry knew they were searching for the same toxic thing. Charles had made his case in earnest, spewing poetic nonsense, making lying promises that fell from his lips like poisoned daggers. Promises like how he would use the magic of the stones to cure poverty, abolish the monarchy, save dying babies and all that malarkey. As always, his brother was transparent as a well-polished pane of glass. Henry saw directly through him. Charles wanted the stones for the person he loved the most in all this wicked world—himself. He would take by force the power, his status as a second son, and their father had always denied him.

Henry hadn't had the time or patience to deal with his brother's verbal flatulence. The same went for Nora and Louis. For his interference, the evil little pup was currently sleeping off a well-aimed blow to the head. Henry hoped that sooner rather than later the priest would find the wastrel and send up a much-needed prayer for the boy who was seconds from being a father.

Rage, irritation, and throbbing knuckles assailed him as he threw open the door to Nora's bed chambers with little finesse. It swung in on its hinges before banging hard against the wall. He caught the door on its swift return. His nose had taken enough of a beating. He stepped into the room; it was surprisingly silent. The dark, violet curtains had been drawn shut, the orange flames leaping in the decorative sconces along the wall had been turned low. There was a breeze rushing through the room, that moved the hair hanging over his brow. He shoved the hair away while closing the door quietly behind him. His heart, soul, and his eyes found her almost instantly. She was a glittering diamond, glowing in the darkness. His heart twisted at the sight of her. She stole the very breath from his lungs. The queen of France, Marie, his love, his wife, his bane. She lay in the cloud of her golden hair, a smile on her flushed lips and a baby in her arms. He watched her breasts rise and fall on a sigh, felt the lust, the need, the desperate, all-consuming want like a kick in the gut. Even in sleep she enchanted him, tore at his insides, and made him want to fall to his knees and beg her for what he now feared she would never willingly give to him.

If he put these stones in Devon's hands he could give her brother back to her. It was what she wanted since the first. He could do it, but there was this nagging fear that he would be damming himself in the process.

There really was only one choice and wasn't that a damn shame? To save his best friend, the man that had been more than a brother to him, yet at the same time give the girl he loved more than life the deepest desire of her heart. One life willingly given —that life had to be his. It was obvious and painful. Henry still didn't think he feared death, not the way a man should, but leaving her would be like ripping off then stepping away from his own skin.

Henry took a single step closer to the bed, to her. The darling was embroiled in the most poignant scene he had ever witnessed. Nora's head rested on Velvet's shoulder, a tiny little girl lay between them, her head cradled in the crook of Velvet's arm. The child was beautiful, with a full head of peachy-gold hair, and lips like some angel stamped a heart on her face. All three girls were holding hands and wearing the softest smiles.

The sight made Henry ache in places he never knew existed. The feelings it invoked slayed him. In his mind, for a horrible, life-changing moment, it was their child Velvet held in her arms. The thought was so soul-twisting, Henry was forced to turn away from them all to keep himself from reaching for her, gathering her up in his arms and never letting her go, not even when their bodies turned to earth and dust. Thrones and crowns be damned. Henry wondered if he would be like Katie when he died. Always hovering on the fringes of Velvet's reality, coasting along the boundaries between worlds, living a life of mists and ghosts, of grey silence filled with untouchable things. Existing through the impossible just for a chance encounter, a glimpse, a hope, a single look at the girl he loved, the one left behind.

Henry spun on his heel and reached for her. He couldn't help it, the action merely instinct over thought. The fingertips of his left hand stopped inches from the brilliant spill of her silver blonde hair. His breath twisted in his straining lungs. Firelight always had a way of transforming her from human to angel. Standing there with his trembling hand hanging in the ether between them, Henry's life flashed through his mind in a series of colorless pictures. The traumatizing day his mother and baby sister died, the men he killed during those years in the Americas, and all the bullshit king and country had demanded of him. Even with and through all of that, leaving this tiny slip of a girl would be the hardest thing he ever had to do.

Dying was easy, any man could do it. The pain of walking

away from her would be infinite, eternal. His fingertips reached inches closer. His right hand closed tighter around the bag of stones. Lightning shards of pain shot up his arm, encasing him in invisible lighting and rooting him to the spot.

He couldn't move, could hardly breathe. All he could do was listen to the racing beats of his heart as it memorized every detail of her. Every line, each gorgeous curve of the face which had enchanted him from the very first moment he clapped eyes on her. Henry drew back his hand and dragged it through his hair as he turned to walk away. He paused on a backwards glance, every muscle in his body tense and shaking. "Goodbye, Marie. You should know I've loved nothing so well as you. I'll keep the image of your smile and leave you my heart in fair exchange."

Stones clutched tightly in hand, Henry left the palace and made his way through the silent gardens, still marred by the remnants of Nora's midnight ball. He felt a moment of medium rage when he realized he would not be able to take Nora to task for glibly handing the love of his life off to another, younger man. One who was not so battle stained and road weary as him. What made it all the worse was that the handsome bastard was probably the perfect fucking choice. The thought of that man peeling the silks off Velvet's beautiful body put Henry in a killing rage. It was bad. In that instant he would have happily murdered a whole battalion with his bare hands, then licked the blood from his fingers, because if it wasn't that simpering duke, eventually it would be someone else.

He turned the corner and walked the dark path leading through the largest labyrinth of Versailles's many mazes. All the torches had been extinguished, and the way was dark. God! There was still so much he wanted to say to her. He wanted more than anything to kiss her lips one last time, wanted to watch her eyes as she whispered his name. He would take the beautiful sound of her voice to the grave.

Breathing in a deep sigh that trembled as it went down, Henry took one last look at the star-soaked sky, one last glimpse at the watching moon. It was only imagination, but he could hear her speaking to him in the screaming silence, begging him not to do it when he upended the bag of glittering gems in the dew-soaked grass. Multi-colored light speared the darkness true as any well-aimed lance. Onyx, jade, amethyst, and gold, the stone of Tamora, equal parts murky and brilliant as cat eyes in the dark peering into the deepest recesses of his soul.

Henry reached for Tamora. Something struck the back of his head, hard. Henry pitched forward with a choked cry, barely managing to catch himself with both hands before his teeth hit the dirt.

"What in god's blood!" Henry shouted. He pulled himself up and spun on his knees. When he faced his attacker, shock dropped his jaw. Black clothes, black cloak with hood drawn high. Devon was hardly distinguishable from the common night shadow.

Devon made a tisking sound and shook his head. "Good evening, your grace, I know you're not out here trying to steal my glorious sacrifice."

"God damn it! Devon, get out of here. This death has always been meant for me," Henry grated, staring at Tamora glimmering from the corner of his eye.

"Don't even think about it," Devon said, stepping closer to the gem, and the violent end it promised.

"Eden, be reasonable. We've protected each other since we were children. You didn't honestly think I was going to fetch the stones like a good hound, then stand by and watch you die?"

Devon drew back, aghast. "You said it was my choice."

"I lied. It would make all the times I save your worthless hide, damn irrelevant."

Devon laughed. "Not at all. You kept me from all the others, helped me save myself for the right death."

"I won't let you do this. Do you think I want to die? Trust me, I had other plans, but you've been my best friend forever, this old world wouldn't be the same without you."

Devon raised his fists. "Touching sentiment, your grace, but how do you propose to stop me? You know I've always been the superior fighter, or have you forgotten? Come at me then, I'm happy to knock you on your ass if it will help refresh your lagging memory."

"I don't have time for this," Henry growled. He reached for the stone again, any stone. Devon rushed him like a battle stallion bearing down on an enemy. The sound of their bodies slamming together woke the birds peacefully sleeping in swaying branches of the surrounding willows. Henry drove a knee into Devon's thigh. Devon responded by smashing his forehead against the bridge of Henry's nose. They rolled across the grass, cursing like sailors at war. Henry sunk a fist deep in Devon's gut, then took an elbow to the jaw. Stars imploded in front of his eyes. Devon took advantage of Henry's brief moment of disability to grab both his shoulders and slam his back down into the grass and hold him there.

"God damn it, Henry! Give over! Katie is worth more than my life. If you make me live, I will never find anything like her again. Everything will always be second best. Don't condemn me to such a wretched a fate. Give me this."

Henry fought like a cornered panther, swinging his fists blindly and roaring something that sounded like *NO!* His knuckle clipped the underside of Devon's jaw snapping his head back. Henry shoved Devon's weight aside, then struggled to his feet.

"Wow!" Devon exclaimed brightly, fingering his jaw. "That was a solid hit. Good to know you still have it in you."

Henry opened his mouth to fire off a pith drenched reply, but Devon's iron fist closed his lips and titled his consciousness on its unstable access. Henry shook off the hit and dove blindly for the stones. A fraction of a millimeter from his target, Devon stepped on his hand, then bore down with all his weight. Henry howled. He swung his leg, and his shin connected with the backs of Devon's ankles. Devon's feet flew out from under him. A second later, his face hit the grass with a dull thud. Then they were rolling again until Henry hoped to hurl all over Devon. Their wild, scrambling progress was finally halted by a stout boulder crowned by a gold-plated, crystal fountain weeping streams of moonlit diamonds.

They broke away with winded groans. Henry, for his part, was spent. Devon had always been lightning-quick. His greater strength meant nothing when the man could dance around him like a ballet darling on her tip-toes. On his knees, Henry took a single moment to catch his breath. The broken ribs, which had come from dancing with gypsies, screamed on every inhale. The stabbing pain from the old wound was the kicker.

Henry had to acknowledge that he was furious at Devon, at the whole damn world. Every moment he fought to die further weakened his resolve to do so. Velvet's face was a thousand brilliant stars painted across the dark skies of his mind. He wanted her with a vengeance, and it seemed the physical pull between them stung when stretched, which made him wonder, briefly, if she would survive the break, live through the loss of him. If positions were reversed, he knew he could never live through the loss of her. Did she love him? If she did, as she had once said, then how the hell could he do this? How could he not? He closed his eyes, rubbed them in an attempt to wipe her away, but her image only grew brighter. Haunting, flawless, precious, loved.

Henry opened his eyes and looked up at Devon, meaning to plead, beg for his own death. *Kill me now,* he wanted to scream, *kill me before I run from the clutches of this maze like the coward my father named me.* He never had a chance to say a single word. Devon's knee was a blur before it slammed into Henry's right temple, and it was lights out. Henry had a vague notion of the back of his head smacking the boulder, but the truth of the matter was swallowed up by an enveloping cloud of darkness.

When sound and sight made their prodigal return, the maze had undergone a dramatic transformation. Purple mists writhed over the ground, sliding along the backs of curled vines with thick black thorns that seemed to have magically sprouted during his brief stint of unconsciousness.

Strange figures moved through the hedges, feet-less apparitions who glided like sparrows on a strong breeze. A strange collection of undead travelers who looked to be wearing white sheets over their heads that were made of dreams and smoke. The listless figures ghosted through the river of colors, pouring from Devon's hand and gushing across the ground as if a dam had broken. Devon stood beside his glimmering girl made of grave dust. The smile in her eyes clashed badly with her bloody, slit throat. Macabre didn't begin to cover the panorama of unreality that met his eyes.

The amethyst in Devon's hand was visibly killing him. Sapping the life from his veins sure as any thunderstorm sucked the colors from a summer day. Henry felt a knifing pain lance through his gut and recognized it as fear. He stood, meaning to charge at Devon, and put a stop to this horror before it was too late.

Devon's head snapped up. He met Henry's eyes, then shook his head. "No! It's done," he said, and stretched out his left hand. Henry saw a glimmer of the ruby before it rendered him completely immobile.

"I have to do this. For Katie, for Nora, for Velvet and you. This is my fate, so let me meet it."

Henry felt hot tears burning his eyes and didn't care. He battled the enchantment, keeping his feet and arms locked in place. It was useless, as if he had been frozen in a block of ice from the neck down. The magic of the pulsing ruby infused his blood and made him weak. "I'm begging you, Devon."

"And I'm ignoring you," Devon retorted. "Can't you see how beautiful she is?" he asked, turning his head to let his eyes melt into Katie's brilliant gaze.

He could see her, and she was beautiful. That was the most terrifying thing of all. If Velvet was standing like that in front of him, murdered and transparent, he would have done all in his power to get to her. He knew Devon would do no less. That knowledge brought a finality that sickened him. Henry struggled again against his invisible bonds, but it was useless, like battling a force of nature.

There was nothing he could do save watch Devon's life force drain brilliant color, slowly turning his skin grey as a mason's grinding stone. Devon swayed, teetered, then crashed down on his knees. His breaths shortened, turning shallow, and weakening by the second.

Katie moved like smoke in the wind to stand behind her dying man. She placed her hands on his shoulders. Henry could see the hedge through her face, as he watched the dark leaves rustle in her eyes. The sight was nostalgic, endearing and the most downright terrifying thing he had ever seen.

"Devon! Devon, stop this!" he raged through clenched teeth.

Devon smiled. "My...my life for the French king..." he gasped. "My choice, my soul willingly given."

"*Damn it! No!*" Henry roared. No one was listening to him. Every single thing around him was tuned to Devon's earth-shattering words. The amethyst responded. It siphoned more color, draining the life of his best friend with no remorse.

Colors ran over the ground like blood from an artery. All the varied vibrations of an individual human life. Henry followed the rainbow river of light with his eyes. It rushed toward Louis's glow, hovering near the maze's largest entrance. A distinguishable outline surrounded the prince, a glittering line of light which Henry was sure hadn't been there before. As Devon's life faded, the outline strengthened until Henry could see hints of the prince's face, and golden locks of hair, moonstruck and wind tossed. It was slight at first, like a portrait emerging from puddles of oil paint.

"Henry," Devon gasped, and the papery quality of his voice was another blazing knife slicing through his insides. "Henry, do something for me, will you?"

"Yes. Anything."

"Tell Nora, how...how much I love her."

"Don't make him your messenger, you bastard! Tell me your damn self!"

Henry slowly turned his head toward the irate sound of Nora's tear-soaked voice, but his eyes went to Velvet standing beside her in a pure white nightgown, her eyes on his face, pools of fathomless brilliance. Nora's nightgown still carried the stains of her triumph. She leaned on Velvet's free arm, her other arm cradling the baby who was sleeping, blissfully unaware.

"I couldn't stop her," Velvet said silently. Henry read the words off her lips and nodded. Nora was unstoppable.

"Ah Nora," Devon sighed. "I didn't want you to see this...see me like this."

Nora threw up her hands, openly sobbing. "You're rude enough to be dying despite my express commands, and you don't think you owe me your last moments? I would kill you if...if..." her voice broke. She swayed against Velvet, and Henry reached out to steady her, but there was no need. Velvet caught the girl around the waist and kept her from falling.

"I knew you would only try to stop me," Devon said. Amethyst tears ran down his own cheeks.

"Don't you think I know that? Could I? Could I stop you?" Nora asked miserably. Henry knew the truth before Devon spoke it with a single word.

"No. No Nora, there is no stopping this."

"Do you know what this will do to me, how raw it will leave me?" Nora demanded as she broke away from Velvet, hands held toward Devon.

Velvet sank to her knees, holding the sleeping baby close to her heart. She rocked them both back and forth, and Henry felt something inside him break. His fingers twitched and his arms literally ached to hold her.

Henry struggled hard, felt his muscles bulge and his veins pop—felt that he did not move at all. "Let me go to her, Eden," he almost begged.

Devon hesitated for a single breath, then gave a brief nod of assent. He dropped the ruby. It fell silently to the earth, vanishing into the long grass, its glow all but extinguished by the swaying dark green blades.

The enchantment's hold loosened instantly, and Henry was running to her. If Marie protested his touch, he didn't hear it as he bent and lifted her and the baby both into his arms. Velvet buried her wet face in his shoulder. Her body shook, long, wracking shivers that coursed through her to him.

"Darling," he groaned. He pressed his lips to the top of her head and watched as Nora stumbled to Devon, fell on her knees in front of him, and reached for Katie's hand. Nora's flesh and bone passed through Katie's ghost like water through air. The touch sensed but not felt.

Devon wrapped his free arm around her as Nora clasped her hands behind his neck and cried against his chest. Smearing tears on the red coat Devon had worn since he was eighteen. For a moment, Nora's sobs and Velvet's soft breaths were the only sounds in the dark maze.

CHAPTER 24

HIM, ALWAYS HIM, ONLY HIM

*V*elvet clung to him. Her body seemed to remember none of their past earthquakes, bloody sabotages, or black misery, so it melted against his. The baby was cradled between their bodies. Her fingers dug into his shirtfront like all the air in the world would be snatched away if she loosened her grip even for a single second. It appeared he knew and shared her feelings because he clutched her just as close. She could hear the way he breathed her in.

"You were going to leave me," she accused. Thinking of the scene she had witnessed before the ruby and Devon's fist had rendered him senseless. Henry kissed her heated brow. His lips lingered.

"Thought I'd take a page from your book," he finally said.

"Oh really? How so?"

"You've been trying to run from me since the day we met. Useless, really. Fight me till we die. I don't care. I'll never let you go."

Velvet wanted to hate him. Truly wanted to fight him and the whole damn world, but those were some of the best words she had ever heard, and they drained all the battle from her heart. Henry's words had the flavor of a blood oath, so she stayed silent, kept her teary eyes on the unfolding scene and prepared her heart to watch Devon die.

The reaper was close. Devon's skin and bones were now transparent as a thought. Nora's tears were a river that threatened to wash him away. Only a year. She had known him only a year, Katie not even that, and she had loved them both. There they stood, martyrs in her crusade. The stones had demanded more blood and price was being paid.

Thunder rolled across the star spattered sky. The incoming, ink-black storm clouds burped and spit lightning, sending crackling shards to earth. They hit the wet grass and sizzled, like drops of water sprinkled over a vat of boiling oil. Steaming darkness intensified the pure colors of magic rushing over the ground and pooling around Nora's knees and Henry's feet. It swirled beneath them all like a midnight whirlpool of rainbows.

More deafening peals of thunder shook the ground, and in the moments between the reverberating booms, Velvet imagined she could hear the very heartbeat of the earth.

"It's the stones. They always bring the storm," Henry said. Velvet nodded because it was true. If someone put their mind to it—those stones could break the world.

"Alfonso is right. The stones need to be destroyed. Or cast into the deepest part of the sea."

"It's nearly over," Henry said. Velvet heard the catch in his voice. He was watching the way the twisting colors all seemed to funnel toward, then settle on something she had not seen before. Something unbelievable, undeniable. A profile made of light, a hint of sea-blue eyes, and golden curls. There was a body, too. A man's arms and legs of a stag. The body appeared to be composed of a substance that resembled a million shards of crushed crystal. The form was celestial, nearly divine. Velvet felt her jaw drop. She saw Henry's faint, sad smile from the corner of her eye.

"Louis," she nearly shrieked. Her nails dug deep in the

muscles of Henry's chest as the baby let out a wail at being so rudely awakened. She hardly heard it. "Henry! It's Louis."

"I know, love. I know. He would've already been fighting Devon, but he was held as immobile as I was. Spells are flying tonight. I never imagined Devon would be the caster. See?" Henry pointed to the colors rushing around Louis's hooves like a pair of fairy manacles.

Together, she and Henry watched, speechless, as the stone stole what remained of Devon's color and gave it to Louis. After what felt like a thousand years and no more than seconds, it was over. Louis soaked up all the colors like a sponge in a bowl of hot water. Louis's chains of color disappeared, and Velvet saw his face, unfettered by enchantment for the first time in eight years. Half man, half stag, the king of France roared like a lion and charged at the soldier on his knees currently in the process of giving his for him.

"Louis, no!" Velvet cried, making little Katie fuss again. Her brother didn't hear her, but it didn't matter. It was too late. Velvet suspected they all knew it, even Louis.

Louis was shockingly large and looked strong as some ancient minotaur. His attack was well aimed. Again, it didn't matter. His fist went straight through Devon's smiling face. Devon was between worlds, Katie could touch him, they could not.

"No! I forbid you to do this!" Louis shouted.

Devon's smile was tainted with sadness. "Be honest, you've gone back and forth," he said, then coughed out a mouthful of blood. In the night light, it looked grey and poisoned.

Louis's eyes blazed like twin sunspots. "I don't want anyone else to die for me!"

"It's my honor," Devon said.

Nora sobbed loudly, still on her knees; arms wrapped around her stomach as if she could somehow hold all her sorrow in. Velvet felt more hot tears pour down her cheeks. In her heart, she knew those were the last words lord Eden would ever speak.

The spell pulled the flesh from Devon's bones and tossed it in that other realm.

Farewell, farewell, farewell, Velvet thought. Nora started to scream as the final pieces of Devon faded to grey, then nothing. Nora reached down and gathered up the few bones that clinked against the ground, then rocked what remained of Devon.

It was done. *Farewell. Forgive me. Goddess, forgive me.*

Fireflies flitting, stars dancing, glitter in the wind. Velvet watched as what remained of Devon's body floated away on a sigh, perhaps a prayer. His essence dissolved into the air until only the four of them remained. All of them on their knees, eyes glued to the place where they had last seen him. A nursemaid had come at some point to take little Katie away and toss a cloak around Velvet's shoulders. Velvet hardly felt the added warmth; her blood was frozen, her bones were made of ice and tears.

None of them twitched, they scarcely dared breathe until the rising sun moved the giant courtyard dial, and pinkened the dusky sky. Nora was the first to speak. She wiped tears and dirt from her eyes, then fiercely blew her nose on the hem of her nightgown. She scrubbed her hands on the grass, then on the skirt of her gown. Slowly, hardly breathing, she turned to face Louis.

Velvet stared at the tears staining her brother's face. Light exploded in her brother's eyes when they fell on Nora.

"Hello," Nora said huskily, a thousand shades of misery tainting the timorous joy in her voice.

"Hello, ma chérie," Louis whispered as his hands found the sides of her face. "I'm so sorry. I've wanted to touch you more than anything, but I...I never meant...never wanted—"

"I know. It doesn't matter now," Nora said thickly. "It was his choice. I hope...I hope he's with Katie," she finished, then started crying again. A guttural sound came from Louis's throat. He leaned down and spread covetous kisses across Nora's face, her fresh flowing tears glittered on his lips. He dragged his hands through Nora's hair and pulled her closer. Nora hesitated for a single second, then her eyes flashed, and they crashed together. Louis's lips locked with hers. Their breaths rushed out in rhythmic bursts. Nora was wild as she gasped and twisted against Louis's still changing body.

Velvet turned away from the poignant scene. She was swamped with pesky self-pity, but let it go. There would be time for her later. She had waited this long; she could wait a few hours longer. Winded by misery, exhausted by emotion, Velvet started to stand, but Henry was quicker, and he lifted her like she weighed no more than a wet feather, which—after nearly a month in the palace—slowly eating her way through every jelly stuffed pastry ever created—truly wasn't the case. Velvet tilted her head back over his arm and closed her eyes. "The stones, Henry," she said weakly. "We need to get the stones. We can't let anything else happen because of them. I don't know if they can be destroyed, but maybe in the cave they'll cause less harm, at least for a couple centuries."

"I'll get them," Henry said, setting her lightly on her feet. Velvet kept her face averted as Henry combed through the grass for the ruby, then reached past the intertwined prince and his lady, for the amethyst which had fallen in the place where Devon died.

The glow of the stones was diminished, as was their custom after they took a life, but Velvet could still feel their dark energy rippling over the ground, creating tiny quakes beneath. This place would be forever changed. Magic would always infest this maze—perhaps all of Versailles would be affected. The ladies and men of court would do well to watch what they said here. Velvet knew better than anyone that some wishes should never be fulfilled.

◆

Velvet watched Henry as he walked back to her. The sun rising behind his midnight hair turned his eyes to glowing sapphires. She knew her own eyes exuded emotion that was impossible to hide. There was too much roiling under her calm exterior, like her pale, unblemished skin was skillfully hiding a mortal wound.

Henry stopped in front of her and took her hand. Velvet hadn't known that she reached for him. He gave her hand a squeeze, then dropped it and ran his thumbs gently over what Velvet was certain were bruise-like shadows under her eyes.

"You need sleep," he finally said.

"Thank you for noticing. Is that a nice way of saying I look like hell?" she asked, unable to squelch a small smile. The searing delight of his hands on her skin was something even the stones couldn't take from her.

Henry returned her smile. "Yes," he said, then kissed the tip of her icy nose. His smile faded quickly.

"You feel it too?" Velvet rubbed her hands up and down her arms trying to dispel the clinging chill. "It...it feels wrong somehow—happiness of any kind. I can't help it though. Louis is alive, and you—" Her voice cracked, and her mouth felt as if it were filled with dust.

Henry raked both hands through his hair, which was already in wild disarray. "It's horrible, but our misery isn't what Devon wanted. We, the four of us, set out on a quest, and he meant to see it done. He's a hero. Louis is safe. He's king of France now, and you—"

"I'm finally free," Velvet finished. A shiver trembled her bones until her teeth chattered.

Henry tugged the blanket draping her shoulders, tucked the ends under her chin, then ran his warm hands down her back, and she shivered again. She opened her mouth to say something but broke off with a startled squeak as Henry bent at the knee and once again lifted her in his arms. Her blood sizzled, and it took all her strength not to make some helpless, needy sound.

Henry looked down at her, his eyes sparking in his austere

face. She stared up at him helplessly, trying to hold herself stiffly, but a moment was all it took for the warmth of his touch to seep through the barrier of her nightgown, and she was melting against him. Right and wrong. Ice and fire. Life and love.

"Where are you taking me?" she asked, not caring at all. Long as she could stay in his arms, she would go anywhere.

"To bed. With me," he said curtly. "To sleep," he clarified, staring at her like a jaded sultan, and misunderstanding the small sound she made.

"I don't want to sleep. I don't want to dream," she said, because it was the truth.

"Fine. We're still going to your bed. I don't give a damn what we do when we get there," he finished, his hard stare relentless.

"Will you give the amethyst to Alfonso?" she asked, much to change the topic before her blush caught her lashes on fire. Bed and him. A scalding concept. Images of his firelit skin assailed her. The feel of his body atop hers, between her legs. Goddess! She could almost hear all the hot things he whispered in her ear. Heat pooled. The tips of her breast started to ache. Damn him. Her hands crept up his shoulders, and she stared at him word-lessly while he seemed to consider her question.

"Yes," he finally said, his voice thick. His dark head lowered. He was tight lipped, as if undergoing some exquisite torture. Velvet wondered if his thoughts were as filthy and wonderful as hers. "I promised Devon," he finished, and she watched a small muscle tick in his cheek. His eyes burned blue fire. Then he looked away. Velvet dropped her eyes to her to stare at a piece of skin she had been picking on the corner of her thumbnail. It was bleeding and achy. She focused on the small pain so she wouldn't stare at his lips and start panting, or something equally as embarrassing.

Neither of them said another word until they were engulfed by the silence of her darkened rooms. He set her gently down beside her bed, held her while she awkwardly found her feet. His hands were on her waist, her breaths were all tangled up in her throat, butterflies danced in her stomach, keeping her cheeks hot and her hands shaky. He stared at her for a moment that rang like the crescendo of an orchestra. A tortured look sapped some of the warmth from his gaze. He looked desperate. Starving, like he could pin her down on her bed, take what he needed and apologize for it later. She stared up at him. Speechless. Feeling all that he was not saying. The silence became a living, prowling creature. There was a hesitation between them. Together they were pleasure and pain. She suspected they both craved the pleasure but feared the pain. She sensed Henry's inner struggle and, for a second, his eyes flared. It seemed he would lose the battle and rip off her clothes with his teeth. She would let him. Stars, she would beg him.

His hands dropped from her waist with a reluctance that was almost palatable, Velvet held her breath as he turned away and went to light the lamp on her vanity.

It was a wonder she was still silent while flying apart inside. So much. Too much. Absent his touch, there were only memories, silence, and the taste of death on her lips. The night came back to her in broken pieces. While Henry rummaged for a match, Velvet tried to contend with the sickening guilt, changing the golden butterflies in her stomach to stinging scorpions.

Brave stupidity and well-meaning folly. She had indulged in plenty of both. The actions she set into motion nearly a year ago had last night come to fruition and killed the best friend of the man she loved. She had a million contrite words on her tongue but was too ashamed to say any of them. She was a walking disaster, and a tornado of misfortune haunted her every step, and it battered all who came too close. Not him. She couldn't hurt him. Not anymore. Not ever again.

The only choice was for them to stay away from each other, but that seemed to be less possible than a human girl sprouting wings. He walked back to her and stopped a few feet away. Velvet opened her mouth to say something, anything. Her throat worked, but the only sound that emerged was a broken squeak.

The stone cast of Henry's face was a torrent of repressed emotion. Velvet wanted to drown in shame and misery. His stare intensified, apparently waiting for her to spit out whatever she was choking on. He wanted something, a sigh, a single word. Velvet tried to smile at him, it was a fail. She burst into noisy tears, gasping sobs that shook her whole body. Her face dropped into her waiting hands. "I'm sorry, Henry," she cried. "I'm so, so sorry."

Henry made a deep, guttural sound and snatched her in his arms. He pulled her close, so their bodies were pressed flush. He kissed her forehead, temple, the corner of her lips. "No. Hush, Marie."

"It's my fault. All of it. Katie. Devon. He was your best...your best friend. You were ready to die for him—"

"Hush." He kissed the tears off her cheeks. His kiss was gentle, but his hands on her body were savage. "I wanted to. Hell, I might have actually done it, but I'm not so sure. You were loud in my heart and mind. I wanted to save him. I didn't want to leave you," he said, and she sensed the tumult inside of him.

Suddenly, Henry dropped his hands and stepped back like she had burned him.

Velvet caught his arm and clung to it desperately. She felt an involuntary tremor run through him.

"Bloody hell," he breathed. "God damn it. I hate it when you cry, princess." Gently, he extricated his arm from her death grip. Velvet clasped her hands behind her back to keep from reaching for him again.

Their bodies were inches apart, yet there were miles between them. Henry dragged his hands across his face. "Listen, this started before you were born. The stones came to you. It was no accident. You, we did the best with what we had. I know you would have given your life for either of them."

"If you don't hate me, then why can't you look at me?" she shouted, unable to bear the tension stretched taut enough to snap.

Henry's jaw locked. His eyes were blue wild-fire. "I could never hate you. I'm near mad with want of you, but nothing is settled. If I reach for you, and you push me away again, I won't be responsible for the violence of my actions."

Velvet moistened her lips and stopped twisting her fingers before they broke like dry matchsticks. "I won't," she whispered, and once the words started, they wouldn't stop. "I don't care what you planned with the king, or the tricks you played. I don't even care that he sent you to kill me. It brought you to me, and that's all that matters. If you leave me, Henry, you'll take the heart from my body. I don't want thrones, crowns, or palaces. I only want you." Her eyes dropped to study her toes. "I'll stay with you for as long as you'll have me."

Henry moved faster than she could blink. His hands sunk into her hair as his lips traced a path across her face. "Dangerous words vixen, you've just damned yourself to an eternity with me."

Velvet closed her eyes and smiled. "The duke speaks my dreams," she said, then Henry kissed her. She could feel him trying not to hurt her, trying to gentle his hands and lips. It wasn't what she wanted. She spread her fingers through his hair and twisted, tugged, wrenched him closer. She arched into his body and felt herself falling into that whirlwind of impossible color only he could summon.

Her past disintegrated like ashes in the wind, incinerated by his fire, by a touch that wrung the very soul from her body. He lifted her off her feet, and she could feel him, hot and hard against her stomach, stretching his clothes. Heat blazed. She ached for him. One of his hands was splayed across her ribs, his thumb resting beneath the curve of her breast, bare under her thin nightgown. After a dizzying moment, he broke the kiss and looked down. No more guards, no more walls. The light in his eyes, the love that raged in them could only tell the truth. "I love you, Marie, stubborn, courageous, beautiful, wonderful you. If you don't want me as your husband, that's fine. Take me as a friend, as a lover. I don't care so long as you take me. I need you.

I've always needed you. I'm a hollow shell of a man without you. You don't have to be my wife. Just be mine."

"I am your wife, Henry, and I'll always be yours."

Henry cupped her face in his hands. "Do you mean it? Truly?"

"With all my heart," she said as his lips locked with hers, and he kissed her as he carried her to bed. Velvet could hear his shredding breaths, feel the deep, resounding beat of his heart against her breast. She bit at his lower lip; her kiss seemed to drive him to the very edge of madness. The weight of his body settling atop hers was delicious danger. It didn't matter. Let the danger come. With him, she was always safe, always home.

He tugged at the hem of her nightgown, and she lifted her arms so he could pull the slip of cloth over her head. "I want to go back to our cave, Henry," she breathed as his lips found her neck. "I want to stay down there with you until the world forgets us."

"The world will never forget you, vixen. You've more than left your mark."

Velvet laughed and kissed the corner of his smile. "Villain. Will you run away with me?"

Henry leaned back, holding himself on his arms, hands planted on either side of her head. There was no one in the world but them. This moment was the only moment that mattered. The look he gave her seemed to lay bare the very depths of his truest soul, and she saw forever in his brilliant eyes. Heard it in his voice when he kissed the corner of her mouth and made a vow. "With you, I'll run to the ends of the earth."

EPILOGUE

ersailles sparkled with candles and diamonds; every surface was bejeweled the day the people crowned the new king of France. Later that day, it is said he married a princess of England and made her a queen. A bastard princess with a history of piracy, but that didn't matter much in France these days.

And so it goes. Despite the pain, life marches on. No king, mythical, imagined, or historic ever loved a woman the way the king of France loved his red-haired bride. She was the true monarch, fair and kind. The French king often said his only job was to make her smile, which she did. Often.

Because of her, the king of France was not the puppet Napoleon desired. It is said the queen threatened the great general's life on so many occasions that the court musician composed a ballad of her numerous threats, which was sung often by the people. Furious at failure, Napoleon took his soldiers in search of greater, simpler triumphs. In 1815, he was exiled to the island of Sanit Helena. Stories of his death now abound. Some say it was the island sweats that killed him, others blame it on a rare stomach malady. Ajax and Abigail say the truth is not far from the latter. Only the malady in question is not that uncommon and was caused by a well-made pirate blade to the gut.

As for the lost princess of France, and her duke, one cannot truly say. However, the gossips tell strange tales of an underwater cave that has no respect for the parameters of time. Stories say their world consists of passion and starlight. For my part, I hope it's true, for I have loved her always. I often pray that the magic which held me captive for so many years, is safe with her. Well hidden beneath enchanted crystal water. The stones finally lost, and simultaneously returned to the place where they were formed, all save one. A single amethyst given to a Romani lord as payment for a blood debt. My debt.

When I put the stone in his hand, he swore to use it only once to see the brother and sister who died to save me. He swore on a blood moon and lied. He used the stone many times.I hear he now wanders the Moors, skin pale as a shroud, and eyes that see between worlds. Call it his fate, or karma. I don't care. He has his reward.

As for my beautiful bride, we have three children who have all carved a place in my heart, but little Katie managed to capture a piece of my soul. Nora was born to be a mother, and to this day, fourteen years later, I still can't stop kissing her.

Excerpt from the diary, of Louis the XVII

～

Don't miss out on your next favorite book!

Join the Satin Romance mailing list
www.satinromance.com/mail.html

THANK YOU FOR READING

Did you enjoy this book?

We invite you to leave a review at the website of your choice,
such as Goodreads, Amazon, Barnes & Noble, etc.

~

DID YOU KNOW THAT LEAVING A REVIEW…

- Helps other readers find books they may enjoy.
- Gives you a chance to let your voice be heard.
- Gives authors recognition for their hard work.
- Doesn't have to be long. A sentence or two about why
  you liked the book will do.

ABOUT THE AUTHOR

JP Roth is an American Novelist, and owner of Rothic comics, founded in 2012, through which she has produced and published five of her original series. JP Roth lives in Long Beach, CA with her beautiful family, and their adorable Bichon Frise. She spends her days writing fanciful stories, walking on the beach, and attending comic conventions across the globe.

JP Roth was born overseas, and spent her life roaming the world. She still enjoys travelling to exotic locations, but admittedly prefers to stay home, wrapped in a soft fluffy blanket, drinking, tea and penning her next novel.

www.rothic.com

 facebook.com/jprothic

twitter.com/@iamjproth

instagram.com/jprothic